NIGHT RUNNERS

MICHAEL SERRIAN

NEO NOIR
PRESS

Los Angeles

To Nancy

"I first heard Personville called Poisonville by a red-haired mucker named Hickey Dewey in the Big Ship in Butte. He also called his shirt a shoit. I didn't think anything of what he had done to the city's name. Later I heard men who could manage their r's give it the same pronunciation. I still didn't see anything in it but the meaningless sort of humor that used to make richardsnary the thieves' word for dictionary. A few years later I went to Personville and learned better."
— Dashiell Hammett, RED HARVEST

1985

prologue:
FIRST BLOOD

It was all around them. Thick. White. Zip visibility. Maybe they took a wrong turn and ended up in heaven. Or hell. Misty. Steamy. Wet. The windshield wipers worked overtime but only managed to smear their vision. The sweating gray Lincoln bore through the dense fog like a missile slicing into storm clouds.

"We've landed," the driver said as he pulled up along the muddy shoulder of the two-lane blacktop road. The green sign before them read:

Welcome to
HAMMETT

And the sign was splattered with red paint . . . or blood.

The four men in the car — two up front, two in the rear — varied in age but not in temperament. The car almost shook from their anxiety.

The Kid, blond and blue-eyed with a missing front tooth, where he lost most of his words in a slur, cracked a joke. The men erupted in polite laughter — just releasing some steam.

"Well, here we go," said the driver. He was the oldest.

He had raven-black hair with a shock of white in front. A hawk nose and rigid cheekbones gave him a hard, gaunt appearance. He had seen too many bad years. He stepped on the accelerator pedal, pulled back onto the fog-shrouded blacktop, and the Lincoln disappeared.

There was a job to be done.

Elmore Shepard stood in the doorway of the small wood cabin looking out at his wife, Debra, seated on a chair a few feet away. Next to her was a small plastic trash can. She was too immersed in trimming a marijuana plant to notice him. Deb clipped the branch carefully with a pair of scissors, the leaves falling into the plastic bucket. She was surrounded by overhead clotheslines where the branches were hung to dry. The misty gray evening left the crop damp.

Elmore carried an empty can over to her and exchanged it for the full one. He eyed the black plastic trash bags in the corner. They were packed solid. His German shepherd, Killer, guarded them intensely.

It was harvest time.

The bags represented his first batch of the season. In fact, he had a run tonight. He would hide a few sacks somewhere in the deep bush, then rendezvous with Al Romero, his primary buyer. When Romero handed over the cash, Elmore would tell him where to find the batch. They found this exchange method to be the safest.

Elmore went back outside. She was still hard at work. He smiled at himself. She was his old lady and he *liked* that.

"Deb."

She looked up and smiled.

"Call it a night, hon."

"Soon as I finish this." She continued her clipping.

"I have to get ready for the run."

She nodded.

"Lock up the cabin," he said. "I'll leave Killer with you."

She glanced up at him. "Good luck."

He winked. "See you later."

Sheriff Higgins sat with his legs crossed on his spotless desk. He pushed back his hat brim and scanned his watch. Two-thirty AM. "Shit," he muttered. He wondered how *he,* the bossman, got duped into this graveyard shift. It was a favor for his Deputy Sheriff, Harry Oates. A youngster. He wanted to boogie. *Where the hell do ya boogie in a town like Hammett?*

Pushing his lean legs off the desk top, he stood up and wandered over to the coffeepot. He poured himself a cup and slowly sipped the lukewarm gook. He pulled out a Camel and lit up. After a few drags the smoke began to irritate his tired eyes, so he squashed it out and cussed.

He sucked in his swollen gut and dragged his pointed lizard-skin Tony Lama boots to the large window. Peering out into the pea soup, he said to himself, "Jeeze, what a night."

His face, reflected in the window, was creased and all worn-out. His eyes, almost hidden behind thick skin and bushy brows, looked so small. A silver-and-black mustache concealed his lean lips. He picked the skintight gray pants of his uniform out of the crack of his ass and sat down at his desk.

Time for a short snooze.

"*Snap, crackle, pop* — he's dead." Al Romero snapped his fingers to emphasize his statement.

"Just like that, huh?" Elmore whistled as he shook his head.

"That's how easy it is."

"Poor bastard."

"We should be safe tonight; the feds aren't about to strike again so soon."

"It's the President and his damn *anti*-drug crusade."

"Screw the President — he's not just *too* old, he's *brain* dead."

"Is that his problem?"

"Hey, you don't look so good yourself, Elmore."

"Damn rash of some kind."

"*Bad* kind by the looks of it."

"Must've been somethin' I ate."

"Must've been somethin' *dis*eased," Romero cackled.

"Knocked the wind outta me, too."

"Should see yourself to the doctor."

"I'll get over it."

"Just hope *it* doesn't get over *you*. Know what I mean?"

"Worried about my health now, Al?"

"We're business partners, pal."

"Yeah, until a better deal comes along."

"I don't work that way, y'know that."

"Uh-huh."

"You have the first batch ready?"

"Would I venture out on a night like this if I didn't?"

"Bitch of a night." Romero handed the thick envelope to Elmore.

Elmore tucked the envelope into his jacket and walked around his motorcycle. He undid the saddlebag and whipped out a small sheet of paper. On it was a small diagram showing directions to the hidden sacks.

"Ain't ya goin' to count it?" Romero asked of the money.

"Hell, we're business partners, ain't we pal?" Elmore grinned.

The gray Lincoln pulled up across the deserted street from the bar. There was a small cluster of pickup trucks and jeeps parked outside.

The driver broke the silence. "We're here."

The Kid in back pulled out a Snickers bar. He tore off the wrapper and stuck the bar in his mouth. He tried to bite off a piece but it was still frozen. That was how he had lost his front tooth the last time. "Damn — s-s-still hard as a rock!" he hissed.

Ron Sharp, the dark-haired man beside the driver, glared back at the nineteen-year-old youth. "You ready?"

"Yep."

"You?" he asked Red, the redheaded, freckled man next to the Kid. He was a little older, maybe twenty-two, and he hadn't spoken a single word all night. He nodded affirmatively.

"Now we sit," Sharp said.

Elmore was dressed in his skins. Shit, it was cold enough. He felt the thick wad of money tucked inside his black leather jacket. Not bad for a night's run.

Yeah, the money was good and getting better every day.

Why, Elmore just upped and bought himself this Honda Nighthawk CB650SC, a sport-custom, high-tech machine with double-cam, 16-valve, and six-speed engine that punched 650 cc.'s of power.

A Mean Machine.

He opened her up as he cruised down Main Street. The pearl-blue sleek two-wheeler glistened in the bright neon light that shined from Jake Hinton's bar. He pulled up alongside Old Ben's pickup truck.

He climbed off the bike and pitched it. Peeling off his leather gloves he stared at the open sores on his hands. *"Damn* — what is *this* shit?"

Elmore removed his helmet and carried it by the straps as he entered the bar.

"That's him," Sharp said.

"Nice bike," the driver said.

"Do we go now?" the Kid asked, resting his head on his folded arms on top of the front seat.

"Naw, let him have a few drinks for chrissakes," the driver said.

"Then we go?" the Kid asked enthusiastically.

Sharp nodded. "Then we go."

Elmore sat up on the bar stool. Hinton set him up with a mug of brew and an eyecup of Jim Beam. His *usual*.

Elmore eyed the drinks before him with discomfort. He had lost his taste for alcohol in the last few weeks. The aroma alone brought on a feeling of nausea and a painful headache. He raised the beer mug and held it to his mouth, pretending to sip it.

Hinton stood before Elmore. His glass eye always made him appear cockeyed, especially when he was tired. "Messy night," he growled.

"Been on a run, Elmore?" Old Ben, who sat a few stools away, snickered and nudged his buddy next to him.

"Some of us gotta work for a livin', old-timer," Elmore said.

Old Ben was stricken with a long spell of laughter.

"How're your crops?" Elmore asked.

"What's that all over yer face and hands, Elmore, *herpes?*"

"You're showin' your ignorance, Ben."

"Yours must be coming through the skin, Elmore!"

Hinton laughed with the rest of them as he eased down the bar.

Elmore shook his head. Elbows on the bar, his hands hugged the beer mug like a priest's chalice. His black eyes stared back at him from the mirror behind the bar. He was *getting deep* again. Tuning out. The locals respected his privacy — these little moments of contemplation. They called it getting deep. He had been that way ever since he returned from Nam.

The bar held seven men including the bartender. That was a lot for the AM hours in this town. Hammett was located in the asshole of the Southeast. Mostly farmers. But there was a Main Street, and they had their share of big stores and banks — even a 7-Eleven store. A lot of the young folk moved on when they hit legal age, so the town never grew as large as had been anticipated. It wasn't much, but it was home for some. And a good home.

Elmore wondered about his younger brother, Tommy. He was going to school in New York City. Elmore paid for his tuition. It was the least he could do since they had no parents. That made Elmore Tommy's surrogate father.

Elmore was the spitting image of his pop. He was six-feet-two-inches tall and lanky with a smooth angelic face and black droopy eyes. He had jet-black hair that he combed back, the curls flaring out of his collar. Just having turned thirty-five, he appeared somewhat older — maybe it was the way he carried himself. There was a serenity about him, an air of self-assurance befitting a man of older years.

Their daddy had run moonshine in another county ages ago. He had been killed on a run. Elmore followed in his footsteps. But it wasn't moonshine anymore. One had to keep up with the times. He grew and sold marijuana. He had several small patches spread out in tightly camouflaged areas, with less than a hundred plants in each section. Currently, each pot plant was worth fifteen hundred dollars. It was good money. All the farmers were into it. Even the old-timers had given up on raising food crops. *Green Gold* was where the money was, especially in these lean times.

Elmore Shepard was the most successful grower in Hammett. He had the most crops and wielded the most power. He grew only *Sinsemilla* — the cream of the crop. It was stronger and more potent in THC than the best of the Colombian dope.

Elmore had it made. Nobody messed with him. The sheriff and his men got their share and so did the mayor. The feds, well, they were another problem. They'd been cracking down on pot growers across the country, but there wasn't enough of them to combat the hundreds of thousands involved. The feds had yet to show their faces in Hammett. They were up to their ears in capturing drug smugglers — too much so to worry about pot growers.

At least that was what Elmore figured.

Yeah, things were going very well until a strange thing happened a few weeks back. Elmore had found a brown oily substance on some plants in one of his patches. At first, he hadn't thought too much about it. But then he'd noticed that the plants affected began to grow at an alarming rate — they were huge in comparison to his other crops. At the same time he'd broken out in this horrible rash. And there were other symptoms — like loss of appetite, a slew of headaches, and an allergic reaction to alcohol. He was feeling tired regardless of how much sleep he got. And his sex drive was on the skids too — that was *really* unusual.

Just this morning he'd noticed that those once-blossoming plants were now brown and wilted. He wondered what the hell was going on. He was glad it seemed to have affected only one of his many batches. Where had he seen this before? He thought hard. And then it came back to him. In Nam. Hell, they had sprayed everything they could think of to combat the VC. When all the stink had come out about Agent Orange, he'd gone to a Jacksonville vets' hospital to check himself out. They had given him a clean bill of health. Naw, it couldn't be *that*. He shook his head to rid himself of those thoughts. He didn't want to worry about this now. He was happy. He was able to pay for his brother's tuition. He had made a nice home for his wife, Debra, and their son, Sage.

Sage.

He was a beautiful boy. Smart. Smart like his Uncle Tommy. Thank God for that. Elmore didn't think too much of his own intelligence. Sure he knew the score and had normal wits, but he just didn't have what Tommy had. Tommy had smarts. Although he didn't know it. Hell, Elmore had to hogtie him to force him to go to college.

Elmore snapped out of it. He put down the beer mug and saw Hinton standing before him.

"Seriously, Elmore, what's with the sores?"

Elmore shrugged.

"Pretty bad looking — did you go see Hank about it?" Hinton asked.

Hank Crichton was a local doctor.

Elmore shook his head.

"You should — why, you're sweating up a storm right now."

"I'll be okay," Elmore said and gazed back at his mirror reflection. Black eyes on black eyes. Getting deep.

"Put on your masks," Sharp barked at them and then faced the driver. "Keep her running."

"Will do," the driver said.

Sharp slipped on his over-the-head rubber mask. He turned to watch the boys do the same.

The Kid checked his Smith and Wesson Model 76 submachine gun with suppressor. It was ready.

Red checked his Ingram M10 SMG. It was ready.

Sharp pumped his 12-gauge Winchester. "Let's go."

Elmore swore he was dreaming. But when he saw the bottles shattering all around him and then the red stuff — he knew it was for *real*.

He'd seen them out of the corners of his eyes. Three men. Three familiar masked faces. Kissinger held a pump-action shotgun. Nixon took aim with a Model 76 SMG. Reagan, off to the side, had an Ingram in hand.

Then he saw Jake Hinton's glass eye bounce across the bar counter.

It was the last thing he saw on this earth.

Higgins popped his head up when he heard the racket. "JESUS CHRIST!" It sounded like he was back in Korea. He jerked himself out of the chair and hurried to the door where he heard a car screech away. He ran outside and down the street to Hinton's place. It was the only thing still open.

He whipped open the door, and a wall of smoke poured out. The unmistakable odor of spent gunpowder penetrated his nostrils. Bodies were spread out across the bar, draped over the stools, their clothing soaked with blood.

"Holy shit!"

The Lincoln cut through the fog going ninety miles per hour. The men tugged off their masks with sighs of relief.

The Kid pulled out the Snickers bar and bit into it. A sharp pain ripped through him as he let out a yelp. He yanked the candy bar from his mouth and saw that his only front tooth was stuck in it.

His redheaded partner, who hadn't uttered a single word all night, gazed wide-eyed at the tooth and said, *"WOW!"*

part one
THE SEEDING

chapter 1

Tommy Shepard, dressed in his nylon running shorts and tee shirt, was working on his sixth lap around the Central Park reservoir. His blue-and-white Nikes kicked up a dusty trail behind him. His roommate, Matt Reeves, tagged alongside him. It was very hot for an October day.

Tommy was running hard. He was feeling good this morning. His blue cotton shirt stuck to his sweaty back like a second skin. He took in deep, steady breaths.

Push harder, wimp!

He enjoyed running when he had a lot on his mind. It helped him think things through. Tommy called it therapy.

He was thinking about his brother, Elmore, and his home in Hammett. Although Tommy had been going to school in New York for some time now, he still considered Hammett his home. He knew it was just a small hick town in comparison to the Big Apple. And though he was having a good time in the big city, he still felt out of place. He longed for the simplicity of small-town life.

Elmore.

Tommy was concerned about him. When Elmore had paid him a visit the week before, he appeared ill. He had this rash all over his body. And he'd looked bloated. He had brought along a sample of one of his marijuana plants. He had discovered a strange brown sap on some of the leaves. He hadn't noticed it before, and he was concerned.

Elmore seemed more unnerved by Tommy than his own condition. He acted strange. Fearful. The thought of Elmore being afraid of anything had never crossed Tommy's mind. Maybe spending time away from Elmore had made Tommy more aware of his faults. Could it be that his older brother was even . . . *human*?

"It's nearly harvest time and this shit has to show up on some of my crop." Elmore collapsed onto Tommy's bed.

"Screw the plants, what about *you*?" Tommy asked.

"I'm okay," Elmore said unconvincingly. "It's this brown shit that I'm worried about."

Tommy held the sample leaves that were inside the plastic pouch. He was about to open the bag when Elmore stopped him. "*No, don't open it!* Who the hell knows what it is."

"You think this stuff has something to do with your condition?"

Elmore avoided Tommy's inquiring gaze and said nothing. His silence answered the question.

"Has anyone else seen this on their plants?"

Elmore shook his head. "I've asked around. *No*body's noticed it."

"That's strange . . ."

Elmore nodded. "I talked with Mayor Carpenter about it. Gave him a sample and all. He told me that he would get back to me. I waited a week and didn't hear a word from the son of a bitch. So I confronted him. He told me not to worry. It's just a kind of sap. Well, lemme tell ya, baby brother, I'm worried. Look at me, for chrissakes. What's happening to me?''

Tommy took in the sores on his brother's face. They were like pimples with open heads. "Could be some kind of allergic reaction . . . maybe just nerves from worrying about this brown shit.''

Elmore grinned. "I didn't start worryin' until *after* I got the sores.''

"How're Deb and Sage?''

"Fine.''

"No one else in town has this . . . *this* problem?''

"Hell, no.''

"What do you want me to do with the sample?''

"Get it tested here on campus. Y'know, some bio student. Got any friends that are into biology?''

Tommy shook his head. "I don't have too many friends. Besides, this stuff's still illegal, you know.''

"Tell me about it, baby brother. I grow that stuff under the goddamn feds' noses. Sure I know it's illegal. But in New York they think differently about things. Hell, I smell them smokin' this shit wherever I go in this town.''

"What the hell do you know about New York City?'' Tommy snapped.

Elmore inhaled deeply, nodding all the time. "You're right, Tommy, I don't know much about it. That's why I'm here.''

"Why are you here?''

Elmore stood up and went to the window. "You're still sore.''

"I don't know what you're talking about.''

He faced him. "About me makin' ya go to school. Jeezus, Tommy, hasn't it sunk in yet, for chrissakes. I want more for you, baby brother.''

"More for me or more for you?''

"For you!'' Elmore shouted. "You're too fuckin' dumb to know better, that's your problem, Tommy.''

"I thought you said I was smart," Tommy said. "That's why you sent me here."

"You don't have to be here. You're old enough to think for yourself."

Tommy nodded with a grin on his face. "That's right . . . so why am I here?"

"To better yourself."

Tommy shook his head. "Nope. I'm here because of you. I just want you to know that, Elmore. I want you to know that I'm only doing this for you."

"Sometimes . . ." Elmore smacked his fist into the palm of his other hand. "Okay, Tommy, I'm here askin' ya for help. Can't ya do that much for your big, dumb older brother?"

"Yeah, I guess. It's just that I don't know anybody . . . maybe Matt knows someone."

"How is Matt?"

"Out on a date tonight."

"That's what *you* should be doin' — gettin' laid," Elmore joked.

Tommy shook his head. "One-track mind."

Elmore sat down again. He squinted up at Tommy with a sinister grin. "Ya know you've changed, Tommy."

"Oh yeah?"

"Givin' me a hard time like you're doin'. I get it. I know where it's comin' from."

"I just wanna know why you came to me with this," Tommy said.

"I didn't know what to do. Who to turn to. I've been tryin' to put it out of my head, y'know. Maybe if I didn't think about it, it would go away. Some shit like that."

"That's stupid."

"I realize that now." Elmore started to drift off.

"Snap out of it, Elmore." Tommy snapped his fingers. "Don't go hiding into yourself again." He hated to watch his brother escape from reality whenever he was faced with a problem.

Elmore said, "I'm sorry, Tommy. I came here because I needed your help. You always handle yourself better in bad situations."

"*Me?*"

"Yes — you. You're stronger than me in some ways. And now . . . Jeezus, you're way ahead of me. Man, have you grown."

"Proud of yourself?"

"How's that?"

"Since it was your idea to send me off to school."

"Gimme a break."

"Okay, I will. I'll see what I can do about getting this shit tested. But you have to promise me something."

"Sure."

"You take yourself to the doctor's in the meantime."

"The *doctor*? I don't need . . . "

"Hell you don't."

"Come on, Tommy."

"Is it a deal?"

Elmore thought it over. He didn't appear too happy. "Yeah, sure."

"Go to that vets' hospital in Jacksonville."

He nodded.

"You have to promise me, Elmore," Tommy pleaded. "Your word of honor."

"Yeah, yeah, yeah."

"Elmore."

"Yep?"

"I'm worried about you."

"Stop it. You know me. I can take care of myself. Been doin' it a long time now."

"Doesn't look like you're doing a very good job."

Elmore stood up and looked into his brother's eyes. "Love you, baby brother."

Tommy went to hug him, but Elmore shook his head. "Don't want you to catch anythin', Tommy."

"You think it's contagious?"

"Wouldn't want *you* to be the one to find out the hard way. Haven't been sleepin' with Deb . . . and stayin' clear of Sage. You never know."

"Jesus Christ." Tommy shook his head. "I don't believe *this.*"

"Who knows, it could all clear up tomorrow."

Or it could get worse. Tommy didn't want to think about *that.*

"Can't you stay the night?" Tommy asked.

"Nope, gotta catch a midnight flight. Have a run in the AM."

"Aren't you spreading yourself a little thin?"

"Business is business — somebody's gotta pay for your education."

"I could always quit."

"Not while I'm still alive and kickin'."

Tommy smirked.

Elmore said, "Call me if you find out anythin'."

"Keep in touch . . . *and* go see that doctor, man."

Elmore was already out the door.

Tommy heard some static in his thoughts. Somebody was trying to break through. He snapped out of it.

"You haven't been listening to me," Matt complained.

"Sorry . . . just thinking." Tommy slowed down to a walk.

"Elmore again?"

"Yeah."

"Have you heard from that chick yet — what's her name?"

"Mandy Cronenberg. No, I have to give her a call. It's just, you know, I don't want to push her. She's doing *me* the favor."

Mandy was a journalist working for the national rock music publication *R & R Express.* Tommy had attended a lecture she had given on campus a few weeks before. He'd recalled her mentioning that her husband was a chemist for a major pharmaceutical firm. He had hoped that she might be able to get her husband to test the brown sap for him. It was a wild shot, but he had nowhere else to turn.

Her journalistic instincts had been aroused. She'd offered him a deal. She'd have her husband do the tests *if* she could interview Elmore for a story on marijuana growers. Tommy had reluctantly agreed.

That had been a few days ago. Tommy hadn't heard anything yet. It was probably too soon, but he was so anxious to hear something . . . *anything* . . . that might aid his brother.

Tommy and his friend jogged out of the park and across 110th Street. They shared an apartment just off Broadway on 112th Street. It was an old walk-up building. The apartment was a floor-through job with windows front and back. It wasn't much, but it was a roof over their heads. Elmore wanted him to live in a more expensive high-rise, but Tommy wouldn't have any of that. He'd felt like an outsider as it was. No, he'd wanted to be like the other students — roughing it. He'd decided to find a roommate. A fellow student. Matt had entered the picture. He was an undergrad studying communications.   They hiked up to their landing and undid the numerous locks. Once inside, they both rushed to the kitchen sink for some cold water. Matt beat Tommy to the faucet.

"Hey, that's a first," Matt beamed.

Tommy waited thoughtfully until he finished.

"You okay?" Matt asked.

"Yeah."

Matt handed him a glass of water. "You must really be out of it, man."

Tommy gulped down the water.

"I never saw you like this, Tommy."

"Like what?"

"So . . . so preoccupied."

Tommy shrugged.

Matt pulled his wet tee shirt over his head. "Last one in the shower is a pussy!" Matt hurried into the bathroom.

Tommy heard the shower going as he walked through the inner rooms towards his bedroom. As he began to peel off his clothes, the phone rang. He let it ring three times before he picked it up.

"Yeah?"

"Tommy?" It was Deb's voice. He closed his eyes. It was the phone call he had been dreading. Something was seriously wrong with Elmore. He just *knew* it.

"It's Elmore."

"I knew it."

"He's dead."

At first, the words didn't register. They had to sink in. It wasn't what he'd expected to hear. He'd thought she was calling to say that Elmore was in the hospital. That he had some exotic virus.

He sat down on the floor, his back up against his platform bed. He could still hear his brother's voice. The way he'd called him *baby brother* with that slight twang of an accent. Tommy had never liked it when he called him that. Hell, he was thirty years old — not somebody's *baby brother*. In time he would miss those words the most.

"Why didn't you call earlier to tell me he was getting worse?!"

"You don't understand, Tommy."

"Didn't he go to the doctor like I told him to?"

"Tommy."

"Answer me, *dammit*!" Tommy snapped.

"He didn't die from *that*."

"What are you telling me?"

"He was shot . . . killed . . . *murdered*." Debra broke down and cried.

"What?" Tommy shook his head. Did he hear her right — *murdered*? "I—I don't understand . . ."

"At Jake Hinton's place . . . a shootout," she said. *"Oh, Tommy!"*

"A shootout?" Tommy asked. "God*damn!* Did it have to do with the dope?"

"I don't know . . . I guess."

"Just Elmore get it?"

"No." She snuffled. "Six of them in all. Jake was taken to Jacksonville. He was hurt real bad."

Tommy had trouble focusing on this. A shootout. Six dead. Jake hurt bad. He took deep breaths. *Calm down.* THINK.

"Tommy, are you still there?"

"Yeah . . . I just don't believe it. Elmore. Gone. My God."

"I don't know what to do, Tommy," Deb sobbed.

"I'll be right down . . . the first flight I can get. I'll take care of everything."

"Thank you, Tommy."

"How . . . how's Sage?"

"I couldn't tell him . . . not *yet.*" Her voice broke again.

"Take it easy . . . I'll see you later." Tommy hung up.

He got to his feet and walked back to the kitchen. Matt was just coming out of the bathroom, a blue towel wrapped around his trim hips. His wet hair lay flat against his skull. He brushed by Tommy who stood in the middle of the room motionless. "Your turn, pussy."

When he didn't hear a response, Matt swung around and eyed the back of his friend. "Tommy?"

He ventured around him and took hold of his bare shoulders. "Tommy?" He shook him.

Tommy blinked out of it. He looked into his room-mate's cornflower-blue eyes. Matt was waiting for an explanation.

"It's Elmore."

"Huh?"

"I just got the call."

"Elmore?"

"He's dead, Matt."

"I don't believe it." Matt shook his dark-haired head. "He was just here."

"Yeah, he was just here." Tommy said.

chapter 2

She'd thought he was a handsome young man. Tall.
Blond. Green eyes. Stubbly reddish beard. A wry grin
— probably felt self-conscious about his crooked front
teeth. He had said he was from the Southeast. But he
didn't have an accent. In fact, he had no trace of any
accent at all. He told her he had worked a long time to
erase his slight Southern drawl. She'd wondered why he
would want to lose it. Because it made him sound dumb,
he'd explained.

"Where did you say we met?" Mandy Cronenberg
asked Tommy Shepard the day he'd come to her office.

"At Columbia. You gave a lecture on journalism. I
thought you were good."

"Thank you." She smiled. "Are you studying journalism?"

"No . . . not exactly. My roommate, Matt, he's into
it. I just tagged along."

"Oh . . . so what can I do for you?"

"I need to ask you a favor."

"I can't get you or your roommate a job — I'm sorry — even my own job is in jeopardy. The paper is running on red ink now, and I hear we're up for sale."

"It's nothing like that."

"Oh, no?"

"Can I trust you?" He whispered as he looked around. Her white partitioned cubicle seemed secure enough.

She gave him the once-over. "I really don't have the time . . ."

He pulled out a plastic bag that was hidden in his shirt. There were green leaves and stems inside. Those leaves were unmistakable. She'd sure as hell smoked enough of it in her time to recognize it as marijuana.

She couldn't help herself. She threw her head back with laughter.

"I don't think you understand . . ."

"Like hell I don't!"

"Really. It's not what you think."

Mandy stood up and went to the coffee counter just outside her cubicle. "I need some caffeine." She poured some into her stained Styrofoam cup. "You want a dose?"

"No, thanks."

She returned to her desk and plopped down on her swivel chair. She pushed herself away from the white formica desk and leaned back in the chair. The blinking cursor on the computer monitor caught Tommy's eye.

He gestured to the screen. "You write on *that*?"

"Yep." She stirred in a packet of Sweet 'N Low. "We may not be as profitable as *Rolling Stone,* but we still run a legit, high-tech operation here," she said sarcastically.

He laughed out of politeness. She wondered what the hell he had in mind. Was he trying to sell her some of his dope? He seemed so preoccupied. Like he was a thousand miles away.

Finally he said, "Your husband . . . he's a chemist."

"Yeah, that's right, how did you know that?"

"From the lecture."

"I didn't mention anything about my . . . oh, now I remember. Oh, yeah." She smiled at the thought. "Some cute kid asked me if I was married."

"That was my roommate, Matt. He has a thing for older . . ." He caught himself. "For more *mature* women."

She grinned. "You were right the first time — *older women.*"

"You're not so old."

"Older than you . . . what are you—twenty-four?"

"Thirty."

"Well, I'm thirty — " She paused. *"Something."*

"See — you're not so old."

"Hey, aren't you a little too old to be an undergraduate?"

Tommy looked away and shrugged. "Started later . . . believe me, it wasn't *my* idea."

"Your parents are making you go?"

"My parents are dead."

Mandy cleared her throat and decided to change the subject. She obviously had hit a sore spot. "Okay, you better tell me what you want."

"I need your *husband's* help."

"My husband's help?"

"You see, these leaves, they're from a marijuana plant my brother grew."

"Stop right there — your *brother* grew it?"

"That's right. My brother. He lives in Hammett."

"Hammett?"

"In Florida. There's a lot of that going on there."

"Yes. I've heard that. Farmers do better growing dope than food crops."

"It's the times."

She had to laugh; this guy was sharp. "So?"

"Well, he found this brown stuff on some of his plants."

"So?"

"Brown stuff. It can't be a sap. Saps are usually clear or milky but never brown."

"Yeah, yeah — go on."

Tommy filled her in on the rest. She listened intently as she dragged on a cigarette, her blue eyes never leaving him. The story really intrigued her.

"Your brother, what's his name?"

"Elmore."

"Right, Elmore. He thinks this brown sap is responsible for his sickness?"

Tommy nodded.

"And you want my husband Howard to test this brown stuff for you?"

"That's right."

"And what do *I* get out of it?"

Tommy was perplexed. "Hit me with that again."

"What's this got to do with me?" she asked.

"Well . . . *nothing*," he said.

"Exactly, so why should I stick my neck out for you?"

"To save my brother's life."

"Your brother is a criminal."

Tommy shrugged. "Maybe. But he's still a human being."

"To be honest, this whole thing, especially the dope growing, interests me. I might want to do a story on it. Pretty exciting stuff. *The new moonshiners.* Yeah, I like it," she mused. "Listen, if I do this thing for you, then I get to talk with your brother. An interview. A whole series of interviews . . . anonymously, of course. I want to know the whole deal — the foundation, the growers, the buyers, the whole *shtick*."

Tommy raised his hands defensively. "Hey, now hold on here for a second," he said. "That could be dangerous for Elmore."

"I won't use his name."

"If anybody ever found out . . . Elmore would be dead," Tommy said gravely.

"That's my price — take it or leave it."

Tommy stood up and put his hands on his hips. "Listen, lady, we're talking about my brother here, okay? With you snooping around, it might fuck up things down there something fierce. Besides, I thought you just did interviews with rock stars or some such thing."

She narrowed her eyes at him menacingly. "Hey, pal, stuff it. You're asking me to stick my neck out . . . *my husband's neck* no less . . . and you expect me to do it out of the goodness of my heart? I'm a journalist!" She pounded her chest.

"I don't know about this." Tommy rubbed his forehead. "I didn't mean to insult you. I'm sorry if I did. You just have to understand that I'm worried about my brother. You know what I mean?"

"You know my terms — that's the best I can do, pal." She scanned her watch. "I really have to get back to work."

He returned to his seat. "I appreciate your taking time away from work for me. I mean that. But this article thing. It could be a problem. It could really be dangerous, not only for my brother, but also for *you*," Tommy said with concern.

Mandy hit him with a stern gaze. *"Me?"*

Tommy grinned. "Shit — yeah. I'm talking some heavy-duty action here. There's a lot of mean fuckers down there who protect their crops to the death."

She smirked. "Believe me, I can handle myself."

"I don't think you realize . . ."

"Deal or no deal?"

Tommy let loose with a long sigh of defeat. "Okay — it's a deal."

They shook hands on it.

Before Tommy was about to leave, Mandy asked,

"Does your roommate *really* find me attractive?"
"Very much so."
That made her day.

"Are *you* crazy?!" Howard shouted at Mandy.
"Just a little test . . . after work."
"With all the problems we're having down at the plant
— give me a break, Mandy." Howard tramped out of
the living room and into their bedroom. He sat down on
the edge of the bed. Indeed, Savitch Laboratories was
having its woes. Their antacid tablets, Tummy Savers,
had been recalled from the stores because of several
deaths. Arsenic had been found in some bottles of the
product. Package tampering had become the new con-
sumer concern of the eighties. It would end up costing
Savitch millions of dollars.
Mandy, dressed in her white nightgown, sat down next
to her husband. "I'm sorry, Howard, I should've con-
sulted you first."
"You always do this to me." He shook his head in
disgust.
She held his hand.
He peered into her blue eyes. It was difficult for him
to resist her. He ran his fingers through her wrinkled red
hair.
"I think this could be something big, Howard."
It was *always* something big. He ran his fingers along
her white, creamy face, wanting, as he always did, to
count the millions of rusty freckles sprinkled there. He
placed his finger on the bridge of her straight, narrow
nose and worked his way down to her thin lips.
"*Hey* — what're you doing?"
Howard made her stand up before him. He held her,
his hands against her hips. She had a nice figure. Not
too thin, not too fat — just right. She was too self-
conscious about her weight. *I guess all women are,* he
thought. He adored her body. It was covered with a

zillion freckles. Half of them were clustered on her chest in the valley between her breasts. There were so many concentrated there that it looked like one large freckle.

"You know that I don't like fighting with you," Howard said.

She pulled herself away from him and lit a cigarette.

There had been too much fighting lately. They both sensed that. Howard knew that living with him was no holiday, but she didn't help things run too smoothly, either.

Howard was a recovered alcoholic. He hadn't touched a drop in two years, since he first joined the Alcoholics Anonymous program. Mandy had been good for him — before *and* after. She'd never pushed him when he was a drunk. But if it hadn't been for her, he would never have stayed dry — he knew that much.

Even though he no longer drank, he still had an alcoholic's personality. The ups and the downs. The constantly shifting moods. They fought. They had fun. They brooded. They talked. The whole carousel ride. Round and round they went.

"You smoke too much," he told her.

"And you worry too much," she said.

"I don't know, Mandy," he sighed. "I don't know if I can do this."

"*Yeahhh . . .*" She exhaled a whole breath of smoke.

"It won't be easy."

"You don't have to do anything." She walked around to the other side of the bed and got under the covers.

"Don't be *that* way."

"What way?"

"Angry."

"I'm not angry, Howard."

"Yes, you are. I can tell. When you say: '*I'm not angry, Howard*' — you're angry." He got under the covers next to her. He put his hand under her nightgown and groped for her large breasts.

"I'm not in the mood," Mandy snapped.

"I'll try — okay?"

"Don't let me force anything on you, Howard."

"How is it that you always manage to turn the tables around whenever we get into an argument?"

"What do you mean?"

"I was pissed off with *you*, and you've managed to make *me* apologize for it."

"I didn't hear any apologies."

"You know what I mean."

She sat up and looked into his brown eyes. She brushed away his dirty blonde hair from his brow and smiled wryly. "You really don't have to do the tests. You're in the right. I'm sorry."

They kissed.

He lay flat on his back staring up at the ceiling. He followed the decorative molding with his eyes like it was a roadway. The geometric forms, the curves, the imperfections of its handmade craftsmanship. They don't do work like that anymore. And they certainly don't make apartments like this anymore either. It was old and charming. Sure, it was drafty in the winter — so they had to cuddle up closer to try to stay warm. He gave Mandy a sideways glance. Her eyes were closed. He wondered what had happened to them. The older this place got, the more charming it became. The older their marriage got, the broader their dissension became.

He always felt like she was using him. When all hell had broken loose with Tummy Savers, she wanted him to give her the inside scoop on the whole story. Hadn't she realized that he had certain responsibilities to his employers? They knew that she was a reporter — they would have known he gave her the facts if she had written the story. Yet when he'd refused to cooperate with her, she snubbed him for days. He was right, yet she'd made him feel guilty. It just wasn't fair. She was doing it again tonight. Of course, this was a different situation, he reasoned. He looked at her again before shutting off the light.

"I'll do it," he said.

"I had an inkling."

It was too dark for him to see her triumphant smile.

Although she was looking at a photo of Rick Marlowe, Mandy was thinking about her visit from Tommy and her subsequent discord with Howard. She had been working on the Rick Marlowe case before Tommy entered the picture.

Marlowe was a rock singer who had disappeared while flying over the Bermuda Triangle in a private jet. There had been no trace of him or the aircraft since. It had been an intriguing story before this dope-growing number broke her concentration.

It had been days since she'd heard from Tommy. She wondered how his brother was doing. Howard had yet to start testing the brown substance.

She took a deep drag on her cigarette and exhaled into Marlowe's photograph. He was dressed in tight leather pants and shirt. Black boots. His hair was long, dark, and combed straight back. It was still from his last album cover, *Victim*.

Marlowe was a ballad singer/songwriter, but he could never be accused of being a folk singer. A rocker to the bone. Hard, angry lyrics. Loud, angry music. His new album, *M.I.A.*, had been due to be released a week after his disappearance. The title was ironic: *Missing In Action*. It was so ironic that many cynics had begun to suspect the whole thing was a publicity stunt. But the distributor had yanked the album when it happened.

"Cronenberg!"

She heard the unmistakably "sweet" voice of her editor, Rob Manville, cry out behind her.

She ignored him.

"Cronenberg — get your ass in here!"

"Fuck off," she muttered as she got up and clenched her cigarette defiantly between her teeth.

Manville was standing by the door of his office. He was short, stout, and pushing forty, with thinning brown hair. He had an olive complexion and hard chiseled features. A real villainous type, her boss.

"Inside," he thumbed.

She sat down on the chair before his messy desk.

He went around his desk and stood there, staring deeply into her squinting eyes.

"You smoke too much," he said.

"That's what my husband tells me."

"Whaddaya got on the Marlowe story?"

"Nothing concrete," she admitted.

He nodded vigorously. "Nothing *concrete*."

"I'm working on an angle.

"Don't even have the angle yet."

"It's a tough nut, Rob."

"Uh-huh."

"I'm getting close."

"All I've seen you doing these last few days is moping around," he said. "You having problems at home?"

"No."

"You on the rag?"

She rolled her eyes. *"No."*

"Then what the hell's up, baby?" he asked.

"I have this *other* thing I'm working on," she retorted.

"What?"

"It's very interesting."

"Who cares, Mandy?"

"Hear me out."

"Did you happen to see *Rolling Stone* today? The cover story?" He picked up the magazine and threw it into her lap. "They're turning Marlowe into another Jim Morrison, for chrissakes, and you want an angle."

"Rob."

"Jim *fucking* Morrison — and you don't have an angle. So simple. Am I right?" he asked nastily.

"Rob."

"You're taking a little trip, Mandy," he said.

"Oh?" she asked, perplexed.

"Key West."

"What about it?"

"It's the place to go," he said.

"On vacation?" She beamed.

He threw his head back and scanned the ceiling. "GOD HELP ME! A *vacation?* That's what you've been on these last few days, hasn't it? You moan to me that I don't give you any feature stories, and what do you do when I throw one in your lap. Nothing." He pointed his finger at her. "I want your ass in Florida working on the Marlowe story P.D.Q."

"Florida?" She wrinkled her nose.

"Key West," Manville said. "The last place Marlowe was seen alive."

"My angle?"

"I'm sure it will come to you."

"This other thing . . ."

"There is no *other* thing until you hand over the Marlowe story."

"But time —"

"No buts!"

Mandy stood up and stamped out her cigarette in the ashtray on his desk. "No butts."

"I wish you would quit those things."

"It's just like working for you, Rob," she said as she was walking out of his office. "A *bad* habit."

chapter 3

She was standing inside the airport terminal. Long, stringy blonde hair hanging down to her bare shoulders. Indigo oval eyes scanning each new face in the oncoming crowd. She wore a blue halter top, tied at the waist, and a pair of denim cut-offs. She was tall and bone-thin, with small breasts and boyish hips. She looked more like a teenager than a mother of a six-year-old child. She certainly didn't look like a widow.

Debra Shepard was twenty-eight years old. And despite her fragile appearance, she was a gutsy woman. She had become hardened through the long and lean years with Elmore. It wasn't easy raising and harvesting marijuana. A great deal of detailed work was involved. Deb had pitched in the best she could. She'd become Elmore's right hand after Tommy split for school. Hell, Elmore couldn't do it all himself. He hired some help from time to time, but he could never really trust them. As soon as he turned his back, they would rob him blind.

She had been responsible for several of the patches.

Each worked their own patches individually. They had only pooled together during harvest time. But Elmore wasn't there to help her anymore. She had to face that fact. How could she do all that work by herself? She still had another half-dozen patches to harvest. She glanced down at her blistered and slashed hands. They were stiff and sore from stripping the branches. She scanned the crowd again and saw Tommy approaching her.

Tommy.

He appeared thinner. Almost gaunt. He was long-waisted like Elmore, his faded black Levi 501's hugging his slight hips loosely. A silver and turquoise western-style belt held them up. His lean, well-built torso was clad in a tight, gray muscle tee shirt. He carried a canvas roll bag on his shoulder.

"Deb!" he called out to her.

"Tommy." She embraced him.

"You look good."

"Yeah, considerin' I've been cryin' for hours." She forced a smile but her red, puffy eyes gave her away.

"Where's Sage?"

"Back home with a friend."

It was a long drive back to her home in Hammett. There were long periods of silence between them. It seemed too difficult to talk. Tommy didn't really know what to say or how to say it. Surely he was as grief-stricken as she, but that was all they seemed to have in common at the moment.

"Any news about Hinton?" Tommy asked.

"He died on the way."

"The sheriff know anything?"

She shook her head.

"He still think it has to do with dope?"

"Well, Elmore had a run last night," she related.

"Oh?"

"But it was with Al Romero — he's okay."

"Sure . . . known Al for many years."

"*But* . . . dope is dope," she stated wisely.

"And money is money." Tommy peered out the window. The scenery rushed by like it did on train rides. It seemed to be moving briskly yet in slow motion at the same time. Tommy felt that way now. He was neither here nor there.

"I told Sage," Deb announced as she dragged on a Marlboro. "Told him daddy went to heaven."

"How did he take it?"

"Just like a little boy should take it. Confused . . . tears. More confusion than sorrow. I think he only cried because I was hysterical."

"It will sink in," Tommy said.

She glanced over at him, her hands firmly gripping the steering wheel. "You seem pretty together."

"Should've seen me after your call. Matt and me, wailing like two kids."

"What seems strange to me," she sighed, "is that I was kinda separated from him for the past few weeks."

"How do you mean?" He eyed her.

"As though he was preparing me."

"I'm not following you." He shook his head.

"His sores and all. He wouldn't . . ." She had difficulty getting the words out. "He wouldn't *sleep* with me. I mean, like *really* sleep with me. And he wouldn't go near Sage. He slept out on the sofa."

"Yeah, he told me that," Tommy said. "Which reminds me, I still haven't heard from Mandy yet."

"Mandy?"

"Her husband is testing the brown sap Elmore found."

She asked cynically, "Why bother now?"

Tommy looked at her. Then it dawned on him. The brown stuff. Could that have been the reason for his murder? But why the other bar patrons? It didn't make sense.

Deb snapped her fingers before his face. "*Hey —* whaddaya thinkin' about?"

"Nothing."
"Must be some *serious* nothing."
"Could be," he muttered. "Could be."

The alarm sounded. Howard shot up and shut the damn thing off. He hated that noisy thing. He should buy himself a clock radio and wake up to Mozart. He glared over at the empty side of the bed where Mandy was supposed to be. He heard the shower.

Oh, yeah.

Off to the Sunshine State. How could he have forgotten? They had had another fight last night. He was tired of her goddamn road trips. Why couldn't she have a normal nine-to-five job like everyone else? *No,* she had to work for that sleazy rock-music rag. Record reviews weren't enough, *no,* they had to have exclusive news features.

Who the hell is Rick Marlowe, anyway? . . . And who cares?

Howard swung his feet out of bed and onto the carpeted floor. Rise and shine. He just loved to get up at six AM so he could commute to New Jersey from their Brooklyn Heights apartment. Yeah, that made his day. Stuck in traffic, sucking in exhaust fumes on a hot August day. *Beautiful.* It was amazing that it didn't drive him right back to the bottle.

He stretched out his arms as he yawned. He looked down at his pot belly with disgust. He reached down and squeezed the flab in between his fingers. *Going soft in your old age, pal.* He flashed back to when he was young — carefree and young. Not an ounce of body fat on him back then. He had been a doper living in an Avenue B walk-up, track marks up and down his arms. Then he'd wised up and traded the needle for the bottle. Hell, it was cheaper and it did the trick. It made him forget, made him feel better.

In fact, he'd forgotten whatever it was that he was supposed to forget. That was when he sobered up.

And Mandy. She was there. Always the observer. She'd smoked some dope, popped a few pills, even drank — but never once did she reach for the hypo. She'd just watched him. Always the reporter. And the constant queries. How did it feel? Why do you do it? Do you want to get married?''

And here we are.

Howard supposed he should be happy now. He had everything a person could ever want. A brownstone co-op apartment on Pierpont Street in a nice, fashionable neighborhood like Brooklyn Heights. An attractive, intelligent wife. He was off the sauce. He was only thirty-eight years old with a promising career. Good pay and benefits.

How come I'm so miserable?

Aren't I too young to be going through menopause? he wondered.

Time to go back into therapy, Howard decided.

Mandy came out of the bathroom wrapped in a towel. She was already buzzing. Howard wished he knew her secret formula for all that energy and enthusiasm. Maybe someday he'd discover it and dump this depression.

"Morning, babe." Mandy walked up to him and they embraced.

He held her tightly, his hands cupping her ass. "Hey, I didn't get *any* last night."

"Well, you were too busy brooding." She tried to pull herself away.

He peeled the towel off her and steered her toward the bed. They kissed, his hands feeling her sticky, wet skin. "I love you, Mandy."

"Couldn't tell that from last night."

"I'm sorry, but you know how I get about your road trips."

"Yeah, like a *baby*," she teased him.

"Come on, let's do *it*," he said, smiling.

"You have to go to work." She pushed him away.

"That can wait."

"I don't know." She smirked. "You still haven't tested that plant for me."

"I will, I promise. While you're away."

"Okay." She fell back on the bed. "Do *it* to me then." She closed her eyes and waited.

They both laughed.

It was an old farmhouse. Elmore had spent a fortune to have it refurbished. It was the finest home in all of Hammett. A huge, gray two-level house with four bedrooms, stone fireplaces, and hardwood floors and trim. There was a big barn out back; all set on ten acres of rustic land. It certainly was a big departure from their last residence — a trailer.

They pulled up to the house, and Tommy got out of the blue-and-silver 300ZX to meet Sage as he ran out the front door.

Tommy picked him up in his arms, and Sage covered his face with kisses.

"How's my big boy doing?"

It felt good to hold his small, warm body. It was strange to feel a human being so tiny and so very much alive in your arms. He was in love with the kid.

"Did you bring me anything, Uncle Tommy?" Sage asked.

"I didn't have time, kiddo. Soon as I heard, I hopped on the first plane down."

Deb came up behind them. "Leave your uncle alone, Sage."

"He's right — I should've brought him something."

"Too bad Daddy ain't here," Sage said with his mother's oval indigo eyes peering into Tommy's. "He's gone to heaven."

It still hadn't sunk in yet.

Tommy closed his eyes. He couldn't bear to look at the boy's face any longer. He put him down.

Deb stood in the doorway and glanced back at Tommy as Sage whipped by her.

They just stood there staring at one another.

Finally Deb broke the silence. "Welcome home."

Mandy entered the Montague Street storefront office of the *R & R Express*. She went to her desk in the poolroom that held eight desks in partitioned cubicles, or toilet stalls as the workers referred to them.

The place was buzzing. Cigarette smoke hovered above the cubicles like storm clouds. She was glad to be getting away from it for a while.

She had to make a few calls before her departure. One name was on the top of her list.

Tommy Shepard.

The phone rang three times before a voice answered. "Yeah?"

"Tommy?" she asked.

"Nope."

"This isn't Tommy Shepard's residence?"

"I didn't say that. I just said it wasn't Tommy."

Mandy took the phone away from her ear and glared at it. She got back on. "*Who* is this?"

"Who is *this*?" he asked.

"Mandy Cronenberg, *R & R Express.*"

"Oh yeah," he said.

"You know me?" she asked.

"Sure, I read you all the time," he said. "You're also doing a little favor for my roommate."

"Who's your roommate?"

"Tommy, of course."

"Well, I'm glad we got that settled," she huffed. "Is Tommy there?"

"No."

"Do you know when he'll be back?"

"Not really."

Mandy sighed impatiently.

"He went back home to Hammett."

"Oh?"

Matt cleared his throat and said, "Yeah, his brother died."

"His brother . . . *Elmore?"*

"That's right."

"From his sickness?"

"No, he was killed."

"Killed?" Mandy exclaimed.

"Yeah, like in *murder,"* Matt emphasized.

"Oh, my God."

"Yeah, the news hit us pretty bad."

Mandy churned it around her head for a while. "I wonder . . . do you have any idea who was responsible?"

"No. Tommy suspected it involved, you know, the drugs."

"Of course." Mandy felt dumb for even asking such an obvious question.

"But it hasn't been verified yet."

"Where is this Hammett?" she asked.

"It's really socked away in the middle of no-man's land. You fly to Jacksonville. It's a few hours' drive northwest from there. Road map should tell you."

"Do you have his phone number down there?"

He gave her the number, and after a few minutes of small talk, she hung up.

Just then, Manville popped his head in. "You still *here?"*

"I have to make a few calls."

"Make them *fast."*

"Yessum, boss." She bowed her head.

"And cut it with the wisecracks, already," Manville snapped, and left her cubicle.

She used the Watts line to call her parents back home in Toronto. Something told her that she wouldn't get a chance to drop them a line for quite some time.

chapter 4

When Tony asked Sheriff Higgins about the shooting, it conjured up thoughts he wished he could forget. But he knew he wouldn't forget . . . *couldn't* forget it, not ever. It would always be there.

Higgins had found Jake Hinton squirming on the floor behind the bar. The sheriff knelt down and asked the still-conscious bartender who had shot him. Hinton struggled some before he could get anything out. Higgins had to put his ear close to Hinton's mouth to hear him. And what he said didn't make much sense at all.

"Whaddaya sayin', Jake?" Higgins asked loudly as he leaned over him.

"*Nix—*" Hinton said.

"Huh? Try it again, Jake. Who shot ya up like this?"

"*—on.*"

"Can't make ya out, partner." Higgins held the dying man's head in his arms. Hinton's good eye was open. A black hole filled his other socket.

"Nix . . . *on.*"

"Nixon?"

"*Nixon?*" Tommy interrupted Higgins' story.

"Yeah, Nixon."

"Nixon who?"

"*The* Nixon, I think."

"The Watergate Nixon?"

"Richard Milhouse himself."

Tommy stared in disbelief at Higgins. "I really don't think he's deteriorated that much that he had to resort to become a hit man, for chrissakes."

"That's what he said and *all* he said. You must understand, poor Jake wasn't all there. He did have a bad eye and all. Maybe this guy *looked* like Nixon."

"Is that *all* you got going on this case?"

"What can I tell you?" Higgins glared at him. *Son of a bitch.*

"Maybe it sounded like Nixon. Nixon — Nixon." Tommy kicked it around inside his head.

Higgins rolled his eyes. College boy from the big city playing detective — *give me a break.*

"Nix. Nick. Nick—son." Tommy persisted with his phonetic theory. "Maybe . . . *Yeah.*"

"Whaddaya got?"

"Maybe he meant *Nick's son,*" Tommy said.

"Nick's son?"

"Yeah, Nick Hill's son, Sam."

"Hey, now hold on there, Tommy." Higgins gave him a sideways glance.

"You know the Hills never got along with us."

"You're just taking a shot in the dark, pal."

"That's more than what *you* got going," Tommy said.

"*No*body living here in Hammett would do such a thing," Higgins declared.

"Why not?"

"Because only animals could do such a thing and we don't have any animals living here in Hammett."

"How can you be so sure?" Tommy asked.

Higgins was losing his patience. This case was going to be hard enough without a smart-ass guy running around making unfounded accusations. "Listen up, Tommy, I'm the law in this town. I don't need any *outsiders* intruding into our business."

"Outsiders?" Tommy ground his teeth in anger. "Who's an outsider? I lived in this town. My brother was murdered in this town."

"You might've lived here *once,* but you ain't one of us anymore. You all change after you leave here. Get all smartened up, then you come back and try to tell us how to run our town. Well, back off, pal," Higgins said, his blood pressure soaring.

"Hey — what is *this*? We're practically family, man. We always took care of you . . . one another. And where the fuck did you come from . . . *Dallas*?" Tommy asked angrily.

"Try Santa Fe."

"You were a cop out there?"

"Process server," Higgins related.

"Oh, yeah."

Higgins took a deep breath. "Listen, Tommy, I'm sorry. I've been up all night and day. I'm bushed."

"I understand."

"But this Hill nonsense — that's all it is — *nonsense.*" Tommy nodded.

"You knew what your brother was involved with. We both knew. It's a dangerous game. There're no winners in that line of work."

"I know," Tommy sighed.

"Listen — I have to ask you to do something for me. I really hate to ask you. I need you to identify the body . . . *Elmore.* I didn't have the heart to ask Deb. Jesus, it's a mess. Makes me believe the killers were mainly after Elmore." Higgins shook his head.

"Why is that?"

Tommy had his answer when Higgins showed him the

body in the back room. Doc Crichton was beside it. H°
was a small, slightly hunched man with thinning gray hair
and bushy eyebrows. The other bodies were in body bags
lined up on the floor. Elmore's body was up on the table.

"This is not the ideal setup for an autopsy, but what
can you do?" Crichton apologized. "I have a medical
examiner coming up from Jacksonville any minute now."

Tommy looked at the body on the table. He recognized
the leather jacket and pants. They were Elmore's, for
sure. But the face. There wasn't any.

"I—I—I *guess* it's him," Tommy stammered.

"It seems they went out of their way to make sure he
was good and dead," Higgins said.

"Looks like a shotgun blast," Crichton said, his hazel
eyes peeking above the rims of his glasses.

"*Two* charges." Higgins shook his head. "They meant
business."

Tommy walked out of the room, through the small jail-
block section, and into Higgins' front office. He stood
before the window, looking out on Main Street. There
were some people across the street at the market.

He heard Higgins behind him.

"Sorry about that, Tommy," Higgins said. "That's
never easy. Why, in the big cities, they have video
monitors for identification. A lot easier that way."

"You said *killers.*"

"That's right," Higgins said as he sat down behind his
desk.

"More than one?" Tommy asked.

"For sure."

Tommy turned around. "Why?"

"There was a machine gun of some kind and the
shotgun. The driver. That makes at least three men,"
Higgins speculated.

"Any witnesses?"

Higgins shook his head. "I heard it . . . woke up the
whole damn town."

"How did they get away without anyone seeing them?"
Higgins shrugged. "I heard a car . . ."
"You didn't go after them?" Tommy asked accusingly.
"I was asleep . . . the racket woke me up. Wasn't any
time. To tell you the God honest truth, I was all shook
up. When I opened the door to Jake's place. *Jesus*. A
real mess." He covered his face with his hands.
"Can I see it?"
"The bar?" Higgins' eyes peeked through his fingers.
Tommy nodded.
"Suppose it wouldn't hurt."
"Let's go then," Tommy said.

It was evening by the time Tommy arrived home. Higgins had been right — it was a mess. The bar had been
torn apart. Blood everywhere. Tommy had never seen
anything like it.

Deb was busy in the kitchen preparing dinner. Tommy
went into the living room and stood by the fireplace.
There was a framed photograph of Elmore and Tommy,
posing with bows and their game trophies, on the
mantelpiece. It was from eight years back. He grinned.

He had had some great times with his brother. They'd
enjoyed hunting and fishing and knocking off some beers
at Jake's. He reached out and touched Elmore's image
with his fingers. The glass smeared at his touch. Now
Elmore's face was all smudgy.

The thought that the Hills might be involved in all this
made Tommy's blood boil. He wouldn't put it past them.
Damn hillbillies. Should've stayed out of the business.
Sam Hill, the oldest boy, had had a mean streak in him
ever since Tommy had a run-in with him a while back.
It had been just before Tommy went off to school. He
had still been helping Elmore out with the crops. Tommy
was standing guard at one of the larger patches. It was
just after midnight. A hot, muggy mid-August night. He
sat by a tree dressed in his camouflaged fatigues, an M-16

in his arms. It was a clear moonlit evening. His face
chalked with coal to eliminate the glare. He heard some
movement in the bush. Footsteps. The sound of a
machete clearing vegetation. He stood up and leaned
against the tree, the automatic weapon positioned in his
arms.

The rocky beam from a flashlight streaked out of the
thick bush. He could make out two human forms through
the sights of his rifle. They came out into the clearing,
the brightness of the moon washing them in a blue hue.
Tommy recognized Hill and his son Sam. Both carried
shotguns.

"FREEZE!" Tommy yelled out.

The two men stopped and brought their guns up.

Tommy sprayed the ground before them with rapid
gunfire, and they hit the dirt.

"I told you to freeze, motherfuckers!" Tommy
shouted. "Now throw out your weapons."

The Hills were on their bellies, their faces and clothes
covered with dust.

Silence.

"DO IT — NOW!"

The elder Hill threw out his shotgun. "There you go,
boy!"

"Now you, Sam!" Tommy commanded.

"UP YOURS!" Sam fired a charge that took a chunk
out of the tree beside Tommy. He rolled into some bush
and squeezed off another round.

Tommy fell to his knees and covered the area with
machine-gun fire.

A dust cloud hung in the air after the short, violent
exchange. Tommy had difficulty with visibility. Before
the air cleared, a loud shriek filled his ears. It came from
the right of him. Tommy advanced cautiously through
the darkness. The painful cries continued as he inched
forward. He found Sam Hill by some trees, his hands

covering his bloody face. His shotgun lay on the ground
by his feet.

Sam had walked right into one of Elmore's booby
traps. He had suspended a fishhook at eye level between
two trees to protect his patch. It was something he had
picked up from the Vietcong.

Tommy came up to him, gun in hand.

Nick Hill followed him. Tommy twisted around and
watched the man run to his wounded son.

"What in hell?!" He pushed his son's hands away from
his face and saw the fishhook embedded in his left eye.
"Keep your hands away — I'll get it out."

"IT FUCKIN' HURTS!" The young man shouted out,
his voice echoing in the night air.

His father removed the fishhook. Sam collapsed to the
ground.

Hill faced Tommy with the hook in his hand. "GOD-
DAMN YOU AND YOUR BROTHER!" He charged
toward Tommy in a blind rage.

Before he made contact, Tommy brought the butt of
his rifle down on Hill's head in a quick sweeping action,
and the man dropped instantly.

Tommy walked over to the suffering son and removed
the shotgun from his reach. Sam glared up at him with
his one good eye. "What did you do to my daddy?"

"He's taking a nap."

"My eye — I can't see!"

"What are you boys doing around here?"

"Whaddaya think?" Sam barked.

Tommy clucked his tongue. "Ain't any of you dumb
rednecks ever going to learn?"

"We're no more redneck than you and Elmore."

"Maybe, but at least we got brains," Tommy chuckled.
"Now get to your feet and shove off."

"I'm blind!"

"That's not all you're going to be if you don't get

moving," Tommy said through clenched teeth.

He got to his feet. His face was red with blood.

"Better get yourself to Doc Crichton something fierce, Sam."

He held his eye. "I'm going to get you for this, Tommy Shepard," he threatened.

Tommy nodded. "That'll be the day."

Deb eyed Tommy as he leaned against the refrigerator drinking a bottle of Coke. He was very quiet. Pre-occupied. He had told her about his suspicions regarding the Hills and just dropped it. She'd wanted to talk it out with him — to have him wait until after Elmore's burial before he went on with his investigation. But he'd tuned her out the same way Elmore did. Sometimes it just made her want to scream

"Higs told you to stay out of it," Deb finally said.

"I still have to check things out," Tommy said.

Deb got up and moved toward him. "I know what you're feeling, Tommy," she said. "I'm hurtin', too. But don't do anything stupid. Let it sit a spell. We have to bury Elmore and harvest the rest of the crop."

"The *rest* of the crop?"

"Yeah, we have six more patches to clear."

"Damn." Tommy shook his head.

She reached up and rubbed his bristled face. "You *are* going to help me and Sage out . . ."

Tommy took in her sweet face. "Of course, Deb."

"I can't do it without you, Tommy."

"I know." He smiled.

She had always like Elmore's baby brother. They were similar in many ways. But the two didn't look anything like one another. Tommy was fair and blond; Elmore was dark. They said Tommy took after the mother; Elmore, his father. Deb couldn't say because she had never set eyes on their folks. They were long dead by the time she had come into the picture. "Why don't you sit down and eat some supper?"

"I can't eat . . . lost my appetite or something." Tommy gulped down his soft drink.

"How was it in the big city?"

Tommy shrugged. "It was okay."

"You never seemed too happy up north."

"Just felt out of place. You know how it is."

"You were homesick," Debbie said.

"Something like that." He nodded.

"Did you have a girl?"

Tommy grinned and shook his head.

"How come?"

"I don't know — just didn't happen."

"You're pretty enough." Deb smiled.

Tommy laughed.

"You going to stick around?"

He nodded. "Sure."

"Don't you wanna finish school?"

"Enough already with the third degree." Tommy dumped the bottle into the trash and started to wash his hands when the phone rang.

Deb rushed to answer the wall phone by the doorway. "Shepard residence."

She eyed Tommy as she listened. "Who's calling, please?" She strained to hear. *"Who?"*

She held the receiver out to Tommy. "For you."

"Who is it?"

"Mandy Cronenberg," she said.

Tommy took the phone. "Hello?"

"Hello, Tommy?"

"Yeah."

"This is Mandy. How are you?"

"Not too good," Tommy said.

"I know, your roommate told me the news," she related. "I'm here in Florida."

"Florida?" Tommy was surprised to hear that.

"In Miami. That article I'm doing on Rick Marlowe.
I think I told you about it."

"Yeah."

"I'm sorry, Tommy."

"Uh-huh."

"Listen, I hope I'm not calling at a bad time."

"As a matter of fact . . ."

"I'm still interested in that story about Hammett,"
Mandy said enthusiastically.

"Well, I guess our deal is off."

"*Off?*" She raised her voice.

"With Elmore dead and all."

"There're other growers there . . ."

"I really don't feel like talking," Tommy said in a
barely audible voice, his energy drained.

Mandy took a long pause to think. "My husband is
testing that sample you gave me right at this moment."

"What difference does it make now?" Tommy asked
apathetically.

"I know you're down, Tommy. But try to think.
There's still something going on there. Maybe your
brother's death had something to do with that sap."

Tommy butted his head against the wall. "I don't
know, Mandy. I think maybe the local farmers had
something to do with it. I mean, this is a competitive
racket y'know."

"I understand that. But what about that sap?"

Tommy exhaled loudly. "I'm having problems thinking about anything right now — okay?"

"Fine. I'll call you when I get the results from my husband. Maybe by that time you'll be in a better frame of
mind," she said.

"Sure . . . do that," Tommy said.

"Again, you have my sympathy."

"Thank you."

"Take care of yourself, Tommy," she said sincerely.

"Goodbye." He hung up.

Deb was behind him waiting to hear an explanation. "What did she want?"

"Nothing."

"You sure have a whole slew of nothings," Debbie snapped.

Tommy eyed her.

"Is she gonna write about us . . . about *Elmore*?" she asked accusingly.

"No."

"Then what does she want?"

"Just wanted to give me her condolences."

Deb didn't buy it. "Sometimes you're just like Elmore."

"How's that?"

"The way you keep things inside you."

Tommy glanced away from her intense gaze. "Can I borrow your car? I want to run over and have a little chat with Nick Hill."

"You should stay clear of him."

"I can handle myself."

"That's what Elmore always said." She dug into her tight pockets and produced the key ring.

Tommy took the keys from her hand. "Why don't you take it easy . . . it's been a long day for us all."

Tommy turned to leave but halted when he got to the door.

"Forget somethin'?" she asked.

"I was meaning to ask you about something." Tommy faced her. "Elmore was dressed in his skins."

"Yeah?"

"In the middle of Indian summer?"

"It was a rainy night."

"But *still* . . ."

"He had the chills . . . those sores . . . his sickness," she related, shivering from the thought.

"How bad was he?"

"He looked horrible . . . in pain. You knew Elmore.

He wouldn't go see a doctor." Deb looked away. She knew Elmore was gone, but she just couldn't grasp it. She kept expecting him to walk in any second with that broad smile on his face. "I can't believe he's dead, Tommy."

He went up to her and tried to hold her, but she pushed him away.

"It's just not fair." She glanced up at Tommy with her raw eyes.

"It never is . . . " Tommy said as she ran from the kitchen. "Deb." She was gone. He wanted to tell her: *I feel it, too*. It felt like someone was squeezing his heart and wouldn't let up.

He knew the pain wouldn't go away until he found Elmore's killers.

chapter 5

Higgins sat before Mayor Carpenter in his storefront office on Main Street. It was a modest office, considering Carpenter's wealth. Decorated with colonial furniture, it reeked of Americana.

Talking with Carpenter made Higgins recall his arrival in Hammett. He had been a process server from Santa Fe. Damned good one, too. Mostly divorce papers. But then he had gotten a call from the District Attorney to serve papers on George Carpenter, a local rancher. It had been a subpoena to appear in court as a federal witness in a large-scale horse-rustling scam. Carpenter had sold his land and stock and taken off. Higgins had tracked him down to Hammett. Before Higgins had a chance to serve him the papers, Carpenter offered him a full-time job as Hammett's sheriff. Higgins had agreed, returning the papers to the District Attorney, saying Carpenter was nowhere to be found. Subsequently, the investigation had been dropped. That was fifteen years ago.

"What can I do for you, Higs?" Carpenter asked as

he folded his hands on top of his huge desk.

Higgins eyed the balding, white-haired man. He had a pink complexion and a purple-veined nose — he obviously liked his hooch. "It's Tommy Shepard."

"Yes?"

"He's nosey."

"As I suspected," Carpenter said.

"He thinks the Hills are involved."

"Is that feud still going on?" Carpenter sighed.

"You know these hillbillies."

"Can you keep him in line?"

"I don't know."

"Yes, you do." Carpenter smiled.

"I don't want him to get hurt," Higgins said.

"Don't worry about Tommy Shepard. I have everything under control." Carpenter smiled again. That smile reminded Higgins how much he really hated Carpenter. A real coldhearted bastard.

"I don't blame him none . . . you should see Elmore's body."

"Please, Higs, spare me the details." Carpenter made a face.

"It's not a very pretty picture."

"It's unfortunate what happened." Carpenter put his folded hands in back of his head and sat back in his wooden chair. "I'm trying my damnedest to keep the feds outta this town."

"They could help us with our investigation," Higgins said.

Carpenter shook his head. "This is *our* problem. We have it under control. Understand, Higs?"

Higgins stood up. "How is it that I feel you know more about this than you're tellin' me?"

The smile again. Almost a shit-eating grin. "Just go on with your work, Higs."

"There's a lot of grief-stricken people out there who want answers."

"And they'll get answers."

"Without the feds helping us?"

"Have you any idea what the feds will think of our little town, dear boy?" Carpenter asked. "Come on, Higs, even *you* have something to worry about."

Higgins picked his head up and gazed at Carpenter sternly. "You know, I'm tired of playin' your puppy dog, Carpenter."

"Have a nice evening, *Higs*." Carpenter wasn't smiling anymore.

Tommy drove up to the Hill home. It was a split-level with work shacks built onto the sides and back of the structure. He turned off the ignition and stepped out of the 300ZX. He walked quietly up to the front screen door. On the roof he noticed someone with a shotgun. The Hills were the only pot growers he knew who had their patches on their own property. They were either very brave or very stupid. Tommy voted for the latter.

He knocked softly on the wooden frame.

A few moments later, a face appeared behind the screen. A man's face. The wire mesh of the screen softened his features. He was a big man. White, bushy hair and mustache. Gray eyes. A cleft chin. Burly. A dim light from inside created an aura around his body. He looked like he was glowing from within.

"Hey, Nick." Tommy smiled.

"What can I do for you?" The voice sounded as rough as gravel.

"Can I come in?"

No answer. Just steady, heavy breathing.

"I guess you heard about the shooting . . . about my brother?"

Hill scratched his back and yawned.

"Before Jake Hinton died . . . he named your son his killer." *There*. Tommy didn't want to say it, but he needed some kind of reaction.

"What're you tellin' me, boy?"

"I just want to talk with you a bit."

"Why, you're Elmore Shepard's baby brother, ain't ya?"

"Yeah, who did you think?"

"I'm surprised I didn't smell you comin', boy. Must be that city livin' cleaned you up some." He cackled like a hyena.

"I didn't come here to be insulted."

"Then *why* did you come here?" His eyes turned to slits as he stared down at Tommy.

"All I want to do is talk."

"Well, that's all you've been doin', boy."

"About the shooting," Tommy specified.

"I wasn't there," he said as he threw his broad shoulders back.

"And Sam?"

"He was home in bed . . . sleepin'," Hill related.

"Do you have any idea who might've done it?" Tommy was trying to remain patient.

"Your brother ran with a wild pack."

"What are you talking about?"

"He was no angel and you know it," Hill said arrogantly.

"And what about your little operation, Mr. Hill?"

"Wasn't as big as Elmore's."

"That really bothered you, didn't it?" Tommy sneered.

"Never really gave a damn."

"Bullshit. You did everything you could to make life miserable for Elmore."

"I don't know what you're referrin' to, boy!" Hill shouted.

"How is it that I think you're responsible for the shooting?" Tommy said accusingly.

Blood rushed angrily to Hill's face as he raised his hand and glanced at his watch. "You got a minute to get the hell off my property!"

"You can't just ignore me, Hill."

"Fifty seconds."

"You're being very unreasonable."

"You had me guilty before you got here, boy — who's bein' unreasonable?" he snapped.

"I apologize for that."

"Twenty-five seconds."

"You haven't heard the end of this, Hill."

"Fifteen seconds."

Tommy ran back to the car. He turned around. Hill was gone. He got into the car and started it. He gazed back at the doorway.

Hill stood there, a shotgun cradled in his hands. Above him on the roof stood his one-eyed son, Sam, taking aim.

"Shit!" Tommy gunned the car and burned rubber as he made a run for it.

Sharp and Red were both dressed in dark clothes as they squatted down in the bushes just outside of Hill's property. Red, his face covered with charcoal, took in the small, plastic-windowed shacks attached to the main house. Inside each man-made greenhouse were over one hundred marijuana plants.

"We takin' 'em all out?" Red asked.

"Naw — just one. That big mother just in back," Sharp said as he focused on the larger shack attached directly to the rear of the house. He shifted his gaze upward to the sole figure sitting on the roof, his legs dangling off the gutter pipe. "Must be the son."

"How're we goin' to handle him?"

"We're not touchin' him unless we have to. In a few minutes, the Kid's goin' to keep him busy. Then you're runnin' over there and settin' the blaze."

Red wrinkled his nose. "Can't we just chuck a grenade or somethin'?"

Sharp glared at Red and clucked his tongue. "We got to make it look like that Shepard guy did it. Now, what the hell would a hillbilly be doin' with a fuckin' grenade, Red?''

"I just thought it would be easier," Red said.

"Yeah, you just thought. Well, leave the thinkin' to me, okay, pal?''

"Sure."

Sharp rolled his eyes. He couldn't believe the assholes they stuck him with on this job. Un*fucking*professional.

They watched as Sam Hill stood up and jolted across the roof to the front of the house.

Sharp put his hand on Red's shoulder. "Let's do it."

Nick Hill was rubbing some witch hazel into his skin. Goddamn mosquito bites! It looked like he'd fallen into a whole nest of them. The unbearable itching had awoken him during the night. He got up and went into the bathroom. His heart had almost stopped when he caught sight of himself in the mirror. He was completely covered with open sores.

The alcohol seemed to be doing the trick when he heard his son's irate voice call from downstairs.

"PA!"

Hill ran to the top of the stairs. His son Sam was at the landing.

"A FIRE OUT BACK — ONE OF THE PATCHES!"

A fire . . . one of the patches? Hill absorbed the information slowly. He was still half asleep. Then it sunk in.

That meant over two hundred thousand dollars of marijuana up in smoke!

Hill pulled on a pair of pants and ran down the stairs to help his son. The heat from the blaze made his eyes tear.

How did this happen? *Who* would have done such a thing?

Who?

Then it dawned on him.

Tommy Shepard.

He was responsible. What was it that he'd said: *"You haven't heard the last of this, Hill."* The words echoed inside his skull.

Tommy will be joining his older brother, thought Hill, *real soon.*

chapter 6

Hank Pope, forty-five with small, thick features, thought about the Watergate scandal as he waited for his appointment at the Watergate Hotel. He stood by the water fountain in the courtyard of the hotel complex. It was a dog day for October in the nation's capital — the humidity was unbearable. They were in the midst of a heat wave.

Born and raised in West Virginia, Pope had been groomed for a political career by his multimillionaire father. But after Pope's decorated military service, he'd opted for the intelligence field instead. His father, distressed over his decision, had disowned him. Later, when Pope had risen to the rank of C.I.A. Deputy Director, his father forgave him and had begun to mastermind a political stratagem for his future. He'd promised to support him financially. However, the seventy-five-year-old Pope, Senior, had died before he could alter his will in his son's favor. Another blow struck when Pope had been ousted by the then Democratic administration.

Pope, bitter over losing both his inheritance and intelligence stronghold, had fallen into a deep depression. Breaking up with his wife, he'd begun to drink heavily. Then a crack of sunlight had appeared on the horizon when the Republicans returned to power. Pope had gotten a chance to speak with the new President at a cocktail party. Pope had told the President what he thought would be a good attack plan for cracking down on drugs. The President had liked his ideas. It wasn't long after that that the President named Pope head of his anti-drug program. The campaign was code named *Grim Reaper*.

But the time between his two appointments had changed the man. Fearful that he might lose favor with the administration again, he'd built an impregnable wall of defense around himself.

Now Pope was feared by his peers and was known for his stubborn, ruthless manner. He also liked to fight dirty — an attribute that seemed to come easily to most government officials.

"Even the fountain doesn't offer relief for this *fuckin'* heat."

Pope turned to face the nasal voice. It was Ron Sharp. *Sharp.*

Pope had to laugh. What a name for such a dimwit. But men like Sharp were useful to him. They usually possessed the workingman's pride and were loyal to their employers. Loyalty was most important. That's why Pope never worked with blacks. They weren't trustworthy. They would sell out to save their own asses. Some might think they were bright for doing this. Maybe so, but brains were the last thing Pope was looking for. The dumber the better.

In that regard, Sharp was perfect. He was good at what he did, but he must have played too much football without a helmet.

The two men shook hands.

Sharp peeled off his khaki safari jacket and folded it over his arm. Sweat rings darkened the armpits of his yellow Izod shirt. His bulging belly hid the brass belt buckle that held up his khaki trousers.

Sharp eyed Pope, dressed in his conservative gray pinstripe suit and burgundy tie, and shook his head. "How can you *stand* this heat, man? Even my shirt's alligator is dying from thirst."

"The heat doesn't get to me," Pope said coolly.

The two men began to walk past the many expensive boutiques.

"Tell me something, Mr. Pope," Sharp said.

"Yes?"

"I mean — the Watergate Hotel?"

Pope smirked. "It's the last place I expect to bump into a Republican colleague."

Sharp howled over that one.

"How's the weather in Hammett?" Pope asked.

"Hot. *Real* hot," Sharp hissed.

They both sat down on a bench.

"I hope you're handling things well?"

Sharp grinned ear to ear. "Like I told you, Mr. Pope, I'm a pro."

"Good . . . good." Pope nodded and sucked in his cheeks. He ran a hand through his dark brown hair, keeping a stern eye on Sharp all the while. "Think the weather will change down there now?"

"A cool wave coming through today."

"Everything go according to *my* plan?"

"Without a hitch," Sharp said.

"You do fine work, Sharp. I appreciate that. It's time for you to handle another situation for me in New York. Take one of your boys with you."

"What about Hammett?"

"You're through there," Pope said as he slipped a thick envelope into Sharp's hand. He stood up.

"Does that cover everythin'?" Sharp asked.

"Everything that concerns *you*." Pope dismissed him with a sardonic grin.

Higgins drove the patrol car on the two-lane blacktop
road that led to Elmore's property. He guessed he
couldn't really refer to it as *Elmore's* any longer. He had
always like Elmore Shepard and his family — though it
was he who had brought the marijuana-growing business
to this neck of the woods. Life in Hammett was never
the same after that. Once a sleepy hillbilly town, as soon
as Elmore had returned from Nam and begun cultivating
his land for marijuana plants, a dark element seeped into
Hammett. The mob from Miami had begun migrating
to the local territory. They had financed some of
Hammett's depressed farmers. Men who had been
desperate enough to do *anything* to keep their farms and
equipment going before the banks foreclosed on them.
In that way, the illegal weed was a godsend for most of
the townspeople. It sure helped Higgins out. His salary
as sheriff was pitiful next to the riches bestowed upon
him by the farmers to turn the other way. Carpenter and
Higgins offered more services to the bandit farmers. Like
tipping them off whenever the feds came to town. Or
acting as mediators between rival farmers, as during the
ongoing Hill-and-Shepard feud. He wondered if that was
ever going to cease. He was on his way now to pick up
Tommy Shepard because Nick Hill claimed he set fire to
one of his patches.

Higgins rolled his eyes. He knew he couldn't arrest
Tommy . . . in the *legal* sense. He would just throw him
in a cell and keep him there for a while until the Hills
cooled off. It was really for his own protection. The Hills
were so peeved they might even blow him away.

Higgins recalled the first time he had Tommy picked
up. It was quite a few years ago. Higgins had only been
a sheriff for a few months at that time. Carpenter had
called him into his office and demanded that he track
down the hoodlums who stole his brand-new Lincoln
Continental. After talking with a few classmates at the
local high school, Higgins had found out that Tommy

Shepard and one of his buddies were responsible. Higgins had found them some hours later passed out in the car on a deserted road. They had knocked off a bottle of Jim Beam together. So Higgins had rounded them up and plopped them behind bars. No formal charges were filed because the automobile had not been damaged, but Higs wanted them to learn a lesson. Tommy had gotten his ass chewed off by Elmore when he came to the jail to claim him. But Higgins had always wondered where those two boys ever learned how to hot-wire a car . . .

When he saw the Shepard home up ahead, he cleared his head. He had a job to do. He was here to lock up Tommy. Carpenter had given him a direct order: "Cage Shepard before he causes any more problems!"

And this time, Elmore wouldn't be there to bail him out.

Howard Cronenberg wasn't too happy about staying late at the office. That meant he would have to find a later A.A. meeting somewhere. But Mandy had insisted that he do the tests. The sooner he started, the sooner he would be finished with the whole affair. He didn't like when she got involved with cases like this. Illegal drugs. One time, it had been a story on cocaine abuse at the recording studios. What the hell would be next?

He examined the brown substance under the microscope. It had similar properties to a toxic poison. Maybe it was a new insecticide or weed killer. But it was different from anything he had encountered before. That meant it would take longer to break down the ingredients.

Since it had been found on a marijuana plant, then it *must* be a herbicide. Like paraquat. But it wasn't anything like that.

He wished he knew more about the subject.

That was when he decided to test it on a live specimen.

He injected the chemical compound into a white mouse. It had no initial reaction. He put the mouse away

and tagged the cage: *Project R.M.* for Reefer Madness.
He laughed at his own silly joke but still felt uneasy about
it. He hoped no one would notice it. They had thousands
of projects under way at the moment.

Howard decided to call it a night. Now, where was that
meeting . . . ?

Tommy was on his way back from harvesting some crops
when he spotted Higgins' car parked outside of Deb's
house. He wondered if Higgins had found out anything.
Tommy sprang from the car and ran up to the front door.
Deb was there before he could get the door open.

The expression on her face should have tipped him off.

"Hey, Deb, what's up?" Tommy went past her and
saw Higgins standing in the living room, his hands on
his hips.

"What's doing, Higs?" Tommy smiled.

"Tommy," Higgins sighed, "you have to come with
me."

Tommy looked at Deb, then back at Higgins. "What
happened?"

"Oh, some bum rap Higs is trying to hang on you,"
Deb snapped.

"Nick Hill has accused you of setting a fire up at his
place," Higgins spelled out.

"A *fire*? What fire?" Tommy was perplexed.

"Out back of his house."

"One of his *patches*." Deb added.

"So?" Tommy asked. "What's that got to do with
me?"

"He tells me you two had a run-in last night *before*
the fire."

"We didn't have a run-in. The son of a bitch shoved
me off his property with a goddamn shotgun," Tommy
related.

"Well, he figures you might've gotten pissed and set
the fire."

"*Bull*shit," Tommy said angrily.

"What can I do, Tommy? I told you to keep out of this."

"How can you arrest me for setting a fire *without* evidence and let him get away with growing marijuana — now tell me that, Higs?"

"Come on, Tommy, give me a break."

"Well, fuck you, man!" Tommy backed away. "What the hell gives here? I think all your priorities are screwed up, cowboy. What is it — is Hill paying you more than Elmore did or something?"

Higgins leaned heavily on one foot scanning the ceiling. "You're trying my patience, pal."

"I'm not going anywhere without a lawyer," Tommy said.

Higgins glared at him through angry slits that used to be eyes. "Then I'll carry you over my back, son."

"Deb, call our lawyer."

"*Move it,*" Higgins snapped.

"I'm going to nail your ass to the wall, Higgins," Tommy threatened.

"I'm only doin' my job, Tommy."

"Come off it, man. If you ever did your job you would have to lock up this whole fucking town, including yourself."

Higgins nodded and grinned. "Come on, it will only be for a few days. It'll cool you off."

"I have a funeral to go to. *Several* funerals in fact."

"Don't worry. You can go to your brother's funeral."

"What about my brother's murderers?"

"I'm doin' my best."

"Well, obviously your best *sucks*," Tommy snapped.

Higgins eyed Debra. "Your brother-in-law has a pretty mouth, Deb. A mouth that could get him in a slew of trouble. Trouble even a smart lawyer won't be able to get him out of."

They walked outside to Higgins' squad car.

"I'm sorry about this, Tommy," Higgins said. "I really am. I could've put cuffs on you. Could've come with my deputy and broke a few bones along the way."

"Gee, I'm glad you're on my side then," Tommy said sarcastically.

"Keep cool." Higgins opened the door for Tommy.

"Tommy!" Deb cried out and ran over to him. "I'll call the lawyer. Take care, okay?" She kissed him.

"Take care of Sage."

"Uh-huh."

Tommy got into the car. Higgins walked around the car and peered at Deb across the roof. "Don't you worry none, Deb. I'll take good care of him." Higgins winked.

"You bet your ass you will, Higs. Lay one finger on him and you'll have to answer to me," she threatened.

Higs saw the fury in her eyes. He knew her well enough to know that she would back up that claim. He got into the car and drove off.

Deb watched them go. She had a bad feeling about this. A bad feeling deep inside her. There was something very wrong here. She had already lost somebody close to her — she didn't want to lose someone else.

chapter 7

Mandy had to admit that it felt good to be away. Away
from home. Away from the office. And *especially* away
from Howard. Their constant battles were driving her
crazy. Howard was a dry drunk and they're the *worst,*
Mandy thought.

She felt guilty about her feelings. She knew she should
be happy that Howard hadn't had a drop in years. It
proved he was a lot stronger than she thought. But she
missed their earlier years . . . the crazy times. He had
been so much fun to be with. The parties. The laughs.
They had lived like bohemians in the East Village. It was
the early seventies, and the hippie movement was in full
swing. The *R & R Express* had been a tiny, nothing
countercultural tabloid with zip circulation. But the old
gang had been fun. They smoked dope to the rock music
constantly blasting away in the old St. Mark's Place
storefront office. The whole scene had been such a departure from her bland Toronto upbringing. *Yeah,* Mandy
remembered those days well.

And now it was over.

The music had died.

And Mandy was sad.

She was lying on the bed in her plush Biscayne Boulevard hotel room in Miami. The price was high, so Manville would be giving her hell over the bill. The room was decorated in shades of blue. Dark blue carpeting, light blue accessories. The walls were sky blue. There was a terrace with a breathtaking ocean view. *More* blue.

Blue. Blue. Blue. All this blue was giving her the blues.

That Hammett story was taking up most of her concentration. It fascinated her. There was a whole subculture out there she knew nothing about. She was really hot to write a series of articles on it . . . maybe a book. She hoped Tommy could set up something for her.

Tommy.

She had to lean on him. Make him give in. She knew he was going through a rough time right now, but he would snap out of it. As soon as she relayed Howard's findings on that sap to him, he would be obliged to fulfill their deal.

In the meantime, how the hell was she going to convince old sourpuss Manville that there was a story in Hammett?

She stopped off in Miami before her trip to Key West, because she wanted to meet with an old friend, David King. Former member of the old gang. He had been a reporter for the *R & R Express* before moving down here to join a local paper, the *Miami Tribune.*

She hadn't seen him in five years.

She met him in the lobby of her hotel. He appeared older. He had gained a great deal of weight. His hair was dark brown and cut very short. He wore wire-rimmed glasses that hid nervous brown eyes. He seemed taller than she'd remembered. Well over six feet. And with the added weight, he seemed even larger.

"Mandy." He hugged her affectionately in his huge arms.

"It has been *too* long."

King stepped back to look at her. She was dressed in a pink sundress. Her skin was so white and freckled, it startled him. "Jesus, I haven't seen anybody *so* pale in ages. You look great!"

"Flattery will get you everywhere," she giggled.

He smiled that big, toothy grin of his. He was dressed in blue Levi's, a button-down white shirt, and a navy blazer.

"Do you want to have dinner here?" she asked.

"Are you kidding? I know this nice Cuban place in Little Havana."

They rode off in his green MG Midget. The convertible top was down, and Mandy's long red hair was blowing like a flaming torch.

"You still have beautiful hair." King smiled at her.

"You're really big with the compliments, Dave. What are you — *horny*?"

King laughed. "How's Howard?"

"Fine."

"Just fine?"

"He's great," she said without much conviction.

He gave her a quick glance. "Problems?"

"Yeah."

"I'm sorry to hear that," he said sincerely.

"It happens." Mandy wondered why she was being so candid. Was it getting so bad that she had to unload it on somebody?

"Yeah." King stopped for a red light. "Y'know I split with Becky."

"I heard."

"It's better this way." King shrugged, then changed the subject. "You didn't tell me why you came to town."

Mandy smiled at her friend's obvious attempt to shift the conversation. "I'm looking for Rick Marlowe."

"Rick Marlowe?"

"Yeah, the rock singer."

"Can't say I ever had the pleasure," King said as he shut off the radio tuned to a jazz station.

"You had but you didn't know that you had."

"He was *that* popular?"

"All over the FM waves."

"Obviously not on *my* jazz station," King laughed. "What's the story with this Rick Marlboro?"

"Mar*lowe,*" Mandy corrected him. "He died, but he didn't really die."

"Huh?"

"Some people say he pulled a Jim Morrison. He was in a private jet flying over the Bermuda Triangle. They lost him and the plane."

"I don't believe it."

"See what I mean?"

"Oh yeah, I get it." King nodded. "He died, but he *really* didn't die."

"He was last seen in Key West," she said.

"The Rock. Natch, *every*body was last seen there."

"So you don't know anything about it?"

"Nope." King turned into a parking lot. "I have my nose buried in this place."

"Interesting part of town." She noticed the ethnic feel of the shops and restaurants along the *Calle Ocho* with its bilingual street signs.

"I love these people . . . their food . . . culture."

"You sound like a born-again Cuban."

King laughed as he pulled into a parking space.

"What's for dinner?"

"Moros y cristianos." King got out, walked around to her side, and opened the door.

"Still an old-fashioned gentleman, eh?"

"Give me a break, princess." King smiled.

They entered the small, white stucco restaurant. Inside was dark and cool, dim candles burning at each table.

"Very pretty," Mandy said.

"*And* expensive," King added with a wink.

"Good, then this is on Rob Manville."

"How is old Rob?"

"Still old Rob."

"He never mellowed?"

"Heaven forbid." She smirked.

They sat down at a tiny table, and King ordered a bottle of the house wine.

"So is it over yet between you two?" King asked.

Mandy shook her head. "We're still together." She thought it was bold of him to bring up that conversation again.

"Till death do us part?"

Mandy shrugged. She hadn't thought it through yet. "It's not always easy."

"Tell me about it."

"And you two?"

"Divorced," he said gravely.

"What happened?"

"Didn't you hear?" he asked. "It's the *in* thing to do these days. You know Becky — always keeping up with the times."

"You sound bitter."

King nodded. "It's not an easy thing to go through. Starts out alright but it always turns sour, y'know?"

"A third party?"

"On her part."

"I'm sorry."

"Stop saying that," King said.

"Okay." She eyed him closely. Should she trust him? It had been a long time. People change. "I don't want you to think things are *that* bad between us."

"Is Howard off the sauce?"

"Yep."

"Dope?"

"Uh-huh."

"So what's the problem?"

"We seem to argue a lot. Get into each other's hair. You know what I mean?"

"Growing pains?"

"Maybe." She nodded.

"Take my advice."

"What's that, Doc?"

"Divorce him and marry me," he joked.

Mandy laughed. "I'm serious about this."

"So am I," King chuckled. "Okay. I'll be serious now. Stick with it. Try to work it out. I mean, it's been hell for me. I don't like being alone. People weren't made to be alone. If it has worked this long, there must be something there."

She nodded. "You're right."

"Of course I'm right. Do I look happy?"

"You look awful."

"Gee, thanks. Let's talk about something else."

"How about dope?"

"Dope?"

"Marijuana, remember?"

"Sure . . . the Rock is the biggest importer of the stuff. Tons of it," he related.

"What about domestic-grown?"

"Good business. One of the national weeklies had a cover story on it last year. 'The new moonshiners,' they're calling them."

"I thought I made up that tag: *the new moonshiners.*" She shrugged. "I guess someone beat me to it. Ever hear of a town named Hammett?"

King poured the wine. "Nope."

"Up north."

"What about it?"

"Dope is their leading agricultural product." Mandy sipped her wine. "It's good . . . not too dry."

"Yeah. So what about this town?"

"I'm working on a story up there."

"I thought you were working on the Rick Marlowe piece?"

"That's only my cover." She winked.

"You want to do a story on these new moonshiners?"

"Even more than that."

"Fill me in."

"It's a long story," she sighed.

"We have all night," King said.

"We're going to need it," Mandy said and told him the story.

Tommy sat on the bunk inside the jail cell reading a comic book. It was the only thing Deputy Sheriff Oates had hanging around to read. It was nearly eleven in the evening. Tommy could hear the crickets outside his barricaded window.

"Wanna play cards?" Oates asked from outside the cell. Oates was about Tommy's age. He was short, about five foot six, with a bad case of acne. Oates had always reminded Tommy of that character in *Catcher in the Rye*. They had hung out together back in high school. In fact, it was Oates who had taught Tommy how to hot-wire a car. His old man, an ex-con, had taught him quite a few tricks of the trade.

"I'm about ready to hit the sack, Harry." Tommy stretched with a loud yawn. "Sorry."

"It's okay." Oates sounded disappointed.

"No word from my lawyer yet?"

"Nope, probably in the mornin'."

"This isn't right, y'know."

"I figgered it wasn't . . . but you know how things are."

"My brother's funeral is tomorrow."

"Yep, whole town'll be out for Elmore's funeral. You can be certain of that, Tommy."

"What's with Higs?" Tommy asked.

"Whatcha mean?"

"He seems uptight."

"That shootin' really shook him up," Oates said.
"First time he ever had to deal with anythin' like that.
You know Higs, he's gettin' old and tired."

"You think so?"

"Sure do. Time for some *new* blood around here."

"Something tells me you're getting ambitious, Harry,"
Tommy commented.

"Got myself hitched, y'know. Wanna raise me a
family. A sheriff's salary sure would come in handy."

"I guess I should get some sleep now."

"Higs will wake you first thing in time for the funeral,"
Oates said. "Good night now, Tommy."

"Good night, Harry."

Being in jail wasn't so bad, Tommy thought. At least
it gave him some time to think. He wondered what his
next move would be. It dawned on him that Higgins was
probably right about the Hills. They were real backwards
people and weren't the type to mastermind that shootout.
It was too fast. Too clean. Too professional. And the
weapons that the killers had used — automatic submachine guns — were out of the Hills' league. Maybe
the mob was involved.

That was his next move — to see Al Romero. Maybe
he knew something about all this.

Tommy closed his eyes.

He had trouble falling asleep and thought about
Elmore. Elmore *and* his father. Someone he hadn't conjured up in ages.

It was a hot, muggy black night — the kind that only
Georgia could produce. The air was thick and rancid, not
a breeze stirring. They were together in the pickup truck.
Tommy, dressed in his shorts and hugging his naked legs,
rode between his dad and Elmore. There was a black
snake of road before them. The auxiliary gas tank was
filled with moonshine. Daddy was making a night run.

Tommy couldn't recall the reason his father had
dragged them along with him. But he did know that it

had made Elmore angry. The tension in the air was as dense as the humidity. Tommy felt uncomfortable sitting between the two — his father and Elmore exchanged glares every few minutes.

Elmore had looked very much like his father, Tommy thought — tall, hard, and tough. The only difference between them was their temperament. Their father was a mean drunk but a real coward when sober. He'd often beat the boys after his long drinking sprees. But as Elmore grew older, he also grew taller and stronger. So by age fourteen, he was nearly as big as his father. Now, whenever daddy came after them, Elmore fought back.

At one point, after a sharp curve, a dark sedan pulled onto the road and stayed close behind them. Its headlights glared into the rear-view mirror.

The elder Shepard twisted his head around and peered out the back window. "Who the hell . . ."

"Trouble?" Elmore asked.

Shepard eyed his eldest son. "Could be."

"I told you, dammit!" Elmore snapped. "Bringin' us along on one of your goddamn runs!"

"Shut up, Elmore — you're scarin' the boy."

Elmore took the shotgun off the rear window rack and pumped it. "Feds or foes?"

"What's the difference?" Shepard growled.

"So lose the hooch." Elmore referred to the emergency drainage valve that would empty the tank.

Shepard shook his head. "I can't afford to lose it, son."

Elmore pointed the gun at his father, across Tommy's chest. "Lose it or I swear to God I'll blow you all the way to hell!"

"You ain't about to kill yer old man, Elmore. Besides, what if they're just ordinary folk?" His father tried to reason with him.

Shepard shrugged. "They usually travel in pairs."

"I think we shouldn't take any chances if they're feds."

"There's only one way to find out . . ." his father said as he gunned the truck.

They left the car behind in a heap of dust.

The truck screeched as it took on the sharp curves.

"Slow down. They're not tailin' us . . ." Elmore said.

"I want more distance to play it safe," Shepard said.

His foot pressed the accelerator pedal to the floor. Elmore took hold of Tommy and squeezed him close.

"SLOW DOWN!"

On the next curve, the truck skidded off the road and turned over several times as it rolled down a rugged incline.

The pickup truck landed upright at the bottom of the hill, the engine smoking. Elmore had a gash across his brow. He grabbed hold of Tommy and carried him out of the truck.

Tommy saw their father pinned against the steering wheel.

"Daddy!" Tommy called out.

His father opened his eyes and cried out.

Elmore held Tommy tightly in his arms as they backed away from the blazing truck.

"HELP ME!" Shepard screamed out in a painful voice.

"Elmore—Daddy's in there!" Tommy struggled to free himself.

"Daddy's dead," Elmore said as he put Tommy down.

The two boys watched the fire consume the truck.

"But he's still alive!" Tommy said.

"He's dead," Elmore said as he took Tommy's hand and both walked off into the darkness.

Suddenly, an explosion ripped at them. Tommy could feel the heat on the back of his bare legs and neck. They turned around and saw that the pickup truck was now a burning inferno.

"See — I told you Daddy was dead," Elmore said.
From that point on, Elmore had become the focal point
of Tommy's life. He was his childhood. Their mama had
died a year later from a broken heart. Elmore had said
she didn't have anything to live for after their daddy's
death. She was born to be his woman, and when he died
she died.

Elmore used to think like that.

But Elmore wasn't really Elmore anymore after he had
gotten back from the service. He was strange. Aloof.
Always preoccupied. The local people had thought he was
bonkers. Maybe he was. Tommy thought it was the
opposite — that Elmore had been too smart. That he saw
the world like no one else did. The time in Nam must
have scrambled something inside his head. It was like he
could read minds or something. Like he had a direct line
with a higher power. The way he'd started the business
was fascinating to watch. Tommy had wondered what
he was plugged into. It just seemed to flow out of him.
He had it all planned. He had absorbed everything he
could to realize his dream. "Ya gotta know the enemy,"
he kept chanting. Tommy never did find out what he'd
meant by that.

But Elmore had sure turned that town around. Before
long everybody had gotten into the business. Competi-
tion had become fierce . . . and *violent*. Along the way,
Elmore had taught Tommy everything he knew. The
seeding. The nurturing. The harvesting. The trimming.
The selling. And the *killing*. Elmore had always said that
Tommy was the best shot in the state — second only to
Elmore himself. He'd educated Tommy in how to shoot
various weapons, build bombs, and set booby-traps.
Tommy had been the perfect pupil.

And Tommy had enjoyed helping his brother and Deb
run the family trade. That was why he was so hurt when
Elmore had sent him off to college. He didn't want to
go. He wasn't even interested in school. He knew more

about life than anyone could ever learn in college. But Elmore had insisted and "bought" Tommy a seat in school. It was back when the feud between the Shepards and the Hills had been really hot. Right after Sam Hill had lost his eye. Elmore feared for Tommy's life and thought it best to shove him out of town before the Hills retaliated. Tommy had understood and accepted Elmore's concern, but it still hurt. And those three years spent in New York City had been *long*. He'd missed Deb, and especially his little nephew.

Now he had returned to Hammett. His home. And he wanted to make sure he never left again. Elmore was gone, and Tommy felt like an orphan. He needed something. Family. Roots. And Hammett had all those things — Deb and Sage and the family trade. Tommy was determined to carry on.

For Elmore.

And that brought to mind something he wanted so much to block out.

Tommy Shepard had to bury his older brother tomorrow.

Matt Reeves walked home from the Broadway luncheonette where he worked the counter on weekday evenings after school. It was a shitty job, but it gave him some pocket money.

It was a nice night, and a cool breeze was blowing. He was looking forward to the following evening when he was going to try to see free Shakespeare in the Park. It meant waiting around all afternoon until they gave out the ticket vouchers. But he was going to be with his girlfriend, Jane, and another couple. A whole day and evening out. A few bottles of wine and a picnic-basket supper. It should be fun.

He ran up the front stoop and checked the mailbox before going to his second-floor apartment. He missed

Tommy. He didn't like coming home to an empty apartment.

When he got to the door he noticed that it was slightly ajar. "Oh, shit, not another robbery!"

They had already been hit a few months before. Luckily they didn't own anything too valuable. It was just that the robbers had made such a mess. He wished Tommy were here — he handled these situations really well.

With his heart pounding in his ears, Matt kicked open the door.

Before him stood a man holding a long-barrelled pistol aimed right at him.

"What the *fuck*?" Matt's feet were frozen with fear. *Run,* he told himself, *run!*

"Come in and shut the door behind you, pal." The man's voice was coarse but calm. He was very much in charge.

Matt stepped in. An arm came from behind the door and shut it with a loud thud.

Matt looked over at the blond-haired kid. He was missing his two front teeth.

"Who are you?" the man with the gun asked.

Matt looked at him carefully. He would need a description for the police later. He was dressed in a lightweight, cream-colored suit that was obviously too small for him. His huge belly hung over his belt buckle. He was wearing a pair of white, patent leather shoes. Real tacky.

"My name is . . . M-M-Matt . . . Reeves," he stammered nervously.

"You live here?"

"Yep."

"With Tommy Shepard?"

"That's right — we're roommates."

"Oh yeah?" The man grinned and gave his toothless partner a nod. "You two queers or sumtin'?"

The blond-haired kid burst out in laughter.

Matt glared at him.

"That's enough," the man snapped.

Matt took in the ransacked apartment. "Is this a robbery?"

"Sit down." He pointed his gun to a chair at the kitchen table.

Matt went over and sat down.

"Where's your friend?"

"Out of town." Matt tried to sound like he wasn't scared, but he looked down and saw that his hands were shaking.

"What's he up to?"

Matt swallowed hard. "His brother was killed . . . he had to go to his funeral."

"Did you know his brother?"

"Hey, *who* are you?"

He put the gun barrel into Matt's ear. "I'm askin' the questions, pal."

Matt shut his eyes and took a deep breath. "Yeah, I knew him . . . Elmore was his name."

"He came up here last week, didn't he?"

Matt wondered how he knew that. "Yeah, I wasn't here . . . Tommy spoke with him."

"What about?"

"How should I know? I wasn't there."

"You and Tommy didn't talk about it?"

"No."

"He's lying, man," the Kid said.

"I'm telling the truth," Matt declared.

"Sure you are, son," The man said, then frowned at his partner. "I knew I should've brought Red along, at least he keeps his hole shut."

"Oh, come on, Sharp, we're wastin' our time with this dildo. Pop him and let's go. Told you he was goin' to come home and interrupt us."

"*Hey.*" Matt stood up. "Listen, I won't tell anybody about this. I don't know anything."

"Whaddaya think, Kid?" Sharp asked as he pushed Matt back into the chair.

"He knows sumtin'."

Sharp eyed his partner.

"I'll get it out of him." The blond-haired kid smiled his toothless grin that made him look like a vampire.

chapter 8

Howard had tried to call Mandy the night before. She wasn't in, the hotel switchboard operator had told him. It was midnight and she wasn't in? He wanted to tell her about the mouse. He had just checked on it. The mouse had appeared bloated with oozing sores spread all over its body. He had taken a blood sample and examined it under the microscope. The blood was completely infected with the toxin. It seemed that the chemical had reproduced at an alarmingly rapid pace. Most unusual, Howard had thought.

He lay in bed looking up at the ceiling. The early morning rays of sunlight streaked across the room. He had left a message — why didn't she call him back? He looked down at the textbook he was reading about dioxins and their side effects. It was like reading a horror novel — only this was for *real*.

He sat up and picked up the phone. He slammed it down again. *She* should call, not him.

The phone rang.

Finally.

"Hello?" Howard asked into the phone.

"Hi, Howard. Sorry I couldn't get back to you until now. I had a late night." Mandy's voice sounded unusually groggy to Howard.

"Where the hell were you?"

"I had dinner with Dave King," Mandy told him. "He sends his love."

His love. "You had dinner until *after* midnight?" he asked accusingly.

"Well, we got to talking and drinking — you know how it is."

"I knew how it *was.*" Howard said. "Was Becky there — how's she doing?"

"You knew they split up."

"Split up?"

"I told you ages ago."

"So you two were *alone.*"

"Howard, don't pull that jealous number on me. Dave is a friend. Besides, you should see the size of him. He's gained a lot of weight. And he's very depressed over Becky."

Howard fell back on the bed, his eyes scanning the ceiling. "So what did you talk about?"

"The old times . . . Rick Marlowe . . . Hammett."

"Oh, speaking of Hammett."

"Yes?"

"The mouse. I injected that chemical into the mouse. It's some form of dioxin. Nothing quite like I've ever seen before. Well, the mouse is bloated and has these oozing sores all over it. Chloracne they call it."

"So *what* is this shit?" Mandy asked.

"A very dangerous chemical," he said.

"Dangerous to plants?"

"Dangerous to *all* living things."

"Jesus Christ," Mandy said. "Who would've used it on those plants?"

"I wouldn't know." Howard thought about it for a while. "Maybe the government."

"The *government?*" Mandy sounded surprised. "You mean the U.S. of A.?"

"Could be. Who else would be fooling around with dioxins?"

"Are you sure it's really a dioxin?"

"Chloracne is the primary symptom of dioxin poisoning," he related. "I've been reading up on it. Pretty frightening stuff. This chemical has very similar properties to a dioxin."

"Why was it sprayed on the pot plants?"

"Maybe it's a new form of enforcement against dope-growing. Though the use of dioxin has been outlawed in this country, so I don't know. If they are using it as a herbicide, they're going to have a whole lot of problems with this stuff," he said.

"Why?"

"Remember Agent Orange?"

"It's *that* powerful?"

"Even *more* so. It seems to act more swiftly than Agent Orange."

"Will it cause cancer like Agent Orange?"

"If you manage to live that long after exposure to it."

"Is it . . . *contagious?*" she gulped.

"Well, it can be absorbed through the skin . . . ingested through water and food. In this case, smoking the infected pot would do the trick. But the pot plant would die before anyone would pick it, so nobody's about to smoke it. But anybody working near the plants — the farmers — they'd get infected. Eventually the soil will be poisoned. Deep water wells . . . vegetation . . . wildlife — you name it — all will be infected. I'm talking about for years and years — even *decades.*"

"My God!" Mandy exclaimed. "How much of this stuff is lethal?"

"How much — you mean quantity? — a mere drop could kill. This stuff is so toxic that a few ounces poured into a major city's water supply could kill off the whole population."

"Do you know what you're saying, Howard?"

"I'm afraid so."

"I can't believe the government could be behind this," she said.

"Maybe they're not," Howard said. "Maybe it's organized crime. Or — " Howard laughed, "the good ol' Russians."

"The *Russians*?"

"What with stuff like *Yellow Rain*—they're really into chemical warfare. Why not start on pot plants? The youth of America would be infected, don't you see?"

"This sounds like something from the fifties."

"Only speculating."

"What about the Martians for that matter?" she joked.

"The possibilities are limitless."

"I wish it was as funny as all that. But this is really happening."

"That's what frightens me, Mandy. You better stay away from that town."

"But I have to find out what's going on, Howard . . . those poor people."

"Please, Mandy, drop it. It's too dangerous to mess with."

"How can you tell me to drop it? There are innocent people involved in this."

"It wouldn't be the first time, Mandy."

"What do you mean?"

"Legionnaire's Disease . . . unknown venereal and immune deficiency diseases. Who knows how they all started?"

"You mean . . . ?"

"They could be experiments . . . like I said, it wouldn't be the first time," he said.

"Using those poor soldiers as guinea pigs during the atomic-bomb tests."

"That's one of many examples. Remember how they used those black people in the South for studying untreated cases of syphilis? Come on, Mandy, it has all been documented *somewhere*."

There was a brief pause for thought. Her head was reeling from the excitement of stumbling upon such a powder keg of a story. All the juices in her body were overflowing. And the probability of danger only added more to it. She hadn't felt this way since her exposé on cocaine abuse in the recording industry. That series of articles had given her more recognition in the business than the twelve previous years of her rock-personality profiles combined. She knew this latest story would be her real breakout.

"Howard . . . what should I do? Who should I tell?" Her trembling voice revealed her elation.

"*No*body."

"But, Howard . . . "

"*No*body. Don't you see, Mandy, if the people who are behind this ever find out you know . . ."

"Oh my God." She flashed on Karen Silkwood. Look what happened to her . . .

"There's no telling what they will do."

"They'll have to silence me."

"Yes."

"They'll have to . . . *kill me*," Mandy said.

"Mandy, I just thought of something."

"What?" she asked.

"I don't think we should be talking about this over the telephone," he said.

The funeral had gone well. There were no incidents. Tommy had been freed due to lack of evidence and his lawyer's irate threats to Carpenter.

Tommy and Deb invited some people back home for food and drink. There, Tommy spoke with an old family friend, Gator Stanton, an alligator poacher from the Everglades.

Stanton was a stout, burly man with a thick crop of white wavy hair and a bandit mustache. He played hard, he worked hard, and he drank hard. Arm-wrestling wasn't beneath him — not even after a funeral. Tommy went along, just to humor the old-timer.

Stanton was married to Betty, a Miccosukee Indian, and they had a ten-year-old little girl, Donna, who was learning to speak their native language, a form of Hitchiti, on the reservation. She was a black-haired little beauty with a mischievous nature. Gator nicknamed her *Okaloacoochee* — little bad water.

"Elmore was the last of the old adventurers," Stanton said after he slammed Tommy's hand against the table. "I won."

He won. He *always* won.

Stanton threw his head back to drain the glass of whiskey. "Elmore was a lot like your dad. Tough. Only smarter. Knew how to make a livin' . . . a *good* livin'. Can't say I liked him gettin' into the *marry-ju-wanna*-growin'. But shit, the kid did all right for himself." He stretched his arms out to show Tommy Elmore's nice spread. "Put you through school. What was it for?"

"Space."

"Huh?"

"You know, taking up space."

"You mean, you studied astronomy?" Stanton asked.

"Not exactly." Tommy didn't feel like explaining it.

Stanton eyed Tommy through his bushy eyebrows. "Do you *know* whatcha wanna do, boy?"

Tommy laughed. "Yeah, I know."

"Could take over where Elmore left off."

Tommy grinned. "I'm working on it."

"Tommy!" Deb called out his name from the kitchen. "A phone call for you — long distance."

Tommy stood up. "Excuse me, Gator."

"Still be here when you get back, Tommy," Gator smiled.

Tommy went into the kitchen, where it was quiet, and took the phone from Deb. "Hello?"

"Mr. Thomas Shepard?"

"Speaking."

"This is Sergeant Argento, New York City Police Department."

"Yes?"

The sergeant asked him if he lived with Matthew Reeves on West 112th Street. Tommy answered affirmatively. *"I have some bad news,"* the cop said.

Tommy hung up after the policemen was through.

Deb was by the stove, her hands on her hips. A fresh ham was roasting in the oven. "Somethin' wrong, Tommy?"

"It's Matt . . . " Tommy was pale and obviously disturbed. "He's dead."

Deb put her hand to her mouth.

"He was killed when he interrupted a burglary in progress at our apartment. I don't believe it!" Tommy punched the refrigerator door angrily.

Deb went up to embrace him.

"I don't *fucking* believe it!" Tommy shook his head. "Just like that, he's dead. First Elmore, now Matt."

He stared into Deb's eyes. He didn't have to finish what he was saying. You didn't have to be a mind reader to know what followed.

Who would be next?

Deb found Tommy going through some of Elmore's things in the den, or what Elmore called *my* room.

He was sitting down with the PSE Mach II bow in his hands. Up on the desk before him lay a nickel-plated Smith & Wesson Model 59 and a Bowie knife and sheath. On the rack above the room's fireplace was a High Standard PPS-12 pump shotgun.

Deb twirled his hair around with her fingers affectionately.

"Whaddaya doin'?"

Tommy seemed startled by her voice as though he had not been aware of her presence all that time.

"What?" Tommy snapped out of it. "Just going through some of Elmore's things."

"I bought that bow for Elmore. It's the Signature Model. He was just aching to use it this comin' huntin' season."

"She's a beauty . . . a big difference from the longbows we used as kids."

"Hey, you better get a move on, if ya wanna make it on time."

Tommy had an appointment with Al Romero.

"Yeah." Tommy stood up to leave, putting the bow down on top of the desk.

"Don't you think," Deb said, "that you should bring somethin' along?"

Tommy looked at Deb, then down at the gun.

"Elmore never left home without it," Deb related.

Tommy picked up the pistol. It glistened in his hand. He snapped in a 14-shot clip and slipped the gun into his jacket.

"I better split." He scanned his digital watch.

Deb grabbed hold of him as he swept by. "Be careful."

He leaned over, kissed her forehead, and left.

Tommy, dressed in black Levi's, motorcycle boots, and a red nylon windbreaker, took Elmore's Honda out for the night run.

It was only the second time he had ever ridden a bike. The first time had been on Elmore's old Yamaha dirt bike. This new one was like something out of a science-fiction movie. Sleek and high-tech, it did everything but fly.

Tommy had called Romero earlier to set up the date.

He told him they had to talk. Romero, a longtime family friend, obliged.

It was eight o'clock by the time Tommy arrived at the meeting spot. It was in the middle of nowhere, at the end of a dirt roadway. Trees and thick foliage all around.

A few minutes later, a dark blue Thunderbird pulled into the clearing. The headlights were off.

It was twilight. A bluish gleam of light fell over them.

Romero came out of his car and walked slowly up to Tommy who was leaning against the hefty bike.

"Jesus, in the dark, you look just like your brother. How are you, Tommy?"

The two shook hands.

Romero was in his mid-thirties. A little plump — he was making a comfortable living. He had long black hair, parted on the side, and wore blue sunglasses. He had long, trimmed sideburns that inched towards the corners of his mouth. And a gleaming smile — he always had that.

"I expected to see you at the funeral today, Al." Tommy couldn't conceal his disappointment.

"I'm sorry, Tommy. I was down south. An important meeting."

"They tell me you were the last man to see Elmore alive."

"No, I wasn't," he said. "His *killer* was."

"Do you know who that might be?"

"Jesus fucking Christ, I don't. If I did the son of a bitch'd be stone-dead by now. I loved Elmore — you know that."

"Any noise out there?"

"Not a sound. Nobody knows from nothing," Romero said.

Tommy sighed.

"But I did hear some static about Hammett."

"What kind of static?"

"I got orders not to purchase any dope coming out of Hammett. Not a fucking ounce."

"Why's that?"

Romero shrugged. "Bad stuff."

"What do you mean it's bad stuff?"

"Poisoned," Romero said. "Figured it must've been sprayed with paraquat or something."

"Who told you this?"

"That's confidential."

"Please, Al, for Elmore."

Romero clucked his tongue. "You're putting me in an awkward situation, Tommy. This guy — he's my *main* man. I sell him seventy-five percent of my stuff. That's a lot of bread, Tommy."

"You can trust me, Al."

"I can't trust *any*body, especially after what happened to Elmore."

"You don't have any idea who *whacked* Elmore?

Romero cleared his throat. "Could've been the feds. They've been cracking down lately. But they wouldn't have done it and run off like that. Must've been the mob. Maybe the fuckin' Colombians. Heard they weren't too happy about the domestic growers eating into their market."

"Elmore didn't have any dealings with the mob . . . except with *you*."

"Come on, Tommy, we're family. I would never have set him up — *never*. I wasn't his only buyer, y'know."

"Who else?"

"I can't give you names." Romero looked around nervously. "I'm dead if I give you names."

"I only want *one*," Tommy said.

Romero swallowed hard.

"Your big man — the one that told you about Hammett's stuff being poisoned."

"I told you — I can't, *dammit*." Romero turned to leave.

"Al!" Tommy pulled out the Smith & Wesson.

Romero faced him and saw the silver barrel gleaming in the near darkness. "You gonna put a hole in me, Tommy?"

"If I have to."

Romero shook his head. "Put that piece away. We're *fucking* family."

Tommy held the gun firmly before him.

Romero tramped up to him, shoved the pistol away, and slapped Tommy hard across the face. "Don't you *ever* point a weapon at a man unless you intend to *use* it — *comprende?*"

Tommy wiped the blood from his lips. He felt the pressure building inside him . . . ready to explode. He looked down at the gun in his hand and then into Romero's dark eyes. "The *name.*"

"I never want to see you again, ever — *understand?*"

The *name,*" Tommy snapped.

"You're as dead to me as Elmore."

Tommy spit out a glob of blood.

"I'm really disappointed in you, Tommy Shepard. Elmore, he would *never* have done something like this. You fucking little coward."

Tommy held his stern gaze into Romero's eyes. The pressure continued to cook inside him.

"Go back to New York with the rest of your kind. We don't act like that down here. We're gentlemen. We're *family.*" Romero sucked in a deep breath then exhaled slowly . . . *slowly* . . . the anger flowing out of him.

A small plane buzzed overhead.

"I have to meet that," Romero said and started walking back to his car. He stopped when he reached the door. He faced Tommy.

Tommy remained as he was, eyes staring dead on, the gun in a loose grip at his side.

Romero said, "Tony Bava — Miami."

And then he got into the car, backed up, and drove off down the dirt road.

Tommy put the pistol into the pocket of his jacket. He started the bike, put on his helmet, and rode off.

As he was about to enter Hammett, he saw a bright blaze burning in the distance.

He stopped the bike, pulled up his visor, and gazed at the burning inferno. He knew what it was. One of Elmore's patches. Nick Hill was still out for revenge.

He pulled out his pistol and started firing in the direction of the fire. He emptied it and cursed. The spent gunpowder penetrated his nostrils. He had come so close to taking Romero out back there. So fucking close. He could almost taste his blood. He stayed there for a while just watching the glimmer a few miles away. He knew he was taking out all his frustrations on Romero. It wasn't right. He understood that. But at least now he had a name. *Bava.* How would he know if the crops were poisoned? The local farmers were going to blow their stacks when it got out that their harvests were worthless. So Elmore's suspicions about that sap had been correct. He wondered if Mandy Cronenberg ever found out anything from her husband. He would have to give her a call. He didn't know if he could really trust her, though. She seemed more interested in obtaining a story than anything else. She was just like all those other selfish New Yorkers. He had never met such a bunch of coldhearted, arrogant folk. Except for the Hills. That brought his attention back to the fire.

He got back on the bike and took off down the dark road, his headlight beaming in the direction of the blaze. The trees swept by on both sides of him as the blackness of the night swallowed up his tracks.

chapter 9

The white mouse was dead.

Howard had to stay even later tonight. There were several co-workers still hanging around after an office party. It had been eight-thirty by the time they all cleared out. Howard hadn't enjoyed himself very much at the party. He had too much on his mind.

Somebody was following him.

At first, he'd thought it was paranoia from his phone conversation with Mandy. But this morning on his way to work, he'd noticed a black Buick close behind him. All the way from Brooklyn to his plant in New Jersey. He thought it was more than just coincidence. He was worried. He had been even too frightened to go out for lunch. What could he do? His uneasiness had made the day drag on endlessly.

After the party had broken up, he went in to check on the mouse and found it dead.

The poor creature had expanded until its insides erupted. The skin was broken, and the poisoned inner organs were seeping through the cracks. It wasn't a very pleasant sight. And the stench was horrible.

Howard shivered when he thought about what this deadly dioxin might do to human beings.

And what about himself?

He had worked closely with it during the testing. Sure, he was extra careful. But *how* careful can one really be, *especially* with this unknown chemical compound?

He might even be infected with it *now*.

He placed the mouse into an airtight container and put it in his briefcase. *Evidence.* When he got home, he would call Mandy, then the authorities. This was much too dangerous to ignore.

He left the building and went out into the hot, muggy air. The parking lot lights were lit, and his blue Volvo was the only car parked. It seemed strange sitting there all by itself. Almost scary.

He unlocked the door, placed his briefcase on the seat, and got in. The car was stuffy and wet with humidity. He started the car and switched on the air vent fan. He sat awhile until cool, fresh air came through the vents.

He put his head back and closed his eyes.

He didn't know if he fell asleep or not. He sure was tired enough. The next thing he knew, there was an arm wrapped around his neck and the nozzle of a gun pressed against his forehead. He saw the man's face in the rear-view mirror. Just a kid, really, with blond, spiky hair and two missing front teeth giving him a big black gap in his grin. His breath was strong . . . like garlic.

"We're goin' for a little ride, Mr. Cronenberg."

He had a Southern drawl and definitely had garlic on his breath.

"W-W-Who-*who* are you?" Howard tried to control his stammering, but the Kid had startled him so.

"Never mind that." The Kid's grip loosened. "I'm goin' to slacken up here, so no funny business, okay?"

"Sure." Jolts of pain shot through his gut. Any nervous reaction had always hit his stomach immediately. His heart pounded in his ears. He had difficulty catching his breath.

The Kid pulled his naked arm away and sat back in the seat. Howard saw the long barrel in the mirror. A suppressor. The Kid handed Howard a quart bottle of Johnny Walker Red.

Howard beheld the bottle in his hand. Scotch. It wasn't his drink. "What do you want me to do with this?"

"What else? Drink it, asshole."

"I don't drink."

"Sure you do." The Kid nudged him with the gun. "Have one on me."

"I really can't . . . I'm a recovered alcoholic . . . I haven't had a drink in two years."

The Kid roared at that. "Then you must *need* one awfully bad."

"You don't understand."

"DRINK!" the Kid commanded.

Howard closed his eyes. *God help me.* "Does this have anything to do with the dioxin?"

"DRINK!"

"I won't drop a word about it — I promise."

The Kid held the gun tightly against the base of his skull. "I'm goin' to blast your brains all over that fuckin' windshield in a minute if you don't start cooperatin'!"

Howard unscrewed the cap. His hands began to tremble.

"Come on, Cronenberg, have one for the road," the Kid sniggered.

Howard put the bottle to his lips and threw his head back. The warm, burning liquor washed down his throat. He gulped it quickly, trying not to taste it. But he didn't have to *taste* it — he *felt* it. The alcohol exploded inside him, spreading its liquid fire through his veins.

He stopped drinking and put the bottle aside. He had a coughing fit.

"More." The Kid nudged him again.
"I can't . . . it's making me ill." The pains in his
stomach worsened.
"I said *MORE!"* the Kid shouted.
Howard drank some more. *"There."*
The Kid grabbed a fistful of Howard's hair and yanked
it towards him. "Come on, asshole. I said *more!"*
And Howard drank more. And more. Until the bottle
was three-quarters empty. Howard couldn't hold his head
up. He was delirious. He felt the cool air from the air
system flowing over him, giving him goose bumps.

Suddenly, he saw a flickering light in the distance. Two
lights coming closer. Headlights. A black car.

He heard the Kid get out of his car. Everything seemed
to be closing in around him. His door opened. The Kid
snatched the bottle from his hand. Then he felt the liquid
being poured all over him. Everything was spinning all
around him. Like the car was caught within a tornado.
Whirling . . . whirling. His stomach swelled larger and
larger. That taste at the back of his tongue. And then
he heard voices . . . laughter.

"I think he has had enough."

Had enough.

Enough . . . the word echoed inside his head.

He felt the eruption inside him. The gagging. The vomit
spewing out with an unnatural force. His scrotum con-
tracting tightly against his body. He was covered with the
foul-smelling discharge. His clothes. The steering wheel.
But the pains soon subsided. The spinning ceased.

It was then that he noticed a rumbling beneath him.
The engine was still running. He gazed outside and saw
the two men conversing some feet away.

Now!

He shifted into drive and punched the accelerator
pedal. The car sped off. He slammed the door shut and
headed towards the exit.

Everything seemed foggy ahead.

But he was away from them.
He had escaped!

Sharp watched the car drive off and went for his gun.
The Kid started to run after Cronenberg's car.
"Hey — come back here!" Sharp shouted after his
partner.
"But — "
"The hell with him."
"What?"
"Look at him, for chrissakes. He'll never make it in
his condition," Sharp cackled.
The Kid hurried back to him. "Yeah, I guess you're
right."
"Makes our job easier." Sharp went into his car.
"Come on, let's make sure he does *finish* it."
They got into the car and started after Cronenberg.

Howard heard the sound of horns blasting all around
him. He kept a strong grip on the steering wheel. *Stay
in the lane,* he kept repeating, *stay in the lane.*
Lights from oncoming cars only made his vision worse.
More horns.
Mandy. I have to call Mandy . . tell her . . . warn her!
He pulled back onto the road when he caught himself
swerving.
Oh God, what should I do?
Howard thought about pulling over and taking a rest,
but the two men would surely be after him. Why didn't
a policeman pull him over?
*Yes, that's it, a cop will pull me over. Then they can't
bother me anymore.*
He had to concentrate. But his mind kept wandering.
The dizziness returned. The feeling of nausea was back.
He tried to think about something else. *Anything else!*
But it was too late.

The truck came up on his right. Howard had been swerving in his lane. The truck sideswiped Howard's car. Howard pulled the steering wheel hard to the left. But he did it too quickly . . . *too hard.*

His auto jumped the center divider and was hit by an oncoming car. Howard's vehicle rolled two times before bending against a guardrail.

The driver of the other car ran to the wreckage. Inside he saw Howard pinned against the steering wheel. Blood streamed down his face.

A black Buick pulled up nearby. Two men got out and wandered nonchalantly over to the accident scene.

"Looks like a goner," Sharp said, standing behind the driver's back.

The driver looked at Sharp and his blond-haired partner. "You think he's dead?"

The Kid gazed over the driver's shoulder and said, *"At least."*

part two
TAKING ROOT

chapter 10

Mandy eyed the New Jersey state trooper slouched behind his desk. He was a young Hispanic with black hair, a mustache, and chocolate-brown eyes. He appeared painfully intense.

He looked like she felt.

She still couldn't believe it. Howard was gone. She had just identified the body lying in the morgue. His cold, purplish naked corpse. Black abrasions on his face. Colorless lips. The ragged stitches lining his chest where the coroner opened him up. His limp penis. His long bony legs. It looked something like him. But the life wasn't there. *He* wasn't there. It was just a body. It could have been made of wax.

"I don't believe it."

"What can I tell you?" He shrugged. "It's a *hard* thing, I know."

"My husband hasn't had a drop in two years."

"Once an alcoholic, *always* an alcoholic," he said. "I've read his record. He'd been picked up a few times.

Vagrancy. Drunkenness. *Even* drugs. Hey, your husband was no angel."

"And he never drank scotch — he hated the taste of it."

The state trooper scratched his head and sighed. "Alcohol is alcohol — y'know?"

"*And* a bastard is a bastard," she snapped.

He pushed his head back and looked down his Roman nose at her. "No need for *that.*"

"I can't believe how coarse you are . . ."

"Listen, Mrs. Cronenberg, I see this day in and day out. Peelin' drunk drivers off the roadways has become routine for us. I don't mind when they kill themselves. It's when they kill or hurt innocent people that burns me. I'm sorry for you, Mrs. Cronenberg, but I have no sympathy for drunk drivers," he said frankly.

"But you haven't been listening to me . . ."

He shook his head. "I *really* don't have the time."

Mandy stood up abruptly. "Okay then, where are my husband's personal belongings?"

"I'll show you."

She signed for Howard's things and then placed them in a paper bag. She turned to leave when she noticed something was missing. *"His briefcase."*

"Excuse me?"

"His briefcase is missing," she said.

"That's all we have except the car, and that's totaled," he related.

"No, he always has his case. He carries everything in it — *especially* his notes."

"That's all our boys found," the state trooper said. "I could have them go over it again, but it's unlikely they missed it the first time — I mean, *a briefcase?*" he emphasized. "They couldn't have missed something like that. Maybe it fell out along the road during the accident. I'll look into it."

"Thank you." She walked away.

"Mrs. Cronenberg?" he cried out after her.
She turned around. "Yes?"
"I *am* sorry — *really.*"
Mandy looked away and nodded. She walked out into
the open air, leaving the police station buzzing behind
her. She looked at the bag in her hand. So this was how
it ended for Howard. A whole life in a brown paper bag.

Deb lay in bed listening to Willie Nelson singing Kris
Kristofferson songs. She was naked except for her
panties, her eyes peeled to the ceiling. The cool air from
the central air-conditioner vent was blowing on her, a
bottle of Jim Beam at her side. Her lips were numb from
all the drinking. She was stretched out across the bed.
It was a king-sized bed. Much too large for one person.
She didn't enjoy sleeping alone.
    That was because Elmore had spoiled her. He had been
too good in bed. He'd tackled everything in life with such
vigor. Their lovemaking had been no exception. It wasn't
one-two-three, boom-boom, good night, dear with
Elmore. There were always long, sweaty sessions of carnal
delight. It had been like the first time *every* time.
    She had met Elmore in a Jacksonville bar while she
was visiting her grandparents. It had seemed like a fun
town compared to Kansas City where she was born and
raised. Elmore had already been at the bar with a buddy
when she entered. She would find out later his friend was
Al Romero. Elmore turned around, and their eyes locked.
He had black eyes that never seemed to blink. And that
gorgeous blue-black Elvis 'do. A *real* hunk. And when
he smiled . . . *wow* . . . she just melted. Without breaking their interlocked gaze, he marched right up to her.
    "Howdy," he said with a local twang in his voice.
    She averted her eyes and smirked.
    "You ain't from these parts — are ya?"
    She shook her head.
    "Thought not. Don't seem to make 'em like you down

here." He picked up her smooth chin with his coarse hand. "Hey — look me in the eye, sweetheart. I'm not about to bite you none."

"I bet," she snickered.

"Why don't you come on over and join my buddy, Al, here for a drink?"

"I don't know," she said softly, pushing the hair out of her eyes with a quick sweeping motion of her hand.

"My name's Elmore." He shook her hand. "Elmore Shepard."

She took in the size and texture of his hand. It was a workingman's hand. A farmer's hand. Her limp hand appeared like a child's in his grip. "Mine's Debra."

They sat up on the bar stools.

"What's your pleasure?" Elmore asked.

"A beer'd be fine."

"Set us up," he told the bartender.

Al Romero nodded at her. "Miss."

Elmore asked, "Where're you from?"

"Kansas City."

"Whew! Long ways from home. I'm from up north a bit myself." He couldn't keep his eyes off her. Finally after shaking his head for some time he said, "Damn, you're beautiful. You ain't never goin' back to Kansas City, honey."

And he had been right.

She had been stuck on him as well. Instant chemical reaction was the way Elmore had always put it. He'd said their hormones were in charge of their destinies. That very evening she had gone back to his motel room and they'd made love. She had never done anything like that before. Hell, she was only a child! But there had been something about him. She knew she could trust him. He had been so gentle. They were madly in love — period. She knew it. He knew it. There hadn't been a doubt in their minds.

She pulled another swig from the bottle of hooch. It burned as it went down. She was hurting something fierce. She wondered when the pain would go away . . .

She heard the roar of Elmore's motorbike outside her window.

Elmore.

She rose and ran out of her bedroom and went to the front door.

Elmore was home.

She swung open the door and saw him. The helmet dangling in his hand. His tight, black jeans. A red nylon jacket. The heavy boots. He was home from a night run.

"Deb."

The voice ruined it. It wasn't Elmore's. She looked down at herself. Her small pink nipples stood out from her breasts like rosebuds.

"Deb?"

She gazed up at Tommy. She wrapped her arms around herself, covering her nakedness. She felt foolish standing there in her panties.

He came up to her. His eyes staring into hers. He put his hand on her shoulder. It was warm . . . sweaty.

She said, "I'm sorry . . ."

"You okay?"

"I thought I heard Elmore . . ." She shook her head, tears streaming down her cheeks. "I feel so silly."

"There's no need," Tommy said as he put his arm around her and walked her back into the house. They stopped by her bedroom door. The record had ended. Silence closed in around them. They stood there for a while. Her arms still wrapped around her. He could smell the bourbon on her breath.

"I didn't mean nothin'," she said.

"I know."

She hit him with her indigo eyes. "You plan on stickin' around, Tommy?"

"I do," he said.

She dropped her arms and took hold of his hand. It

felt coarse like Elmore's. She led him into the bedroom and shut the door behind them.

The noonday sun glared from the outer edges of the drapes. Deb lay naked on her stomach, a sheet tangled about her feet. Tommy was on his back. It had been a long night *and* morning. He had tried to put out the fire, but it was no use. He'd sat down on the ground with his back against the bike and watched it consume the entire patch of one hundred plants. The aroma of the dope had overwhelmed him. He had passed out and woken up at dawn.

Now he was in bed with his brother's wife!

He didn't even want to analyze that. What the hell would the townspeople think? How would Sage take it? The questions raced through his mind.

Was it all just an accident? She was drunk, and he was delirious from the long night of dope. Maybe she wouldn't even remember what had happened after she woke up. He glanced over at her. She would be out for quite a few hours.

He heard the phone ring faintly from the kitchen. He jumped into his jeans and hurried to answer it before it woke her.

He closed the door and flashed a glance at Sage as he sat on the floor watching television in the next room.

Tommy rushed to the kitchen to pick up the phone. "Yeah?"

"Tommy?" It was a woman's voice.

"Yes."

"This is Mandy Cronenberg."

Tommy rolled his eyes. He wanted to talk to her but not *right* now. He had too many other things on his mind. "Oh yeah, how are you?"

There was a long pause before Mandy said, "Howard

of this. Every time he picked up the phone somebody else was dead. "Jesus, I'm so sorry, Mandy — what the hell happened?"

"Drunk driving."

"Drunk driving?"

"I don't believe it, Tommy. Howard hasn't had a drink in years. I think they only made it look that way."

"*They?*" Tommy had difficulty following her.

"Whoever is behind all this."

"Oh, I didn't tell you about my roommate, Matt — he was killed during a break-in at our apartment."

"*What?*"

"That makes three, Mandy," Tommy said.

"Then they're onto us."

"What do you mean?"

"They know that *we* know. They're closing in on us, Tommy," Mandy sighed. "They're picking us off one by one."

Tommy thought she sounded paranoid. "Well, let's not get carried away now. I'm sure there are logical reasons for these deaths."

"Do you really believe that? Your brother and roommate. My husband. What did they all have in common, huh?" she screeched.

"Calm down. I know how you feel. We have to think rationally . . ."

"*Rationally?*" she snapped. "I don't know about you, but I'm not going to sit around and wait for somebody to come gunning for me."

"I'm not saying that . . ."

"YOU'RE THE ONE THAT GOT US INTO THIS!" she cried.

Tommy shut his eyes. She was right. He had come to her for help, and now her husband was dead. "I'm sorry . . . this is like a fucking nightmare. I would really like to know who's behind all this."

"Don't you get it, Tommy? We must already know who they are."

"Huh?"

"We know who they are, but we don't know we know," she said.

"You're not making too much sense, Mandy."

"Look, we *must* know who they are if they're coming after us."

"Or we're getting too close to finding out what's going on. I did manage to get a name — Tony Bava."

"Who's that?"

"I had a little chitchat with the man Elmore sold his stuff to. This guy told me that Tony Bava of Miami wouldn't touch any dope coming out of Hammett. That it was poisoned."

"How would this Bava guy know *that*?"

"Precisely."

"You think he's behind the dioxin?" Mandy asked.

"He's our best bet."

"What is he exactly?"

"I don't know . . . trafficker or something. Maybe the mob."

"In Miami, you said?"

"Yep."

"I'll be going back down there after . . . *after* the burial," she told him.

"I'm sorry, Mandy."

"Y'know, I feel more angry than sad."

"Angry?"

"Yeah, angry that these guys can just murder people like this. Who the fuck are these people?" she asked angrily.

"Sounds like the mob to me."

"I don't know about that, Tommy," Mandy said. "Howard and I talked it over. He thought it might be the government . . . that they were behind the dioxin."

"The *government*!" Tommy said. "You can't be serious."

"Howard tested the leaves . . . he said it was a dioxin

like Agent Orange. Only worse . . . stronger . . . really dangerous stuff. He injected it into a mouse. It developed the same symptoms that Elmore had — the sores and all.''

"What happened to the mouse after that?"

"I don't know.'' Mandy sounded disappointed. "Howard was killed before he ever got back to me. That was the *other* thing.''

"What other thing?"

"His briefcase was missing from the wreckage. He always carried that damn thing. It was one of those aluminum jobs. I used to kid him about it. I called him the Man from Glad. He kept his notebook in there.''

"A notebook?"

"He kept a diary. He would jot down notes. Things that he thought about. It helped him with his A.A. program. And he also kept some of his work notes in there.''

"Like notes he might've had on the tests?'' Tommy asked.

"You got it,'' she said.

"So you think somebody had him killed and took his briefcase?''

"They took his *notes*,'' she emphasized.

"Was there anybody at the scene of the acccident?''

"Hhhhmmm,'' Mandy mused. "There was the driver of the car who hit him.''

"Maybe he saw something.''

"Yeah, you got something there. Listen, let me give you my Miami hotel number.''

"Okay.''

She gave him the phone number. She told him she would talk to the driver, then return to Miami. There she would talk things over with King about Bava. If he didn't hear from her, he should call her in Miami.

"Okay, Mandy.''

"And Tommy, you better stay away from those plants. God only knows how many may be infected with that poison.''

"Yeah, I'll do that," Tommy said. "Should we go to the authorities?"

"What if they're involved?"

"Yeah . . . Jesus, how will we handle it, then?" he asked.

"We'll manage — there must be some honest people left in this country," she said.

"I'm so sorry for involving you in all this."

"Let's just get to the bottom of this before they manage to kill off any more of us."

"Goodbye." Tommy hung up.

Then it hit him. *Stay away from those pot plants,* she had said.

What about last night?

He had slept there before the burning plants, inhaling their potent vapors. What if they were infected? If so, *he* was now.

"Uncle Tommy."

Tommy looked down at Sage. The little boy tugged on Tommy's hand. Tommy yanked his hand away, out of Sage's reach.

"Don't touch me, Sage!" Tommy snapped.

Sage pouted, "Why not, Uncle Tommy?"

"Just in case," Tommy said, more to himself. "Just in case."

He had to get Deb and Sage out of there. As far away from Hammett as he could take them. Too many had died already.

He peered into Sage's innocent eyes. *A sheep ready for slaughter.*

He examined his hands for any sores. What about Deb? She had worked closely with the plants, too.

He hurried into her room where she still slept. She was bronzed from the sun except for the pale patches on her buttocks and back. He sat down on the edge of the bed and looked at her skin. There were a few birthmarks and freckles but nothing out of the ordinary. He gave a sigh

of relief. He covered her with the sheet and left the room.
Sage was waiting for him. "Is Mommy okay?"
"She's fine, Sage."
"Don't you like me anymore?"
"Of course, pal." He squatted down. "I just didn't
want to give you anything."
He rubbed one of his eyes as he stood there in his short
pajamas. "Are you sick with what Daddy had?"
Tommy shook his head. "I don't think so, Sage. But
I wanna make sure first because I don't want anything
to happen to you."
"That's what Daddy told me. . ." he said as he
marched back to the television set.
Tommy stood up. He felt it all deep inside him. The
frustration. The pain. The feeling of helplessness.
If only Elmore were here. He would have known what
to do.
Then Tommy remembered not too long ago when
Elmore didn't know what to do and had come to *him*
for help. Why had he done that? Elmore had told him
that night that Tommy was stronger than he was. Tommy
had to remember that.
I'm stronger than Elmore.
Then that feeling of helplessness evaporated.
I'll get to the bottom of this.
The pain turned to anger.
How dare they do this to me.

chapter 11

His name was Peter Powell. He lived in a split-level house in Short Hills, New Jersey, with his wife and two children. He was a copywriter for a major advertising firm. He commuted to and from Manhattan every workday. That was what the state trooper had told Mandy.

His wife answered the door. The attractive young woman was dressed in designer jeans and a short-sleeved pink knit shirt. Mandy could hear the children splashing in the backyard pool.

She took a deep breath. "Mrs. Powell, is your husband at home?"

The woman gave Mandy the once-over.

Mandy was wearing a black skirt and a white blouse. She had just come from her husband's burial. Although pretty shook up, she was still determined to investigate her husband's "accident." Maybe keeping busy would help her deal with Howard's death.

"Who should I say is calling on him?" The tone in her voice was suspicious.

"Mandy Cronenberg." The name registered on the woman's face.

"Oh . . ." She paled and swallowed hard. "Are you related to . . . ?"

"I'm his widow."

"I'm very sorry, Mrs. Cronenberg. Please come in."

Mandy entered the plushy carpeted entranceway and followed the woman to the huge kitchen. There was a sandy-haired man with dark-rimmed glasses sitting at the table eating a sandwich.

"Pete, this is Mrs. Cronenberg."

He stopped chewing and stood up. *"Mrs.* Cronenberg?" He was wearing an Izod shirt and a pair of white tennis shorts.

"How do you do." She extended her hand.

Powell shook her hand. "Please sit down."

"Would you like a cup of coffee or something?" Mrs. Powell asked.

"No," Mandy smiled. "No, thank you."

Powell eyed his wife as she sat down. Mandy looked around the kitchen. It seemed larger than her whole apartment. "Beautiful home you have here." She pulled out a microcassette recorder. "Do you mind?"

"No," Powell said nervously.

"Go ahead and finish your lunch . . ."

Powell beheld his half-eaten cheese sandwich with distaste. "No, that's okay. I'm not very hungry. What can I do for you, Mrs. Cronenberg?"

"You were at the scene of the accident."

"That's correct."

"Was there anybody else there?"

"Eh . . . well, I was the first. I mean, your husband's car came out of nowhere and ran smack into me. I wasn't hurt, thank God. Afterwards, I ran to him. The car was a wreck."

"Was there anybody else on the scene?" Mandy wondered.

"Yeah, I'm coming to that. I looked in on your husband. He looked bad. Then I heard this guy behind me."

"What did he say?"

"He said something like he looks bad, you know. I can't remember the exact words. I was so upset. I was never in an accident before," he said.

"Did he say anything else?"

"I don't think so. The other one . . . he said something."

"The *other* one?"

"Yeah, there were two of them. They came out of nowhere — just like *that*." He snapped his fingers. "They were in a black car . . . an Olds or a Buick, I think."

"What did this other one say?"

"He agreed with me."

"What do you mean?"

"I asked them if they thought he was, *you know* — " He wiped his sweaty brow.

"Dead?" Mandy asked with a tremble in her voice. Powell averted his eyes. "Yes."

"What did these two men look like?"

"Well, one was older. He looked like he was from around here. Suburban type."

"What makes you say that?"

"The way he was dressed. The stereotype. Seersucker suit, white shoes — that whole number."

"Pat Boone."

"Yeah. And the other one was just a kid. Blond hair, I think."

"How old?"

"A kid. Maybe twenty or so. He had a funny accent. Southern. And he was missing his two front teeth so he had a lisp."

"Did they say anything else?"

"No, that's all I remember about those two," he said.

"It's funny, they weren't even mentioned in the police report," Mandy noted.

"Oh, they were long gone before the police arrived."

"That's strange — isn't it?" She squinted at him, perplexed.

"I don't think so . . . who wants to get involved?"

"What's this all about, Mrs. Cronenberg?" Mrs. Powell interjected. "And why the tape recorder?"

"I just find my husband's accident very suspicious."

"Well, Pete is telling the truth."

"I'm not accusing your husband of anything. The recorder," she said, holding it up in the air, "that's just for my notes. You see, I'm a reporter."

"A *reporter*?" Mrs. Powell asked.

"Yes, I write for *R & R Express.*"

She shook her head. "Never heard of it . . . hey, you don't plan on writing about my husband, do you?"

Mandy said, "No . . . I'm just here to follow up on some things I felt the police were a little vague about. Now, getting back to those two men."

"Yes?" Powell asked.

"Is there anything else you recall about them?"

"No, they were there and gone in a matter of minutes."

"Did you notice if they took anything from the car?"

"Like what?"

"A briefcase."

"No." He shook his head. "I think I would've noticed that."

"Did you see a briefcase in the car?"

Powell kicked that around for a while. "Everything was a blur . . . I mean, I was *really* upset."

"I understand."

"I don't remember seeing a briefcase . . . but I can't be sure." He seemed frustrated by his attempts to recall the details.

"Do you think you could remember those two men? Their faces? Pick them out of a mug-shot book?"

"I don't know," Powell sighed. "I doubt it."

"Maybe we could make a composite drawing from your description."

Powell and his wife exchanged glances. "I don't understand. Mrs. Cronenberg, what is this all about?" he asked, distressed.

"Murder."

"*Murder?*" Powell asked. "The police said your husband had been drinking. I saw it. He was all over the road."

"I think somebody forced him to get drunk," Mandy explained.

Powell raised his eyebrows. "I know you're perturbed, Mrs. Cronenberg, but perhaps you should *re*think this when you're feeling better."

"You don't believe me?" Mandy asked accusingly.

"It's not that." Powell cleared his throat. "I mean, the police will handle this."

"They've already closed the case."

"See — there you are." Powell waved his hand.

"I knew my husband very well, Mr. Powell." Mandy tried to compose herself, but she had an urgent need to cry. She had been suppressing it ever since the funeral. There would be no stopping it now . . .

"Of course you did . . ."

"Thank you." Mandy hurried out of the house before they could see the tears welling in her eyes.

Powell ran after her. "Mrs. Cronenberg."

But it was too late. She hopped into her car and started the engine. Powell and his wife stood at their doorway as they watched Mandy back out of the driveway and take off down the street.

"I didn't mean to hurt her . . ." Powell mumbled sympathetically.

"It's going to take her a while . . ." Mrs. Powell said.

Tommy couldn't help himself. He *had* to tell someone.

It was eating him up inside. Mandy had told him that he shouldn't go to the authorities, but he thought it was beyond their control.

He had gone to check out Elmore's other hidden patches throughout the local countryside. Deb had showed him the way. The plants in two out of the six patches had been brown and wilted. They'd wondered if it was caused by the dioxin. Tommy had worn gloves as he examined the dead leaves and stems. He hadn't seen the brown chemical around. But he had noticed something unusual.

"Do you hear that?" he asked.

"What?" Deb held her breath to listen carefully. "I don't hear anythin'."

"*Exactly.*" Tommy was standing in the middle of the decaying patch looking all around. "No birds. No insects. Not a single living thing."

Deb was puzzled. "What does it mean?"

Tommy came up to her. "It means this place must be contaminated and we shouldn't be *here.*"

"Do you think this chemical not only killed off the plants, but the wildlife, too?"

They gazed into one another's eyes silently.

Finally, Tommy said, "How long can you hold your breath?"

That was when Tommy had decided to go see Carpenter. He remembered Elmore telling him that he had gone to Carpenter for help and had not been satisfied. But a lot of things had happened since. Perhaps Carpenter would be more receptive now.

Carpenter was hunched over his desk when Tommy entered his storefront office.

"Carpenter?"

He glanced up.

"I have to talk with you . . . about something important."

"Of course, Tommy, sit down." Carpenter sat back

in his chair and smiled. "Now, what's on your mind?"

Mandy slammed her office phone down. *"SHIT!"*
    Manville came into her cubicle. "What's up?"
    "Fucking police are useless."
    "I thought I gave you a week off?"
    "I have to work, Rob," she said.
    "On what?"
    "On my husband's murder case."
Manville sat down on the chair next to her desk.
"Mandy, Mandy, Mandy. What're you doing to
yourself?"
    "Nobody will listen to me."
    "Your whole scheme doesn't make very much sense,
Mandy. Come on, we're all sorry for Howard. But you
knew Howard . . . he was *troubled.*"
    "Give me a break, Rob."
    "Why don't you really take a week off . . . spend some
time with your folks?"
    "My folks? They didn't even bother coming down for
the funeral. You know how much they despised him.
They didn't go to the wedding, so why bother with the
funeral — right?"
    "I seem to remember that they weren't *invited* to the
wedding," he reminded her coyly.
    "Goddamn your memory, Rob." She exhaled a long
stream of cigarette smoke.
    "If you want to work, you still owe me the Marlowe
piece."
    "Don't you see — this is *more* important."
    "I won't allow you to dwell on this, Mandy. You're
a pro — pros don't get personally involved. That's rule
numero uno," he said.
    "Rob, three people have been murdered."
    "No, Mandy, *one* man was murdered. A criminal was
involved with drugs. It happens every day. Another was
killed when he interrupted a break-in, and Howard died

from a drunk-driving accident. They are all unrelated deaths. Coincidental — maybe. Conspiratorial? Only inside your *own* head."

She lit up another cigarette and puffed away angrily. "Why is everyone working against me?"

. "It's alright to feel that way, Mandy. You're upset. Your husband is dead. You feel like you're losing control. You need to invent this murder investigation so you can force yourself to deal with it. Don't you see?"

"Are you shrinking me, Rob?" she asked.

"I'm trying to help you, dammit," Manville said.

"If you want to help me, Rob, leave me alone."

"You probably feel responsible . . . guilty."

"Guilty?" Mandy beheld him sternly. "Guilty about *what*?"

"You were away when it happened. Maybe there was some static between you and him before you left."

"Mind your own business."

"Think about it, Mandy. Cope with it, don't invent something else . . . something that isn't there."

"Enough, Doc."

"I care, y'know," he said sincerely.

Mandy took his hand. "I know, Rob."

Carpenter listened to Tommy's story. He went along with the disturbed man. He had to make it look like he was concerned. But then a name popped up and Carpenter got nervous.

Bava.

Tommy Shepard knew too much.

"Well," Carpenter grinned, "you'll have to admit your story sounds pretty farfetched. What with talk of deadly dioxins and conspiracies!"

"You don't believe me, then?"

"I think you're just too emotionally wound up. It's hard for a man to look at things when he's personally involved. I'll tell you what — I'll look into it. As I told your brother, I had the brown sap tested, and it's harmless — *really*."

"But I had it tested up north and was told it was some kind of dioxin," he related.

Carpenter laughed. "The stuff that I had tested for Elmore was no dioxin."

Tommy looked Carpenter in the eye. There was a strange expression on Tommy's face. "There's one way to find out."

"Oh?"

"The autopsy report." Tommy said. "Elmore's *autopsy* report."

Carpenter swallowed hard. "What about it?"

"There must've been some trace of the dioxin in Elmore's body."

"Yeah, that's a good idea. I'll have to give the coroner a call."

"Where is he?"

"Jacksonville."

"Why don't you give him a call right now?" Tommy asked excitedly.

"*Right now?*" Carpenter held up his hands. "Don't worry, Tommy, I'll give him a ring . . . *later*." He picked up his pen. "I'm very busy now."

"I don't know why I didn't think of it before now."

"Yeah . . ." Carpenter agreed. "Me neither."

Tommy stood up. "So I'll be hearing from you?"

"Yes." Carpenter shook his hand. "Have a nice day."

Carpenter watched Tommy leave his office. He walked across the street to his motorbike. He chatted awhile with a passing neighbor. Then he took off.

Carpenter picked up the phone and dialed. He could barely keep his fingers from shaking. *Damn bastard knows more about this operation than I do!*

"Is Mr. Pope there?"

"No, Mr. Pope isn't in right now. May I take a message?" The secretary's voice was husky — evidently an older woman.

"Eh — " Carpenter thought it over. "Never mind."
He hung up and sat there in anguish. *How in hell did
I get involved in all this?*

Hank Pope.

He was so convincing. Of course, the figures he tossed
around had made Carpenter's mouth water. He hadn't
asked for much. He'd just wanted to try a little experi-
ment in Hammett. Clean up the town. Show the President he had been doing his job as head of his anti-drug
program. Pope had promised to drop Carpenter's name
to the President. Just think of the prospects. Why waste
away in this small nowhere town picking up petty cash
when you could move up the ladder politically? *Your
pockets will be overflowing,* Pope assured him with an
all-knowing wink.

Carpenter would have to help orchestrate the pro-
ceeding for Pope. That was all. If he had any problems,
he should speak with Tony Bava in Miami.

Then Elmore had come to Carpenter with that brown
sap. And the poor bastard had looked so ill. Carpenter
had pacified him just like Bava instructed him.

The next thing Carpenter knew, there had been a
shootout in town. A goddamn massacre right in his own
town! That hadn't been a part of the plan. How was he
supposed to cover something like *that* up? He had to convince that federal agent, Frank Bigelow, from Jacksonville that he had everything under control. He still had
doubts that Bigelow bought his story.

Bava had told him not to be concerned about it. Just
make sure that *no* autopsy was performed on Elmore
Shepard's body. *Why not?* Carpenter wondered. Bava
had refused to give him an explanation.

Then Tommy Shepard had come in with this tale about
dioxins and conspiracies and mentioned Bava by name.
There had never been any talk about dioxins and murder.
Carpenter didn't like the smell of this. Things were out

of hand. It was time to get to the bottom of this once and for all.

That meant calling Hank Pope *directly.*

He unlocked his desk drawer and retrieved his black, leather-bound phone book that lay next to one of the last jelly jars of Old Ben's moonshine. He looked up Pope's home phone number. He had sworn he would never call him directly — *ever.* All communications between them would be handled through Bava. Carpenter reconsidered a moment before he picked up the phone and dialed the number.

I deserve an explanation! Carpenter reassured himself and remained on the line.

His wife was the most elegant woman in Washington — there was no doubt about that. The society columns still spoke of her with admiration — Alexis Cosima Pope, the estranged wife of Henry "Hank" Pope and daughter and heiress of Alexander Cosima.

Alexander Cosima, a talented European designer, had numerous boutiques around the world, including New York, Beverly Hills, and Paris. A multimillionaire well into his advanced years, Cosima was a widower with only one child, his beloved Alexis.

She had dark, haunting features, long chestnut-brown hair, and cocoa eyes. Her skin was as dark as a tropical suntan. She was tall and possessed a model's lithesome figure.

Pope was still madly in love with her. She was his only weakness.

Although legally separated, they still saw one another several times a week. He was courting her again, trying desperately to convince her that he had changed.

Alexis had left him during his depressed period when he began drinking excessively. He had been unduly rude to her family and friends. He was only now becoming the person he once was — the man that she had fallen deeply in love with. At least, he was doing his utmost to convince her of that.

They had a long romantic lunch and were now back at his Georgetown town house. It was a quaint but elegant brick structure with a warmly furnished interior. Alexis had decorated it herself and Pope had never altered it — even after she'd left him some five years ago.

They lay together beneath the satin sheets. She was wrapped in his arms, their naked bodies one.

Pope had yet to ask Alexis to return to him . . . to be his wife again. He'd hinted about it enough times, but he always played it gently. He didn't want to push her into anything. He wanted the idea to come from her . . . she should make the decision.

Any phone call alone would have ruined their wonderful afternoon, but when it turned out to be Carpenter on the other end, Pope couldn't restrain his temper.

"What the hell did I tell you, Carpenter!" Pope's voice was trembling with anger. "Never call me *here*!"

"I had to . . . it's an emergency."

"An *emergency*?" Pope repeated sarcastically. "It's *always* an emergency with you!"

"It's about Tommy Shepard."

"How is it that I keep hearing Tommy Shepard's name being batted around?" Pope eyed his wife as she slipped out from under the satin sheets to get dressed.

"He knows too much, Hank."

"How much is *too* much?"

"He knows about Bava."

"*Bava!*" Pope shouted, and then said more quietly, "Hold on." He covered the mouthpiece and smiled at Alexis as she put on a silk blouse over her bare torso, her dark erect nipples showing through the white fabric. "I'm sorry, honey. Damn business problem."

"I understand." She walked over and kissed him, then left the room.

Pope got back on the phone. "Goddammit — how did he find out?"

"I have no idea. I tried to get it out of him."

"Who would have told him?"

"I don't know. He's been nosing around *every*where."

"You're supposed to be watching him."

"I can't watch him twenty-four hours a day, Hank. You pulled your men out. I have no one to assist me."

"I needed my men elsewhere. What does Shepard know about Bava?" Pope asked.

"Nothing."

"He knows his name — that's *something*."

"Yes," Carpenter said.

"Okay — okay," Pope said. "I'll handle it — *as usual*."

"In the meantime, I'll keep an eye on him."

"You better, Carpenter."

"I will."

After a short pause, Pope said, "Time to end this once and for all."

"Huh?"

"I'm not talking to you, dammit!"

"There's one other thing," Carpenter said sheepishly.

"There's *more*?"

"Shepard wants to see his brother's autopsy report. You know I paid off the coroner not to perform one."

"Don't worry about Shepard — I'll take care of him," Pope assured him. "Is that it?"

"Yep."

"Then hang up, for chrissakes!"

Pope stayed on the line to hear the click and then the dial tone. The operation was in jeopardy because of this Tommy Shepard! And because of Carpenter's weaknesses. Both would have to be terminated. He would send Sharp off on a long-overdue vacation. He had done his share in this case. Now he needed somebody with a different approach to do the job. Someone not directly attached to Intelligence. An outsider.

He thought it over as the phone buzzed in his ear. Then it came to him.

George Michael Karb.

Perfect. A Hollywood stuntman, G.M. Karb had been thrown out of several stuntman organizations and lost his SAG card because of unprofessional behavior. Now he worked in non-union exploitation movies and road-tested cars for the major car companies. He had done a job for Pope before and was damned efficient.

Pope wondered where he could find him . . .

Alexis stood just outside her husband's bedroom door-way, her ear pressed to the fine wood door. What were the names he mentioned? . . . Carpenter, Tommy Shepard, and Bava. She made mental notes of Pope's phone conversation. Too bad she didn't bring along a recorder of some sort. But where would she have hidden that?

Then she heard Pope dialing the phone after a long pause. Who was he calling? It was only seven numbers — a local call.

"Fred — this is Pope," he said. "Do me a favor. Run a check on George Michael Karb. K-A-R-B . . . George Michael. Got that? Good. Put a superpriority on this. And one more thing, Fred. Keep this under wraps. That's right. I owe you one."

She heard him hang up. She hurried away from the door and finished dressing. A few moments later, Pope opened his door. He had a big smile for her as he stood there naked. "Sorry about that, dear."

"I understand." She returned his smile.

"We can finish what we started now . . ."

She shook her head. "That's okay . . . I have already finished dressing."

He seemed disappointed.

She was relieved. "Next time, okay, Hank?" She

pecked him on the lips and turned to leave.

Pope watched her descend the winding staircase. Her beauty still sent shivers throughout his body. He wanted her back so bad it hurt.

Mandy sat on the living room sofa. The television set was on, and the stereo was blasting Rick Marlowe's sound. The network news and Marlowe — a lethal combination.

She gazed at her wedding photograph on top of the TV set. It was Howard and her, dressed in antique clothing, standing under a weeping willow tree. It had been a nice affair. Folk music. A hippie service. She didn't invite her folks because they had not approved of them living together. They had never like Howard. They thought she could have done better than a former drug addict.

Howard. She'd miss him. His smile. His sweetness. His anger. His troubled soul.

She had to make a morning flight tomorrow. She had an appointment with King. He had to find something out for her. Something about Tony Bava.

But first things first.

She began to cry.

chapter 12

Like the lunar landscape, a white flat earth for miles and miles in every direction. Utah's salt flats. The sun was bright, the air cool and painfully dry. There was no breeze.

It was a good day for a crash.

He was dressed in a white zippered jump suit and a white helmet with a black sunshade mask. He pressed down hard on the accelerator pedal. The engine roared like a purring panther. The car was red. Sleek and sexy. Satan's chariot.

He heard the green light command buzz in his ear. He shifted gears. The vehicle screeched ahead.

Then he saw it in the distance straight ahead.

A gray wall of cement blocks.

He glanced at the speedometer. One hundred and forty miles per hour.

The wall crept closer. A dryness came to his throat. He felt a tightness in his bad knee.

One hundred and forty-five miles per hour.

His eyes burned from the salty sweat that inched down from his forehead.

The wall was before him.

He was right on course — *dead center of the wall.*

Then he hit it. Within a split second of the impact, the air bag swelled up against him. He heard the agonized cries of twisted metal and breaking glass. And the pressure driving him forward . . . *foward* into the wall. He felt his stomach take a dip, and he vomited violently inside his mask.

Then silence fell over him. Like white noise. A hissing sound filled his eardrums. He was underwater and out of breath — he felt like he was drowning.

"Eh — you alright, Karb?" The voice crackled over his helmet receiver.

The door sprang open and strong, thick arms pulled him out. They dragged him away from the smoking car.

Suddenly, an explosion ripped at them, shaking the ground beneath. His two saviors were knocked off their feet.

Karb yanked off his helmet and gagged on his vomitus. The car was engulfed in flames.

Honda came running up to him and put her arm around his shoulders. "KARB!"

"I'm okay, Honda." She helped him to his feet.

He straightened up, and his back cracked loudly. "God *damn!"*

A technician came up to him. "You okay?"

"Still breathing," Karb grinned. "Come on, girl, let's get the fuck outta here."

They walked arm in arm to his gigantic recreational vehicle parked some distance away.

"How's ya back?" Honda asked.

"Fine," Karb said as he took the tequila bottle she handed him. "It's this damn taste in my mouth." He sucked a mouthful out of the bottle.

The young Oriental girl, dressed in a pink bikini top

and black denim cutoffs, handed him his painkillers.
He popped a handful of pills and washed them down
with the tequila.
She opened the door of the RV and he climbed in. He
went to the back where the shower stall was. She came
up behind him and unzipped his jump suit. He stepped
out of it, completely naked. She ran her slender fingers
over his taut, hairy, scarred torso — a virtual bat-
tleground. "Oh, my poor baby," she cooed as she gazed
deeply into his gray eyes. His white hair was cropped
short and stood like tiny bristles on top of his skull. He
had thick dark eyebrows and a broken nose. His lips were
lean, and his smile gleamed from a brand-new set of
pearl-white dentures. His skin was dark from the Cali-
fornia sun and creased from the never-ending pain. He
was pushing forty but appeared much older. Karb had
been stunting for twenty years and had broken forty-two
bones. He had a plastic kneecap that squeaked when he
walked. There was a metal brace attached to the outer
side of his left leg to keep his bones in place. That caused
him to limp. He had also broken his back once, and it
was never the same since.
Honda, sixteen, with long black hair, kneeled down
and wrapped his brace in plastic for the shower. When
she was finished, she gripped his penis and pressed it
tightly. It grew miraculously in her hand. It was the only
real part of his body left.
She stood up and he undid her bikini top. Her small
breasts came into view, the dark nipples standing at atten-
ion before him.
He unsnapped her cutoffs, and they fell to her feet.
A soft, black mound of hair covered her pelvis. He
hugged her closely, gripping her buttocks in each hand.
"You looked *so* good out there, Karb."
He smiled and kissed her, their tongues darting play-
fully inside each other's mouths. He turned on the shower
and they stepped into the stall. "Did you get it on tape?"

"Of course, Karb."

"Good girl."

Karb washed the sweat and puke off while Honda soaped up his body. *She's a good kid*, Karb thought. He had picked her up on Ocean Front Walk in Venice one morning. She had been on roller skates, dancing to the beat of her headphones, wearing a black micro-bikini. Flat and hard and jailbait. Karb fell in love at first sight. That had been six months ago. She had been with him ever since. He called her Honda, after the Japanese bike he had as a youngster. In fact, it was that dirt bike he had as a boy that got him interested in stunt work in the first place.

They stepped out of the shower and dried one another off. Honda ran naked into the bedroom, giggling all the way.

"You have something in mind, little girl?" Karb went over to the VCR and popped in a cartridge. *G.M. Karb's Greatest Hits.* He switched on the 27-inch monitor he had fixed at an angle on the ceiling, and the screen came alive with images of some of Karb's best work.

He turned on the cassette deck and the new wave group, *X,* vibrated out of the four-foot-high speakers.

Karb stood at the edge of the bed. Honda lay there, her knees up, her sex beckoning to him.

He slowly climbed onto the bed. She held his head as he inched up her body with his tongue. She looked up at the monitor.

A car sideswipes a truck, and the truck goes off the road, crashing into a canyon . . .

He sucked on her breasts.

A chopper falls from the sky and explodes in a burning inferno . . .

She felt him inside her.

A motorcycle sails in the air and misses the landing cliff; the bike falls into the ocean below . . .

Karb's back crackled as he plunged into her . . . *deeper and deeper.*

A man on a hang-glider crashes head-on into a helicopter, and the propeller tears the hang-glider into pieces . . .

"Karb!" Honda cried out as the music shattered her eardrums, as the images assaulted her vision, as her clitoris pulsated into orgasmic waves.

Karb rammed it in harder as he exploded inside her, filling her cavity with his burning motor oil.

He collapsed on top of her with a groan, their sweltering bodies entangled, the stench of sex all around them.

Karb rolled onto his back and took a swig of tequila. He was wondering what his next move might be. He had no other gags planned after this test drive. He thought about going back to L.A. and trying to pick up some splatter movie work. The makeup people had a field day working on him.

"Karb." Honda stood up and took a manila envelope off a nearby table. "This came for you before."

"For *me*?"

"Some guy in a van dropped it off," Honda said.

Karb sat up and grabbed the envelope from her. His name was printed on the front. Nothing else. *Strange,* Karb thought.

He tore it open, and a bound stack of one-hundred-dollar bills fell out.

"What the fuck?" Karb was bewildered.

"Wow — look at all that green stuff." Honda spread out the bills all over the bed.

He peeked into the package and pulled out two smaller envelopes. One envelope held an invitation to an art show opening in Georgetown for the following evening.

"What's that?"

Karb looked into her black eyes. "Beats me."

"What's in the other one?"

He tore it open and there was a one-way plane ticket from Salt Lake City to Washington, D.C. "I guess I'm going on a little trip."

"Where?"

"Back east."

She wrinkled her nose.

He grinned at her. "I was wondering what my next gag was going to be," Karb said and laughed.

"What about *me*?"

"You gotta mind the store, little girl."

She pouted.

He reached out and touched her soft cheek. She was a beautiful girl. She was born in Vietnam. That was what she'd told him. Her grandparents had brought her over. She didn't remember much about the war. Karb remembered it all too well. He'd filled her in. A person shouldn't forget their roots, Karb thought, *especially* the horror stories.

"How long will you be gone?"

He shrugged. "As long as it takes." When he saw the Washington plane ticket, he knew what it was all about.

Hank Pope needed him.

Karb wondered what the old bastard was up to. Their last job together had proved fruitful. Pope had hired Karb to put a little muscle on a political opponent. That had been back when Pope was considering running for Congress. He never did pull it off. But, there was one thing you could say about Pope — he was generous with the government's money. He glanced at his watch. He didn't have much time to drive back to Salt Lake City and catch that flight tomorrow.

He eyed Honda and shook his head. He was sure going to miss her.

What the hell . . . he had time for another round.

Sage straddled Tommy's knee as he sat on the living room sofa. He had just run a few miles and was still dressed in his jogging gear.

Deb came in and dropped off a cup of coffee. She sat down next to them and put her arm around Tommy. "How're my two men doing?"

"We're doing great — right, sport?"

"Yep." Sage was having a good time riding his uncle's knee.

"You've been so quiet during these last few days," she said.

Tommy nodded. "Been thinking."

"About what?"

"You and Sage."

"Oh, *yeah*?" she smirked.

Tommy laughed. "It's not what you're thinking."

"Oh, no?" She ran her fingers through his hair. "Your hair is so light compared to Elmore's."

"Yeah." Tommy smiled at the thought. "Elmore used to kid me about it. Said Mom fooled around with the farm help."

Deb giggled. "Elmore always had a good sense of humor."

"What I was thinking about . . ."

"Yeah?"

". . . was the two of you getting the hell out of Hammett," Tommy said frankly.

Deb sighed and put her hands in her lap. "I don't know."

"Only until all this blows over."

"How come you want us to leave?" She looked hurt.

"I'm just afraid for you and Sage."

"What about you?" she asked.

"I can't leave right now."

"Why not?"

"I'm working on something . . . *something* that has claimed three lives already, and I don't want anything to happen to you guys."

She gave him a provocative sideways glance. "You have any regrets about the other day?"

Tommy sighed. "I don't know. You were drunk. I was stoned. Sometimes I wonder if it really happened."

"It happened all right," Deb said.

"Does it bother you like it bothers me?"

She stood up and put her hands on her hips. "I think it was just too soon. I mean, I liked it. I really needed something. Some contact, y'know? I guess I feel some guilt, too. Was it right what we did?" she asked, her voice trembling.

"Jesus, Deb, how the hell do I know?" Tommy threw his hands up.

"Is that it — the end — no more?"

Tommy averted his eyes.

"Is that why you want us to split?" she asked angrily.

"You know the reason."

"Do you feel for me, Tommy?"

"Very much so," Tommy said.

"I think we can work it out."

"In time, perhaps," he said. "Right now I'm real worried about your welfare."

Deb leaned over and kissed him. "I'll go only if you promise we'll work things out together."

Tommy grinned. "I promise."

"Now where do you want us to go?"

"Remember that old farmhouse my Daddy built?" Tommy asked. "Elmore and I have been renting it out for years. It's empty right now. It will be a nice, quiet place."

"Can I ever come back here?"

"Of course. This is your home."

"*Our* home," Deb specified. "You'll be okay by yourself?"

Tommy nodded.

She didn't really want to leave him alone. She did not know if it was right what they had done. But it felt good to be close to him. She loved him. Maybe it wasn't the same love she had for Elmore, but it was love. Being tight with Tommy made her feel like she was still with Elmore. She knew that didn't make much sense, but emotions never do. She decided to go along with his wishes . . . at least for Sage's sake. "I better get lunch together. How's peanut butter-and-banana sandwiches sound?"

Tommy didn't answer. He was in deep thought again.

Debra shrugged and went into the kitchen.

Tommy was thinking about Mandy. He wondered how she was doing. She must be back in Florida by now. He had an urge to call her. He really didn't have anything important to tell her, so he decided not to. She might get angry with him if he told her he went to Carpenter. He still had a problem trusting her. Shit, he didn't even know her. He could hardly remember what she looked like. She was just a voice on the telephone. But she did lose a loved one, as he had. He knew now that she wasn't in this just to get a story out of it. She wanted to know who murdered her husband. He had to believe that. He had to believe in *her*.

King sat on the edge of the bed in Mandy's hotel room. She had just come out of the shower wrapped in a towel and stood by the dresser, sipping her gin and tonic. He felt embarrassed by her lack of modesty. She had always been so nonchalant. He admired her for that. He wished he wasn't so uptight about everything.

"Tony Bava," King said. "You wanted me to dig up some facts about him."

"What's his game?" Mandy asked. "Drugs?"

"Rumor has it," King said. "Used to be, anyway."

"*Used* to be — are we talking in the past tense here, Dave?"

"Probably present tense, too. Now, that would make it interesting."

"Why?" she asked.

"He's the Business Manager for Cardinal Airlines," King said.

"I'm impressed."

"He used to run a fleet of charter boats off the Rock. That's where the drug rumor comes in. But he was never caught at it."

She leaned against the wall. "The Business Manager of Cardinal Airlines." Her mind wandered at the thought.

"In fact, our man Bava is Cardinal's right-hand man. He doesn't shit without Bava standing by with a roll of tissue for him."

"Intimate."

"*Very.*"

Jonathan Cardinal was a self-made multimillionaire. He had revolutionized commercial flying when he'd introduced his new lower-priced "No-Frills" airline. He had been a successful executive with a major international airline before he invested in forming his own company. The fifty-two-year-old bachelor, married and divorced three times, was also quite popular with the gossip columnists because of his swinging lifestyle of fast cars and faster women. He had dated many famous celebrities and was well received in social circles. He was the last person Mandy expected to be tied up with Tony Bava.

"Very interesting — *no?*" King broke her concentration.

"Do you know what we might have here?" Mandy was overjoyed. "We could be onto the biggest crime caper ever!"

"*Or* we could be dreaming."

Mandy dismissed him with a wave of her hand. "I have a lot of homework to do on Cardinal."

"Hey, now hold on here." King stood up. "You review rock. albums and do performer profiles, not criminal investigation. We're talking pro-reporter stuff here, Mandy."

"I'm not a pro? I did a series of articles on cocaine

abuse in the record industry last year — I know what I'm doing.''

"Mandy, listen to me. This could be very dangerous. If you're right, Cardinal isn't going to appreciate you snooping around.''

"I'm sorry I'm not a hot-shot reporter like you.''

King inhaled deeply and slowly let out a sigh. "I'm not a hotshot reporter. Every good man knows his limitations — you know what I mean?''

Mandy nodded.

"I'm only offering advice. Plugging away on your terminal in the office is one thing. But going out on the fucking street — that's a whole other ball game, Mandy. I went through the wringer to get where I am today. Do you know where I am? *Zip*ville. You want to know why? Because I'm not good enough. And I can admit that. I know my limitations; therefore, I'm stronger for it. I write cultural articles about Little Havana, not interviews with professed Omega 7 terrorists. *Comprende?*" King asked.

"Lesson over?" Mandy snarled.

"Okay, I'll ask around for you. Talk to the boys in research. I'll get the tag on Bava.''

"And don't forget about Cardinal.''

"*And* Cardinal.''

"And what can I do?" Mandy asked.

"I believe you still owe that Marlowe piece to Rob.''

Mandy rolled her eyes. "You've been talking with Rob, I see.''

"He called me. Wanted me to help you out as best I can. That's what I'm doing," King said.

"Did he tell you that I was crazy?''

"He didn't have to — I've always known that about you," King smiled. "By the way, I've been doing my own homework on Marlowe. Interesting fellow. Did you know he was a Nam vet?''

"That's well known, Dave."

"They say he was very depressed lately. What with the political and social climate going on here. I think our man Marlowe was the last of the great liberals. I can't believe his songs ever made it to the top ten."

"Why not?"

"They're so political . . . so bitter."

Mandy shrugged. "Nobody listens to the words, Dave. He made good music."

King shook his head and kissed her on her cheek. "Sounds like he was a helluva guy."

She still owed Rob a piece on Marlowe. She would have to try to work on both stories at the same time. She knew that wouldn't be easy, but what choice did she have? Manville would pull the plug on her if he found out she wasn't down here doing the Marlowe piece. Now she had to come up with some angle on the Marlowe story so she could at least get started on that. "I still need some kind of hook on Marlowe."

"Listen to his *words* this time. Maybe something will come to you."

Mandy watched him leave the room. *Listen to his words.*

"Superstar turned black hole," Mandy said aloud as she recalled some of Marlowe's lyrics. "Man who lost his soul."

Man who lost his soul.

"Hey, I think I found my angle!" she said excitedly to herself.

chapter 13

G.M. Karb lay down on the table. The attendant, dressed in white, attached the electrodes to Karb's chest,
abdomen, back, thighs, arms, and buttocks. He switched
on the console.

Karb felt the tingling throughout his nerve endings.
"Higher."

The attendant increased the intensity of the impulses.

Karb's limbs began to convulse — his left leg rocked
from side to side. He'd had the brace removed just a few
hours previously. He had to get in shape for Pope's mis-
sion. He was too soft. This EMS treatment usually did
the trick when he didn't have the proper time for a
workout. Karb had been using Electrical Muscle Stimula-
tion for years, mainly for muscle rehabilitation after being
laid up with one of his many injuries. Now, "passive exer-
cise" had become a fashionable health program for the
lazy masses. Forty-five dollars for forty-five minutes was
the going rate these days.

Karb had flown in to Washington, D.C., that morning

and checked into his swanky Pennsylvania Avenue hotel room with a terrace that overlooked the C & O canal.

As the current flowed through his body, he wondered what his new gag would be. He recalled that Pope had been ousted from his C.I.A. seat. What the hell was he involved with now — business or personal? He knew there had never been a clear division between business and private life in Pope's spectrum.

Any gag was better than doing horror-movie schlock. In his last film, he'd played a wacko killer of naked coeds. His weapon? A hot soldering iron used to burn out the young ladies' eyeballs. This flick made *Grand Guignol* look like a Saturday-morning cartoon. Jesus, did the red-dyed karo syrup flow in that picture! Even Karb, not known for being too particular about classy gags, had felt dirty and immoral after working on that one.

The attendant shut off the console and detached the electrodes. *Gee, that was forty-five minutes?* Karb stood up and flexed his muscles. *Yeah, they were back again.* He was feeling good, his veins like taut cables, running up and down his thick arms.

He scanned his Rolex — he didn't have much time until the art opening.

Alexis Cosima Pope was dressed in one of her father's luxuriously designed evening gowns. She sat across the dinner table from Barry Nulls, Assistant Attorney General. He was meticulously attired in a black tuxedo and bow tie. His sandy hair, parted on the right side, was softly coiffed. His catlike green eyes glowed in the candlelight. He couldn't keep his attention off his beautiful date. The noise of the five-star restaurant didn't seem to interfere with his concentration.

"Do you like the champagne?" he asked.

"Very much so."

"I'm glad we finally made it out in public," he said sincerely.

It was a rarity that the couple ventured out on the town for all the world to see. Alexis did not like the limelight. She had grown up in it because of her father, and when she'd married Pope it had intensified even more. She hated reading about her personal life in gossip columns. It was nobody's business what she did with her life. And the tongues would wag when it got out that she was having an affair with the handsome, thirty-six-year-old Assistant Attorney General. But she knew how much it meant to Nulls to go out for dinner like any other couple in the nation's capital.

Although not yet divorced, she considered her marriage to Pope finished. She had actually grown to hate the man. She despised the way he tried to charm his way back into her life. He was a selfish, power-hungry snake. She only continued to see him to spy on him for Nulls. Pope was working far too independently for a government employee. He answered to no one — not even the President. This alarmed the Attorney General's office. They did not want another J. Edgar Hoover running around Washington. And that was exactly who Pope was beginning to resemble. People were becoming increasingly fearful of him. He seemed to possess enough dirty linen on important governmental officials to intimidate them. The Attorney General would not stand for that and had assigned his assistant, Nulls, to keep an eye on him.

Before his assignment, Nulls had already been emotionally involved with Alexis. She had planned to ask Pope for a divorce to marry Nulls. But when his new assignment had come up, they discussed a different stratagem. It was *she* who had suggested that she act as spy on Nulls' behalf. Pope would never suspect her of any wrongdoing. She knew it might mean becoming closer to him . . . even sleeping with him. That had bothered her and almost dissuaded her. But she'd decided to go ahead with it. She would do anything to hurt that bastard.

Pope was a mean drunk. It wasn't beneath him to antagonize his wife with violent verbal abuse. He had also resented her family fortune. He treated her father with total disrespect. The man that she had married was a warm, docile, even-tempered man. But when things had begun going badly for him, he couldn't cope with it. He'd become a horrible Mr. Hyde. And even now when things were going well for him again, he remained a nasty, poisoned man. He trusted no one. He treated his staff coarsely. He became a tyrant. No matter how hard he tried to show his "good side" to Alexis to win her back, she saw the monster lurking inside him, ready to pounce on anyone who disagreed with him.

Barry Nulls was the complete opposite of Pope. Yes, he was ambitious. All the men in Washington were ambitious. She liked that in a man. Her father possessed more ambition than anyone she had ever known. But he also had a heart and soul — two things Pope had lost a long time ago. Nulls also cared. He really cared about his country. And he loathed men like Pope who took advantage of their power. Pope loved to stamp out people like they were insects.

Nulls slipped on his tinted, wire-framed glasses and began reading the menu. Alexis observed him lovingly. She had not told him of her latest rendezvous with Pope. Though he appreciated her assisting him in watching Pope, it upset Nulls for her to have any contact with him.

"Hank is involved in something deep, Barry," she said.

Nulls glanced at her over the top of the menu. "You saw him?"

She nodded. "Yesterday." She saw that he was hurt. "Nothing happened," she added.

He put down the menu. "What do you mean he's involved with something?"

"I overheard a phone conversation," she related. "It seemed to have distressed Hank. I wrote down as much as I could remember."

"Did you get any names?"

"Quite a few."

"Good."

"What the hell do you think he's up to?" she wondered aloud.

"When it comes to Hank Pope, God only knows," Nulls said. "We know he's involved in something way over his head. We just have to pinpoint the location. You don't know where the call came from?"

She shook her head.

"Every time we tap his phone, he uncovers it. He's always one step ahead of us. He has calls coming through so many different outlets that they are impossible to trace back."

"I wonder . . ." Alexis mused.

"What do you have?" Nulls asked.

"The call he got. He was annoyed about receiving it. It seemed to have been an emergency."

"Which means it didn't go through the usual channels. The phone company will have a record of it. Yes — that's it!" Nulls was grinning from ear to ear. "It's a good chance we will find out the location. And with your list of names . . . this could be it, Alexis."

"We caught the big rat?"

"Oh — not yet. Soon. First we have to set the trap." Nulls waved over the waiter. "A phone, please."

"Very good, sir." The waiter left to get a phone.

"I'll have my office check with the phone company."

She saw how excited he was. "You seem to be glowing."

He whipped off his glasses and beamed at her. "Did I ever tell you that I love you?"

"Many times." Her eyes sparkled. "Many times."

Pope, dressed handsomely in a black tuxedo, sipped his champagne as he stood before a huge canvas depicting a large black face, a subway car, and the artist's tag,

Snatch. Graffiti had now become an art form. Pope shook his head. Modern art. *What would a self-professed savage like Gauguin think of this shit?* Pope smirked at the thought.

Pope drifted around the room, catching snags of dialogue. It seemed most of the people favored this crap art. They should take a ride on the New York City subway system and see this precious art form in all its glory.

Just then, someone caught Pope's eye. He was wearing a black leather suit and a black tee shirt. His crop of white hair and deeply creased face didn't seem to belong to the hard and lean body. He glanced through the program, passed up a glass of champagne, and wandered about the room.

Karb had aged in the last ten years. His appearance was a shock. Too many years of painkillers and booze. Pope seriously wondered if Karb would be up to what he had in mind.

Their eyes locked. Pope nodded. Karb averted his gaze and coughed into his program booklet. They made contact. Pope briskly left the room and went outside into the thick, hot air.

Karb lingered awhile, drifting by the canvases. The dazzling colors danced in his eyes. He liked the feel of this stuff. It was raw. It reeked of protest and energy. It captured the youthful spirit perfectly. All it took was a repressed environment, a spray can, and some imagination. You could keep your fucking computer graphics. This was where the heart and soul lay.

Karb wasn't a pretentious man. But he always considered himself an artist. His work was his art. His tools were his own flesh and blood. He proved that man could go beyond his natural physical and mental boundaries. One could s-t-r-e-t-c-h. *Break down the barriers* was Karb's battle cry. His head was filled with the teachings of Nietzsche and Wilhelm Reich. Both probably madmen. Maybe so, but at least they strived for something more.

There had to be *more,* Karb thought . . . *hoped.*

He blinked out of his concentration and hurried outside. The door transported him from a cool, white environment into a tropical, dense, polluted street. The heat hung heavily in the air, the unseasonable heat wave still with them. Karb immediately began to perspire. He turned the corner where Pope's stretch limo was waiting. Without missing a beat, Karb entered the back door. The luxurious black car took off.

The two men shook hands.

Pope was smiling broadly as he held a scotch on the rocks in his hand. "What are you drinking these days, my friend?" He waved his hand over the open bar.

Karb poured himself a glass of Jack Daniel's. He pushed his head back and drained the glass. He poured another.

Pope was amused. "I hardly recognized you, Karb — the years haven't been too kind."

Karb sat back in the seat, stretched his legs, and wiped the sweat from his brow. The air conditioner felt good. He coughed and said, "I don't have a desk job, Hank."

"No, you don't."

"Unusual weather for October," Karb announced.

"Yes, it's been crazy. We'll probably have the first frost by next week," He tittered. "What did you think of the art show?"

"Interesting."

"I'm not into this modern stuff. When I look at something, I want to be able to recognize it right off."

"It just takes a deeper form of concentration," Karb said. "I like challenges, Hank."

"I have a tough one for you, Karb."

"What is it this time?" Karb asked as he glanced out the window.

"A little departure from our last job together."

"Oh? What exactly are you doing these days in D.C.?"

"Watching my ass very carefully," Pope grinned.

"You still with the Spooks?" Karb asked, gazing at Pope.

"No-no . . . I head the President's anti-drug program."

Karb tossed that around for a while. "Could make yourself a small fortune, Hank."

"I plan on making myself a large fortune . . . a *very* large fortune." Pope smiled.

"To finance your presidential campaign?"

Pope threw his head back and laughed. "No, my political aspirations have waned."

"You just want the big bucks, right?"

"Well said, Karb. Yes, I'm after the *big bucks*," Pope said.

"Speaking of big bucks, how's Mrs. Pope?"

"I'm afraid we split up a few years back," Pope said gravely. "I've been working very hard on getting her back."

"Sorry to hear about that — I know you think the world of her."

"Yes. I lost her when I went through this change of life or whatever they call it." Pope gave Karb a sideways glance. "You never bothered getting hitched, did you, Karb?"

"You know I'm not an monogamous animal," Karb said. His relationship with Honda was one of his longest affairs.

"I envy you in a way, Karb," Pope said with admiration. "You're the last of the great American primitives. I don't mean that in a negative way."

"I understand."

"But your kind is almost extinct. You should pass on your genes to carry forth your vitality . . . your frontier spirit. This country's going soft."

"I must have half-a-dozen bastards tucked away somewhere," Karb said, grinning.

Pope chuckled. "I guess I should tell you why I recruited you."

"Yeah, the suspense is killing me." Karb poured himself another drink.

"I'm afraid I need your expertise for a liquidation."

Karb froze as he was about to take a sip. The rim of the glass was resting on his lower lip. He brought the glass to his lap. "Are you talking about assassination?"

Pope nodded.

"Where?"

"Domestic," Pope said.

Karb shook his head. "Can't you recruit one of your old hit men from the Company?"

"This isn't governmentally sanctioned."

"You're flying solo on this one?" Karb asked, surprised.

"Does that bother you?"

"Damn straight," Karb snapped. "That means you can't protect me."

"There are ways," Pope said confidently.

"Who am I terminating?"

"Two properties."

"*Two?*"

"Yes," Pope said.

"How much?"

Pope noticed the mercenary look in Karb's eyes. "You know I pay well."

"Well, now you're going to pay even better."

"Name your price."

"Let me think about it."

"The job or your price?"

"My price."

"Then you will do it?" Pope asked.

Karb smiled. "A gag is a gag."

chapter 14

It was one of those black-glass monoliths, the roof somewhere in the clouds. Cardinal's office was on the penthouse floor. Mandy was concerned that her nose might bleed while riding up the express elevator. She exited from it on unsteady feet. The receptionist sat behind a clear-glass, kidney-shaped desk. Behind her was a large plaque depicting the company's trademark — a big red bird. She had also seen the insignia in the lobby and elevator.

Man, that bird shits everywhere, Mandy thought.

She wobbled over to the desk.

The receptionist, a cool gorgeous blonde with teeth instead of a smile, acknowledged her. "May I help you?"

"How do you do *that*?"

"Do what?"

"Talk without breaking your smile?" Mandy asked in awe.

The young woman didn't bat an eye. "Do you have an appointment?"

"Mandy Cronenberg, *R & R Express.*"

"Do you have credentials?"

Mandy rummaged through her leather handbag and found her wallet. She pulled out her press card. *"Here."*

The receptionist compared the photo on the card to Mandy's face. "You don't take a very flattering photograph, Ms. Cronenberg."

Mandy snatched the card back and put it away.

"Please have a seat."

Mandy deposited herself onto the black leather sofa. It was then that she noticed the Hispanic security guard by the elevator. He looked straight ahead, his facial expression engraved in stone.

The receptionist leaned over and spoke into the intercom. "A Ms. Cronenberg to see you, sir."

"Send her in." The voice was low and sexy.

The young woman flashed her teeth. "You may go in, now."

"Thank you." Mandy stood up and gathered her stuff together. Just before she reached the door, the security guard was on top of her. He passed a metal detector over her body and bag. Mandy shot a glance at the receptionist. "I'm not boarding a plane, am I?"

"It's just a security measure," she said behind a frozen smile.

After the guard was through, Mandy said to the receptionist, "You better be careful, your face may stay that way." And with that, she went through the door into a gigantic office. The ceiling was a sheet of glass; the sunlight flooded in on them. Cardinal stood behind his crystal desk. The whole room resembled an ice palace with its windowed walls and white carpeting.

Mandy strolled towards the desk — it took an eternity to get there.

She couldn't see his face in the glary light that washed the room. He extended his hand to her. She took it. He gave her a firm handshake.

"A pleasure to meet you, Ms. Cronenberg."

"Well, I think it's a pleasure for me, too, if I could only *see* you."

Cardinal laughed. "Please sit down."

She sat down on a chrome-and-leather chair. She pulled out her notebook and microcassette recorder.

He pressed a button on his desk console and the windows darkened. She could see him now. He was dressed elegantly in a white linen Giorgio Armani suit and blue satin tie and collar pin. His pale-blue eyes appeared like two pools of cool water in his bronzed face. He had gray hair, parted on the right side and neatly trimmed. He was clean-shaven and had a dazzling smile to match his pretty receptionist's.

Mandy had difficulty pretending not to be overwhelmed by his presence.

"May I get something for you — a drink, perhaps?"

"Whatever you're having."

"Well," he grinned, "I, myself, don't indulge in liquor or soft drinks. Just chilled spring water."

"Sounds delicious."

He stood up and walked to the bar across the room. He brought her back a tall glass of water. She looked down at his feet — he wore no socks beneath his taupe Bally shoes. "Thank you." She took the glass.

Cardinal leaned against his desk. "Now, what can I do for you? I believe you mentioned something about doing an article on me?"

"Yes. I write for *R & R Express.*"

"That's what I found curious — a rock periodical's interest in a man like myself."

"Well, we're trying to emulate *Rolling Stone* and expand into more mainstream material."

"Oh? *Rolling Stone* did a profile on me last year."

"Yes, I read that."

"I didn't know *R & R* was a national magazine," he said.

"Oh yeah. We don't have as high a circulation as *Rolling Stone,* but we're working on it."

"Wall Street seems to hold a different opinion," Cardinal said.

Evidently he has done his homework, Mandy thought. She cleared her throat. "Do you mind?"

"No, go on."

She switched on her tape recorder. "Instead of asking you all the usual questions about how you started out, I thought we could start off with the current situation."

"That's fine with me."

"The Wall Street reports about your company haven't been very promising, either." Mandy had done her homework, too. It seemed Cardinal Airlines was having some financial woes due to stiff competition and the recession.

"True. We were hurting somewhat in the previous fiscal year, but I'm happy to report that our finances have improved greatly, and we estimate to be in the black very shortly."

"That sounds like a press release," she said directly.

Cardinal sighed cheerfully. "It's very difficult for me to relax in front of a reporter. I apologize."

Mandy nodded. "How do you account for your company's recent recovery then?"

"A new business manager, for starters."

"Oh?"

"Anthony Bava," Cardinal said. "He's been a breath of fresh air around here."

"Yeah, a very interesting man with a mysterious background."

"I beg your pardon?"

"His background — he's managed a fleet of charter fishing boats off Key West."

"Yes, what's so mysterious about *that*?" Cardinal asked.

"How does a small businessman like Bava manage to

come on board and turn a major corporation around? He has no corporate experience."

"Yes, that was the breath of fresh air I spoke about. He didn't bring with him any of the overloaded luggage most corporate men carry around with them — that political self-preservation defense mechanism."

"I still can't comprehend an uneducated man running a major company," Mandy said.

"He doesn't run it. *I* run it. He assists me. And what he lacks in a formal education, he makes up for with *genuine* on-the-job experience."

"What about his criminal record?"

"Now *I* don't understand, Ms. Cronenberg," Cardinal said with an edge to his voice.

"He was suspected of drug-trafficking."

"The key word there is *suspected*. The authorities have no evidence against Mr. Bava."

"They brought him to court," Mandy said.

"The case was dropped due to lack of evidence." Cardinal spoke in an irritated voice. "I really don't appreciate this line of questioning."

"How does a man of your stature meet up with someone like Bava?"

"Obviously, you don't have a very high opinion of Mr. Bava." He arched his eyebrows.

She smirked. "He's not in your class."

"Well, if you honestly researched my background, Ms. Cronenberg, you would have found out just what class I came from."

"Everyone knows about your middle-class, blue-collar background. You're a self-made man. You proved the American Dream exists."

He held his head up. "I'm very proud of my heritage. Bava is a man not so different from myself. I'm now giving him a chance to capture his own American Dream."

Mandy realized she was not going anywhere with her inquiry. She really didn't know what good all this was going to do — but she had to take a stab at it.

Suddenly a buzzer rang out.

"Pardon me," Cardinal said politely as he pressed the intercom button. "I thought I told you that I didn't want to be disturbed." He spoke firmly into the box.

"Mr. Bava has asked to see you in his office, Mr. Cardinal."

"Tell Mr. Bava I'm in the middle of an interview with a charming young lady." He winked at Mandy.

"Mr. Bava insists — it will only take a moment."

"Very well." He sighed as he addressed Mandy. "I apologize for this — must be something on the burner . . ." He stood up. "I'll be just a few minutes." He walked around the desk and out the door.

Mandy shut off the tape recorder. This was her chance to check out some of Cardinal's things.

She shot up and ran to the other side of his desk and began going through the papers.

The short, round man with the black hair and mustache sat before the video monitor watching Mandy Cronenberg going through Cardinal's desk.

"So bloody obvious," Cardinal said as he stood behind Tony Bava.

Bava nodded. "It makes you wonder." Bava had summoned Cardinal to inform him that Pope had just called to warn them about Mandy Cronenberg. Cardinal and Bava were not aware of the reporter's involvement in this affair. Bava briefly filled him in as they watched Mandy go to work in Cardinal's office. Both men were concerned about the breach of security.

"What're we going to do with our little redheaded friend here?" Cardinal asked.

Bava swung around in the chair and peered up at Cardinal with his big brown eyes. "Call her boss."

"Her boss?"

"Let's handle this diplomatically at first," Bava suggested. "If that doesn't work, *then* . . ."

Cardinal sighed heavily. "I don't like this. What the hell is Pope up to? He's supposed to be handling security."

"There was a little slip-up in the operation. Pope is ironing out the wrinkles."

"It only takes a nosy bitch like this one to bring us all down."

"Don't concern yourself, Jon."

"She came here to see *me*, not you, Bava," Cardinal said through clenched teeth.

Bava folded his hands in back of his head and leaned backwards in the chair. "But her questions were about me, not you."

"You're supposed to be my business manager, remember? The whole fucking world knows that, Bava."

"Don't push the panic button yet, Cardinal. I think you handled yourself very well in there. She knows she can't break through. She doesn't even know what to look for. She's taking shots in the dark."

"I hope you're right."

"I know I'm right," Bava said.

They watched her on the screen as she returned to her chair.

"Looks like you can go back in there now."

"So bloody obvious," Cardinal repeated in a hushed tone.

A pale Manville left the publisher's office completely drained. He hurried into his office and slammed the door. He sat down behind the desk and picked up the phone.

"Get me Cronenberg!" he screamed to the office operator.

A few minutes later, he heard Mandy's voice on the other line.

"Hello?" Mandy asked.

"Cronenberg?!"

"Yes?" Mandy didn't recognize the incensed voice.

"Manville here."

"Oh, Rob."

"Don't *'oh, Rob'* me. What the fuck are you doing down there, for chrissakes! What the hell does Jonathan Cardinal have to do with Rick Marlowe?"

"Jonathan Cardinal?" Mandy asked.

"Yes!"

"How did you know — "

"Never mind that, Cronenberg!" Manville cut her short. "I want my piece on Marlowe, or I'm pulling you off the story."

"Pull me off?"

"Not only will I pull you off — I'll throw you out in the fucking street!"

There was a short pause before Mandy said, "Is that any way to treat a recent widow?"

Cardinal pulled out of the building garage in his silver Mercedes 380 SL convertible. He drove north on Biscayne Boulevard and hung a right onto 195 where he would pick up A1A and drive north to his Palm Beach residence. It was a long drive, and he caught himself wandering off in deep thought.

He recalled running into Hank Pope at a White House cocktail party. Pope had managed to corner Cardinal as he stood off alone sipping his chilled water and snacking on fresh vegetables.

"Mr. Cardinal?" Pope asked with a slight Southern accent.

"Yes."

"My name is Pope." They shook hands. "Hank Pope."

"Don't I know you, Mr. Pope?"

"Yes, we've met before. I'm the former Deputy Director of the C.I.A."

"Ah." Cardinal nodded.

They had crossed paths years before while Cardinal was still with the international airline. Pope, then with the C.I.A., had approached that company with an offer to purchase their Asian airline affiliate outright for C.I.A. undercover operations. Since the Asian airline had been in existence for quite some time, it wouldn't be suspected as a C.I.A. property. Cardinal and Pope had met several times to strike a deal. But the parent company had to obtain permission from the board of directors before approving such an agreement. The impatient Deputy Director Pope had decided instead to approach another airline, and the deal with Cardinal never materialized.

"I now head the President's anti-drug program," Pope said.

"Oh?"

"I have great respect for a man like you, Mr. Cardinal."

"That's very kind."

"You did it the hard way," Pope said as he sipped his scotch. "Me — I'm from a comfortable background. But since I disengaged myself from my family, I had to go it alone for most of my adult life."

"Oh?"

"Yes. So I did it the *hard way* as well, I suppose."

Cardinal agreed.

"But I hear your business interests have been slipping lately."

Cardinal, always a gentleman, smiled wryly. "That's the nature of the beast, Mr. Pope."

"That would be a shame . . . you know if *it* fails," Pope said.

"I haven't given it much thought, Mr. Pope."

"Hank," Pope said. "Call me Hank."

"Hank."

"Look what happened to that Freddie Laker fellow."

Cardinal remembered how uncomfortable Pope had

made him feel. "I assure you that that's not about to happen."

"There are ways, you know, ways to *prevent* something like that. It's all a matter of cash flow — am I right?" Pope asked.

Cardinal nodded in agreement.

"Too bad there isn't a way to pump in a cash surge of some kind."

"A cash surge?" Cardinal raised his eyebrows.

"Yes, a way of raising capital more quickly."

Cardinal laughed. "I wish I knew *that* secret formula."

"I have the ingredients," Pope said and smirked.

Cardinal recalled, all too well, the business tactics Pope had employed with him when they negotiated for the Asian airline purchase. "Do you have a proposition for me, Mr. Pope?"

"What's your sport?"

"My sport?"

"Yes, what sport is your pleasure?"

"Polo," Cardinal said.

"There's not much polo playing going on here in Washington," Pope laughed. "How about a game of golf?"

"I prefer tennis."

"Then tennis it is," Pope said. "I'll call your hotel."

Pope walked away, leaving Cardinal bewildered.

The next day they had their tennis game, and Pope dropped his main ingredient for instant cash surge.

Drugs.

At first, Cardinal had laughed him off. But then he realized that he had been serious. That had frightened him. He had gone this far working legally for the most part. You cannot run a large company without indulging in some kind of questionable business tactics. But to step into the drug market — there was no doubt there as to its legality. Cardinal had shaken his head vigorously. He would never stoop that low.

After Pope left him, he'd wondered whether he was being set up for a trap. It wouldn't be the first time a government agent entrapped a successful businessman. The ABSCAM trial had still been fresh in his memory.

No, Pope hadn't hooked him yet. It would be some months later when Cardinal's company had taken another turn for the worse. Pope had come back and asked him again. He sounded more secure about what he had in mind. After much thought, Cardinal had accepted Pope's offer.

Then Bava came on board. He'd distrusted him. He was all wrong for the role he was to play. The Business Manager of Cardinal Airlines. Imagine, this hoodlum involved with complicated corporate business! Cardinal would become the laughingstock of Wall Street. He had to present Bava in a different light. That was when he had come up with the dogma he'd laid on Mandy Cronenberg — that Cardinal was giving him a chance to obtain his own American Dream. Wall Street had bought it. That had come as a surprise to Cardinal. Of course, since the cash flow increased with Bava's arrival, the financial analysts thought Cardinal had taken a very bold business venture that paid off.

But now Mandy Cronenberg, the Lois Lane of liberal newspaper reporters, had stumbled onto their little scheme. Cardinal didn't like that. He hoped his heated phone call to her publisher would detain her. He hated to think what would happen if she persisted in her inquiry. Men like Bava and Pope resorted to levels far below what Cardinal considered normal human virtues. He had a bad feeling about all this. He should have never gotten involved with these gangsters in the first place. Now he had to see it through to the end.

But he saw no light at the end of the tunnel.

chapter 15

Deb sat behind the wheel of her 300ZX with Sage next to her in the passenger seat. Tommy was leaning on the roof of the car, his head tucked in the open window. The back seat was down and packed clear to the hatchback with suitcases and boxes.

"I'm goin' to miss this old place." Deb had a tear in her eye. "I can still feel Elmore — y'know?"

Tommy nodded. "You'll be back soon — I promise." He wished he knew that for certain.

"Where're we going, Mommy?" Sage asked as he played with his Rambo toy gun.

"Goin' for a little vacation, Sage. Don't ya remember?"

He shook his head vigorously.

Tommy laughed. "Sure you do."

"Nope," he said.

"Don't be difficult, Sage," Deb said as she patted his head.

"I'll take good care of the place," Tommy promised.

She craned her head around for a last look. She sniffed as she put on her sunglasses and started the car. She gazed up at Tommy over the top of her shades. "Make sure *no*body messes with it, okay?"

Tommy grinned. "Scout's honor." He held his heart.

She wrapped her arm around the back of his neck and brought his face to her. "I love you, Tommy." She kissed him firmly on the mouth. She pulled away and shifted gears. "I gotta go, baby." Her nose was red, the tears streamed down her cheeks.

Tommy stepped back. "Deb."

She sped off quickly.

Tommy waved at the car as it disappeared with a cloud of dust behind it.

The Kid aimed the shotgun microphone at Tommy and transmitted his last words to Karb and Red back at the van some miles away.

"I love you," Tommy said softly to himself.

Red, who sat behind the receiver and tape-recorder modules, grinned up at Karb who stood just behind him. "Like a fuckin' soap opera."

Karb nodded. "That's two less we have to worry about."

Red said, "Yep, now comes some heavy action — am I right?"

Karb picked up the microphone. "Kid — you there?"

The Kid's voice crackled over the speaker. "What the hell do ya think? Over."

"Come on home. Over and out." Karb put down the mike. "Asshole."

Red removed his headphones and sat back in the chair with a heavy sigh. "The Kid's okay."

Karb ignored Red's statement. He couldn't believe how incompetent these rednecks were. "Why don't you take a walk?"

Red screwed up his face sourly. He stood up and stared defiantly into Karb's gray eyes.

Karb returned his gaze. "Don't test me, boy."

"I ain't testin' nuttin'." Red slid open the side door and slammed it shut.

Karb picked up the phone connected to the blue box and placed a call to Pope. It took a few minutes to transmit through various stations across the country so that the call would not be traceable.

"Hello?" Pope finally answered.

"It's me," Karb said. "Just listen up. First off, where did you find these monkeys you got helpin' me?"

"They're Bava's men."

"Boys — they're Bava's boys. I don't think one of 'em has even grown whiskers yet. I don't like them," Karb said frankly.

"Sharp had no problems with them," Pope said. "They're good and loyal. A little dumb, maybe. Where in hell can you find good *white* help in that area anymore? The young one, he's good with weapons. The other guy, Red, he's a pro when it comes to surveillance. He rigged up that van you're in."

Karb looked around the high-tech interior. "That hick set this shit up?"

"Yes. He's a wiz. He just has a problem with field-work. That's where the Kid comes in. He's certifiable, but he sure can shoot. Bava swears by them."

Karb sucked in a lungful of air and slowly exhaled. "Okay-okay. Spare me."

"When are you pulling off the operation?"

"Tonight."

"Tonight? Damn, you work fast. That's why you're the best."

Karb scratched his head and rolled his eyes. "I'll be in touch."

"Good luck," Pope said and hung up.

Karb opened the door and went outside. Red was

sitting on a lawn chair with a beer in his hand.

Karb folded his muscled arms and leaned against the black van. A camouflaged awning hovered above him. They had set up camp in a clearing nestled in the center of a thickly wooded area. There were two tents alongside the van — one housed the two kids, the other was for Karb.

"What's the word?" Red asked as he sucked on the neck of the beer bottle.

"Tonight."

Red whistled. "You don't waste any time, do ya, stuntman?"

"The sooner I'm through with this, the less time I'll have to spend with you scumbags."

Red sucked in his cheeks and gulped loudly. "How is it you don't like us, Karb?"

"I don't like ignorance in any form."

Red gripped the arms of the chair, his knuckles turning white from the tension. "Well, I don't like workin' with no fuckin' *weirdo*."

Karb grinned.

"Did you hear me, stuntman?"

"Get back in there and monitor Shepard," Karb ordered.

Red shot up, knocking the chair to the ground. He stormed up to him and stuck his face close to Karb's. "I don't like anybody, especially *you*, tellin' me what to do — okay, stuntman?"

"You do as I say, or I'll twist your little head off," Karb threatened.

Red smiled. "I would like to see you try it."

Karb sighed. "Fuckin' ace."

Red was about to make a move when Karb shot a blow to his stomach and he doubled over. Then Karb gripped Red by the head and brought his knee up into his face. Red fell back onto the ground with a bloody nose. He shook his head in bewilderment — he didn't know what hit him.

"Now get in there and do your job, Red." Karb walked off to his tent.

Red held his face as he sat on the ground. *I'm goin' to kill that turkey, if it's the last thing I ever do.* He gripped the awning pole and pulled himself up. He went over to the ice chest and retrieved a cold bottle of beer. He held it against his nose and went into the van. He got back in time to hear Tommy talking to Mandy on the phone.

"So you think Cardinal is tied up in all this, too?" Tommy asked.

"I just know he is," Mandy said. "I can feel it in my bones."

"But why?"

"He needs money to help his ailing company."

"But the guy is rich, isn't he?" Tommy asked perplexedly.

"Rich people don't have real money. Everything is tied up in securities and stuff. When it comes to good old cash, they're as bad off as we are," Mandy explained.

"Someday I'll figure out the capitalist system."

"Don't bother unless you have the money to go along with it," Mandy said cynically.

"One thing still bothers me."

"What?"

"Why Hammett?" Tommy asked.

"That's the missing link we have to figure out."

After some more small talk, they both hung up. Red removed his headphones when the Kid entered the van. Red swung around and put his legs up on the table.

The Kid noticed Red's bruised face. "What happened to you?"

"I ran into a tree."

The Kid threw his head back and gave his partner a sideways glance. "What kinda tree?"

Red took a sip of his beer. "That fuckin' *weirdo.*"

"Karb?" the Kid asked. "Did he do this to you?"

"We had a difference of opinion," Red said.

"Damn — I hate that bastard."

"I thought Sharp was a prick . . ."

"The man is scary," the Kid said.

"I wouldn't mess with him, if I were you. Man, is he *fast.*"

The Kid sat on the edge of a table. "And we gotta work tight with him on this?"

"I ain't sayin' or doin' nuttin' but my job. Then I'm splittin'. I'm goin' to give a piece of my mind to Bava. Son of a bitch." Red suddenly stopped talking.

The Kid turned around and saw Karb in the doorway. He stood up. "I don't like what you did to Red."

Karb entered the van and marched up to the Kid. "Mind your business, boy."

"There's nuttin' holdin' us here — y'know?"

The look on Karb's face sent a chill down the Kid's spine. "We have a little job to do this evening. I'm going to need your help, Kid. After that," Karb said, shaking his head, "I don't give a damn what you do. But you're not taking a walk before this job's done. Understand?"

"You goin' to stop me?" the Kid asked boldly.

Karb eyed Red. "You better have a talk with your friend here, Red."

"There're two of us now, Karb," the Kid said.

"Then I'll have to use both hands this time." Karb smiled sardonically.

"Kid — cool it," Red said.

The Kid faced his friend.

"It ain't worth it," Red said wisely.

The Kid shifted his gaze back to Karb. "We don't mind workin' for you if you start treatin' us decent-like."

Karb laughed. "You two talk like a couple of babies. You'll never last in this business if you're too soft."

"I still think you owe Red an apology."

"Never mind, Kid," Red said. "It was my fault. I started it."

"I wish you two would come together on this," Karb smirked.

The Kid shook his head. "Don't ever come after me, Karb."

"I'm shaking, son, I'm shaking." Karb patted his face.

The Kid whipped out a switchblade. Karb gripped his wrist and squeezed tightly. The Kid's face reddened from the struggle.

"Cut it out!" Red shouted.

The Kid dropped the knife. Karb continued to pour on the pressure. The Kid dropped to his knees, his face twisted up in agony.

"Please, Karb, let him go!" Red stood up.

Karb gave Red a warning look. He backed off.

Karb released his grip and snatched up the knife. He closed it and put it in his back pocket. The Kid remained on his knees holding his sore wrist.

"Now do we know who the boss is around here, boys?" Karb asked.

Red nodded.

Karb looked down at the Kid. "Huh?"

The Kid glanced up at Karb with bulging eyes. He nodded.

"Good," Karb said. "I'm glad we came to an understanding, then."

Barry Nulls sat behind his desk in the spacious office looking over the files on Pope and Operation Grim Reaper. The President's appointment of Pope to head his anti-drug program was a thorn in Nulls' side. Before Pope's installation, Nulls had been in charge of the drug operations. Although Pope was heading only one of several federal drug-reinforcement programs, Operation Grim Reaper was the most visible one politically. And the President's giving Pope a free hand further irritated

Nulls. He had never possessed such freedom. But now
he had something on Pope. The phone call had paid off.
It originated from Hammett in northern Florida — an
area that had been under careful scrutiny in recent years
because of its reputed large-scale marijuana-growing.
Nulls was running a check on those names he'd received
from Alexis. He was also following up on some large
capital expenditures to a pharmaceutical firm for "her-
bicides." Nulls was impatient to hear the outcome of his
inquiries.

He just had a hunch that he would finally catch Pope
at one of his self-aggrandizing acts.

Carpenter slipped on his western-style jacket and adjusted
his string tie. He looked at his wife in the mirror. She
was still dressed in her slip. *Damn, did she take her time
getting dressed.* Carpenter shook his head and sat down
on the bed to pull on his cowboy boots. Huffing and
puffing, he managed to slip them on. His face was all
red from the ordeal. "Do your goddamn feet swell with
old age or somethin'?"

His wife, Madge, giggled. "Only when you put on too
much weight."

He beheld his bulging gut and patted it with his hands.
"Damn, I look like I'm pushin' nine months pregnant."
He howled and stood up. His thick belt buckle was eating
into his skin.

His trim, sandy-haired wife went up to him and
snapped the bottom button of his shirt. He couldn't even
see down that far.

It was Saturday evening — their night out. They always
ate dinner every week at the Cracker's Inn on Fourth
Street just off Main. It was Hammett's only nice
restaurant. It cost more, but the food was exceptional
and with generous portions to boot. The best southern-
fried steak in this part of Florida.

Madge went into the bathroom as Carpenter wandered

into the wood-paneled living room and turned on the color TV set. He sat down on his Leatherette recliner and put his feet up. *The Lord only knew how much longer she would be.*

Carpenter had been feeling uneasy the last few days. He hadn't heard from Pope or Bava. Things seemed quieter in general. That made him worry. He just wished Pope would level with him — fill him in on the real scoop. He hated working in the dark.

His wife came into the room with her pocketbook and sweater.

Carpenter smiled at his wife. "You ready now?"

"I've been waiting for you all this time," she said.

The Kid watched Carpenter's Thunderbird pull into the Main Street parking lot located across the street from the restaurant.

Carpenter got out, walked around the back of the car to the other side, and opened the door for his wife.

The Kid spoke into the walkie-talkie as he sat behind the wheel of the Firebird. "They're here. Over."

Karb's voice crackled over the receiver. "The next time I hear from you, Kid, it will be with the green-light command. Over."

"Roger. Over and out." He put the walkie-talkie next to him on the seat.

Tommy put the paperback novel down and yawned. He got up and checked on the fireplace. The fire was almost out. He yawned again as he looked at the photograph of him and his brother on the mantelpiece. "I miss you, Elmore." He carried himself into his bedroom and plopped down on the bed. He whipped off his sneakers and pulled down his jeans. He got under the sheets and put his head on the two pillows piled one on top of the other.

The house seemed different without Deb and Sage

running around. He shut off the lamp and turned over.

He planned on seeing Carpenter tomorrow about Elmore's autopsy report. Maybe that would help uncover the truth.

Red pulled up just outside of the Shepard house in a jeep. Karb got out. He was dressed in a black jump suit. The two men exchanged glances.

"Go back to base and check up on the Kid. I don't want him dozing off on me," Karb ordered.

Red saluted mockingly.

"Keep cool, Red," Karb said. "Let's get through this in one piece."

Red nodded and drove off.

Karb walked to the side of the house where Elmore's motorcycle was pitched. Tommy's black helmet was sitting on the seat. He put on the helmet. It was too small. He adjusted the inner straps and tried it again. It fit fine. He removed it and slipped on a radio receiver, putting the earplug in his ear. He placed the arm of the mike at his mouth and slipped the helmet over it. He closed the black sunshade. It was too dark for him to see in the night, but it would conceal his face. He walked the bike away from the house.

He had this down to the last minute.

After walking some distance from the house, Karb straddled the motorcycle and started it. The engine roared beneath him.

He rode off into the darkness.

The Kid was leaning against his green car smoking a Marlboro. It was a cool night. A refreshing breeze blew his long blond hair out of place. He eyed his watch. It was just after eleven. *Jesus, was this a dead town on Saturday night.*

He ducked down when he saw the sheriff's car pull up in front of the restaurant. Higgins got out, hitched his pants, and began to stroll along the sidewalk. The Kid could see the orange glow from his cigarette.

The Kid opened the door and slipped into his car. He picked up the walkie-talkie. "Karb."

He waited a few moments. "You there, Karb? — over."

Karb was waiting with the engine off at the other end of town. He was on a side street — more like an alley between two stores. There was no activity. He heard the Kid's voice buzzing in his ear.

"This is Karb — what's up?"

"Higgins just pulled up in front of the restaurant," the Kid said nervously.

"*What?!*" Karb barked.

"He got out and started to walk along the sidewalk."

"Is he in sight?"

"Not anymore."

"Was he holding a piece?"

"No — he looked clean," the Kid answered.

"Keep a lookout. This has to be done quickly and cleanly. Over and out."

Karb shook his head. *Great, just what I needed.* He hoped he didn't have to cancel his plan until next week. No, he would have to do it tonight, even if it meant terminating Higgins.

He scanned his watch. Eleven-thirty. It would be any minute now.

The Kid saw the restaurant door open. Carpenter came staggering out with his wife holding him up.

He held the walkie-talkie to his lips. "The target is in sight. Over."

"I'm on my way. Over and out," Karb said.

Carpenter managed to walk as far as the curb; then he leaned against the sheriff's car. Madge still held his arm.

"Higs — where are you, man?" he called out, then started to giggle.

"SHHHH!" his wife hissed him. "People are sleepin'."

"Bunch of deadbeats in this town," the mayor announced. "Where are you, Sheriff Higgins?" He laughed again.

"Let's go, George." She pulled him by his arm. "I'll drive home tonight."

Carpenter straightened up. "Whaddaya mean *you're* driving home? I do the driving in this family." He punched his chest.

"You can't even walk, never mind drive, George," his wife scolded him. "Now, let's get to the car."

He pushed her away from him. "I can walk by myself." He held onto Higgins' car as he struggled past the curb. His wife stood beside him, her hands all ready to grab him if he fell.

"See, I'm fine." He took a few more steps and was nearly in the center of the street.

The Kid sighed nervously and pulled out his Colt .45. *Come, on, Karb, let's do it.*

He heard the rumble of the engine in the near distance.

"Thank God." He exhaled in relief.

Carpenter froze at the dotted center line when he heard the roar of the motorcycle. He gazed in both directions but didn't see a headlight.

Madge grabbed hold of his arm and began to push him along when the bike appeared out of nowhere.

It all happened in a split second.

The motorcycle ripped by Carpenter in a flash. The wheels rolled over his feet while his body twisted around. Madge was thrown some feet away, landing on top of the trunk of Higgins' car. Carpenter's body collapsed in a mangled pile of bones, blood erupting from his torn flesh.

Higgins heard the motorcycle, then saw it cruise by him on Main Street. He ran out into the street. He saw that it was Elmore's bike. He knew that Tommy had been using it since he was back. Then Higgins turned around and saw the carnage that lay just up the street by his car. His mouth dropped open and he began to run. He stopped when he saw a cowboy boot before him. He bent over and picked it up. That was when he saw the splintered bone sticking out of the top of it. He dropped the boot, his heart pounding in his chest. *Oh, my God!*

He hurried to his car. He saw Carpenter's remains splattered all over the street. He heard a moan. It was coming from behind his car. He went there and found Madge lying on the sidewalk, her face badly bruised and bleeding. He squatted down next to her. "Madge."

She opened her eyes and tried to speak. Her teeth were all cracked, and her tongue was bright red. She gurgled and spit up some blood.

"Take it easy, Madge." Higgins removed his jacket and placed it under her head. He ran to his car and radioed for an ambulance.

Higgins got out of the car and took off his hat, wiping the sweat from his forehead. He swallowed loudly and held his stomach. He started to suck in fresh air, hoping to overcome his nausea.

It didn't help.

Higgins fell to his knees and vomited onto the curb.

The engine started puttering, and the front wheel was out of alignment. Karb pulled over to the side of the road and shut off the engine. "SHIT!"

Karb got off the bike and pulled off the helmet. His face was beaded with sweat, and his wet hair lay flat on his head. He spoke into the mike, "Red."

"Yeah, Karb?"

"The bike gave out," Karb said. "Come pick me up."

"Jesus — what about the plans?"

"Just get your ass over here real fast," Karb ordered, then gave him his location.

Karb had a new plan. He would bring the bike back to Tommy's place and leave it there for Higgins to find. He'd have to arrest Tommy for the crime. It wasn't what he'd originally planned, but it would have to do.

He went up to the bike and kicked it. "Damn modern shit!"

They didn't make anything like they used to.

chapter 16

Tommy was dreaming about Debra. They were strolling
through one of the poisoned patches. It was an autumn
day — cool and sunny. They were checking over the
plants when Deb cried out suddenly. Tommy turned to
her. She was weeping as she pointed to something behind
a thick plant. She started to speak. But it wasn't her voice.
It was a man's voice. *Tommy,* she/he said. *Tommy.*

Tommy opened his eyes and looked up the barrel of
a Smith & Wesson .357 Magnum. Higgins said, "Put
your pants on, boy."

Higgins grabbed a handful of Tommy's blond hair and
dragged him out of bed to his knees.

"What the hell is going on?" Tommy asked painfully.

Higgins yanked Tommy's hair back and he yelped.
Tommy slipped into his blue jeans. Then Higgins threw
him against the wall. Higgins held him by the back of
the neck as he put handcuffs on him. Then he slammed
Tommy's face against the wall, bloodying his nose.
Higgins pushed him out of the room and outside. It was

still dark. Tommy watched as several men loaded Elmore's damaged bike onto a pickup truck.

"Hey, what're they doing, for chrissakes?" Tommy asked. "What happened to Elmore's bike?"

"Like you don't know," Higgins snapped as he opened the rear door of his squad car and threw Tommy in. He slammed the door and got behind the wheel. Steel grating separated the front and back seats.

"What's going on?!" Tommy asked once again.

Higgins craned his neck around and glared at him with angry slits. He pulled out a piece of paper and began to read him his rights.

"ANSWER ME!" Tommy shouted.

Higgins continued to read, then said, "Did you get that?"

"Why are you arresting me?" Tommy asked as he sat there in his white tee shirt and jeans and bare feet.

"For the murder of George Carpenter and attempted murder of his wife . . . who's in critical condition."

"*What?!*" Tommy screamed. "What the fuck are you talking about?"

Higgins drove off.

"Murder . . . " Tommy shook his head to rid himself of sleep. "You think *I* killed Carpenter?"

"I thought I knew you, man," Higgins said disappointedly. "I really did. You and Elmore were good people. First, Jake's place gets all shot up. Now *this*. I never saw the likes of it before."

"Why do you think I did it?"

"I saw you with my own eyes, Tommy Shepard. On Elmore's bike. You didn't even have the brains to skip town. You mow over two people and ride back home and go to bed." Higgins shook his head. "Never saw the likes of it . . . *NEVER!*"

Tommy sat back in the seat. He gazed down at the handcuffs. "This must be a nightmare . . . " He looked up at Higgins through the bars. "Tell me this is all a dream."

"It's all too real," Higgins said. "When I picked up George's boot and saw his foot still in it . . . God, it's all *too real.*"

"Why would I ever want to kill Carpenter?"

"I know he wasn't the easiest man to like . . . but Jesus Christ, man!"

"I swear on Elmore's grave I didn't do it, Higs. Somebody must've stolen Elmore's bike to make it look like I did it. Don't you see?"

"Why would anyone want to do that?"

"The same reason they shot up Jake's place and killed my brother. If you ever bothered to solve that case you would know why," Tommy said sarcastically.

Higgins pulled up in front of the station house. There was a small crowd of people gathered outside. Tommy saw rifles and baseball bats in their hands. Oates stood just outside the door with a shotgun.

"What the hell?" Tommy asked.

"Some people don't want to wait for a trial, Tommy," Higgins said and got out. A few men clustered around the car. Tommy saw the Hills and a few of his neighbors.

"Okay, boys, let's take it easy," Higgins said. "In this country, men are innocent until proven guilty." He stood boldly by the car, his hand resting on his holster. He pushed back his Stetson. "*No*body lays a hand on my prisoner without going through me first — understand?"

Nick Hill, his face pimpled with sores, said, "That kid don't deserve to live after what he done."

"A judge will decide that, Nick," Higgins said as he chewed on a toothpick. "Now — everybody — home to bed. I'm in charge here." He shot a glance at Oates. "Harry."

Oates walked to the car, shotgun at the ready.

"If anybody starts anything they'll be answered with 12-gauge worth of buckshot," Higgins threatened. "Now move on!"

Oates started to push the men back. "Come on, boys, let's call it a night."

Higgins whipped open the door and pulled Tommy out.

As soon as the crowd set eyes on Tommy, they charged through Oates waving their weapons. Higgins stood before Tommy and pulled out his revolver. He shot up in the air. "The next bullet is for the first man who so much as takes a single step towards me."

The crowd backed off.

"Harry — next time use your weapon!" Higgins ordered.

"Yes, sir." He pumped the gun.

Higgins grabbed Tommy by the arm and walked him into the building. Oates backed up behind them, his eyes on the crowd. When he reached the door, he said, "Now, go home!" He shut the door after himself.

Higgins removed the cuffs from Tommy and locked him in the cell. Tommy stood there with his hands gripping the bars. "I SWEAR TO GOD I DIDN'T DO IT!"

Oates went up to him and shook his head. "Man, you're in a slew of trouble this time, Tommy."

"Stop conversing with the prisoner, Harry," Higgins said as he sat behind his desk. He picked up the phone and dialed Jacksonville. "I'm goin' to need some help here. That crowd out there may get out of hand."

"Who're you calling?" Oates asked.

"Who else?" Higgins said as he picked his teeth with the toothpick. "The feds."

Tommy sat down on the bunk. His feet were cold. He buried his face in his hands. There was a knot in his stomach. His head was spinning. He didn't know what to do. What to think . . .

He felt so alone then. Without Deb . . . and Elmore. He had to calm down. To think it through. Higs was calling in the feds. How should he handle that? Tell them the truth? But would they believe him?

And what if the feds were *involved* in all this? What if it was their operation all along?

His spirits sank even lower.

Federal agent Mike Bishop was sipping his morning coffee out of a cardboard container while scanning the sports section of the newspaper. His desk was completely covered with files and reports. He couldn't even remember what the hell the top of the desk looked like. Some kind of gray metal with a cardboard blotter, he thought. He ran his hand through his fine, yellow-white hair to neaten it. He felt like lighting up a cigar, but he knew that its pungent odor perturbed his secretary. He would have to wait until he went out for lunch to have one.

Just then his phone rang. He waited until it rang twice before picking it up. His secretary's voice said, "There's a Sheriff Higgins on the line from Hammett."

"*Hammett?*" Bishop kicked that around for a while. He had just spoken with the Assistant Attorney General about Hammett yesterday. Bishop had filled Nulls in on what was going on up there. How he had sent one of his agents, Frank Bigelow, to investigate illegal drug activity in Hammett. Before long Bishop had gotten a heated call from Pope and was ordered to pull Bigelow out. Pope had said they were interfering with his operation there. So Bishop had recalled Bigelow and that was that. First the Assistant Attorney General's call and now this one from Hammett's sheriff. He wondered what the hell was going on. He hated the way Washington kept him in the dark about these things. "Okay, put him on."

"Hello?"

"Mike Bishop here. How can I help you, Sheriff?"

"Listen, Mr. Bishop, this town is comin' apart at the seams," Higgins said urgently. "I have a young man

locked up here who just upped and murdered our
mayor!''

"Murdered your mayor?'' Bishop asked.

"That's right, sir,'' Higgins verified. "Ran him down
with his *motorcycle,* he did.''

"Who have you arrested?''

"His name is Tommy Shepard — a local. His brother
was murdered up here not too long ago.''

Bishop was writing it all down. *"Murdered?* Another
murder? What the hell is going on up there, Sheriff?''

"The Lord only knows, sir,'' Higgins exclaimed. "The
whole town's outside ready to string up my prisoner. I
need assistance.''

"Okay, calm down, Sheriff. I'll send some help. In the
meantime, protect your prisoner.''

"I will, sir.''

"I'll be in touch.'' Bishop hung up and digested the
information he had just received.

He picked up the phone again, and his secretary was
on the line. "Get me the Assistant Attorney General in
Washington *pronto!''*

Mandy drove up in her rented white Camaro and got out
of the car. She walked to the front and leaned up against
the hood. She lit a cigarette and folded her arms. She
watched Cardinal as he played polo on an auburn mount.
He really got into it. He played hard and seemed to be
a favorite among the spectators in the stands, who
cheered every time he took control of the ball.

When he dismounted, he gazed over at her. She
removed her sunglasses and waved to him.

He didn't bother to wave back. His dazzling smile
vanished. An attractive blonde came up and put her arms
around him. But his gaze was fixed on Mandy.

She wanted to let him know that she was watching him.
She hoped his friends had gotten back to him about her
interviewing them. She'd told them she was writing a

story on Cardinal. Most of them had been very eager to open up to her. Cardinal was well liked by one and all . . . a real charmer.

He said something to the blonde and then, polo helmet tucked under his arm, he wandered over to Mandy.

A chain-link fence separated them.

Mandy smiled at him as he gripped the fence with one hand, the mallet in the other. He looked around nervously to make sure nobody was watching them.

"What're you doing here, Ms. Cronenberg?"

"Mandy." She walked towards him. "Call me Mandy."

"What are you up to?"

"I told you I was doing a piece on you."

"Your publisher said his magazine was *not* doing a story on me," Cardinal said.

"Oh, did you talk with my publisher?" Mandy asked innocently.

Cardinal stared at her with his piercing blue eyes. "What's your little game, Cronenberg?"

"I'm not playing any game — are you?"

"I hope I don't have to resort to using more extreme measures to restrain you."

"Extreme measures?" Mandy smiled. "Like the ones you used in Hammett?"

He looked down at his boots and started to knock the dirt off with the mallet. Then he looked up at her again. "Hammett? What are you going on about?"

"I'm talking about the dioxin . . . the shootout. Elmore Shepard."

He shook his head and laughed to himself. "I truly believe you're disturbed, Ms. Cronenberg. I know how one must feel so soon after a loved one's death."

She wiped the smile from her face. "How did you know about that?"

"I did some research on *you.* A precautionary measure.

I never know if people are really who they say they are,''
he said, smirking.

"I know you're involved in all this, including my husband's murder.''

Cardinal said, "Didn't your husband die in some kind
of *accident*?"

"It was made to look that way.''

"But you know better.'' Cardinal nodded. "I can
recommend a very good doctor.''

"Don't think you can get away with it, Cardinal. I'm
onto you. And I'm going to stick real close to you.
Nobody's perfect. You'll slip along the way . . . and I'll
be *there*.''

"I can have you arrested for harassment,'' Cardinal
threatened.

Mandy shook her head. "Not with the tale I have to
tell.''

"Ravings of a lunatic.''

"Oh yeah?'' Mandy said. "Then why are you so
threatened?''

Without missing a beat, he said, "I'm fearful for my
welfare. I get death threats quite often. There are lot of
sick people out there.'' He eyed her accusingly.

She stamped out her cigarette and exhaled in his face.
"And some of them are above suspicion.''

"Precisely, Ms. Cronenberg,'' he smiled. "I never want
to see you again or I'll have you arrested. Do we understand one another?''

"This is going to make one hell of an article,'' Mandy
said and walked back to her car.

Cardinal stood there by the fence watching her.

She got into the car and started it. She put on her
sunglasses, backed up, and drove off.

Cardinal bit his lower lip and said, *"Bitch.''*

Frank Bigelow was sleeping in his own comfortable bed
when the phone rang. He picked it up after the first ring.

"Yeah?"

"Frank, we have a job for you," his boss, Mike Bishop, said.

Bigelow rubbed his eyes and sat up. "A job?"

"You have to escort a prisoner from Hammett to Jacksonville."

"Oh, shit. I just got off a case. This is the first time I got any sleep in three days."

"Sorry, Frank."

"Did you say *Hammett?*" Bigelow asked as he tried to clear his head.

"That's right. It seems the shit has hit the fan up there. I'm under direct orders from the Assistant Attorney General's office to retrieve a prisoner from up there. One Thomas Shepard."

"Shepard — that family runs one of the biggest dope operations up there."

"You remember that, huh?" Bishop sounded like he was proud of one of his best agents.

"I thought we got orders to pull out of there?"

"There seems to be something very big going on. Hush-hush. You know what I mean?"

"Why *me*?" Bigelow asked tiredly.

"Barry Nulls himself requested you. Seems he has been reading up on your files on Hammett."

Bigelow smiled to himself. Maybe he was finally getting a break. Or was he just going to be used for the benefit of a political advancement for Nulls?

"I don't know about this, Mike."

"Just haul your ass in here, and I'll fill you in on the rest."

"Give me an hour." Bigelow hung up and put his feet on the carpeted floor. He stretched and yawned. He had been sleeping since late yesterday afternoon. That meant he'd gotten something like twenty hours. Wow, his wife's Valium sure had done the trick.

He stood up and shuffled into the bathroom. He gave

himself the once-over in the mirror above the sink. His thick, black hair was all out of place. He was in need of a shave. And he had a big pimple on the tip of his nose. *Pimples at my age!*

He turned on the faucet and filled the basin with cold water. He splashed some on his face, wiping the sleep from his hazel eyes.

Just then, his wife, Ann, entered the bathroom. She was wearing a housecoat. "Who was that on the phone?"

"What's the matter," he smirked, "interrupted your soaps?"

"No." She curled her lip.

"It was the office," Bigelow said as he stuck out his tongue in the mirror. "I have to bring in a prisoner."

She sighed heavily. "How about some time off for a change?"

"What does it mean when your tongue is white?"

She shook her head and stormed out of the bathroom.

Bigelow clucked his tongue. She was right. After twenty fucking years he was entitled to more time between jobs. But with all the federal cuts, they had a shortage of agents. What could he do? He was fortunate to still have his job.

What does a forty-three-year-old man do when he's out of work?

He shrugged. He liked his work. He brought home a good income. He had a nice split-level house. A faithful wife. Two kids. One in college. The other, his little girl, a high school junior. Jesus, he couldn't believe how fast they had grown. His boy was on the football team. A quarterback. He had a tremendous arm. He was very proud of him.

He stepped out of his draw-string pajamas and turned on the shower. He looked at his naked body in the mirror. He was a hairy ape. His kids had teased him. God, were they right. He was still in pretty good shape, though, from his football days at Penn State. He still had the thick arms and neck. The chest and stomach were softer now. And he hated the flab that hung from the sides of his hips. He'd tried sit-ups for a spell, but it was no use. He'd have to cut down on the Bud. Someday, anyway. Right now there wasn't time to cut down on anything.

He stepped under the warm spray and lathered up. He'd have to apologize to his wife for being so snappy before. He didn't mean to be. But he detected *that* tone in her voice. She had known very well who was on the horn. What did she want him to do — quit? She couldn't support them on her bank teller's salary. And what the hell would he do? Become a Rent-A-Cop? No way. He was a fed, and that was all he'd ever be. Besides, he was itching to get back into Hammett and clean up the mess.

He stepped out of the tub and wrapped himself in a towel.

His wife was sitting on the toilet bowl.

"Howya doing, baby?" he asked.

"Fine."

He leaned over and pecked her on the cheek. "I'm sorry about before."

She nodded. She stood up and buttoned her housecoat. She was naked beneath. He gave her a bear hug.

"Frank, you're all wet!" She pushed him away.

"Oh!" he laughed. "A little water isn't going to hurt you."

"Never mind." She flushed the toilet.

He grabbed hold of her again and began to nuzzle her neck just the way she liked it.

"Frank."

He bit into her neck affectionately. "It's been a while."

"It's the middle of the afternoon."

"Yeah," Bigelow purred.

"Stop it."

He picked her up in his arms and carried her into the bedroom. Their daughter, Amy, was sitting at her mother's vanity putting on some makeup. She gazed at them in the mirror and said, "Are you two at it again?"

Nulls was seated in the first-class section of the Eastern
Airlines jet. He was hoping to be able to get in a short
nap along the way, but he was too wound up. When he
had gotten that call from Bishop about what was going
on in Hammett, he knew it would only be a matter of
time before he finally nabbed Pope. He had ordered
Bishop to bring Tommy Shepard to Jacksonville. Nulls
was eager to talk to him. He might have the information
Nulls was looking for.

Just before he received Bishop's call, Nulls had received
vital data from a herbicide manufacturer. It seemed that
Pope had ordered gallons of an experimental chemical
called EXP-44. The company had forewarned Pope that
they had not fully tested the product. But Pope had insisted on obtaining the substance. That intrigued Nulls.
Would Pope be crazy enough to use an untested, possibly
deadly herbicide in his anti-drug crusade? Nulls smiled.
Jesus, he could take him out of operation for good if that
were true.

And then a thought entered his head.

A deadly chemical substance?

That would cause an unfavorable repercussion against
the current administration if it got out that a government
official had used a dioxin on American soil. Nulls would
have to tread lightly through this affair. Perhaps he
should brief the Attorney General and, in turn, the President, on this matter. No, he would have to gather more
facts together before he could face them.

He sipped his martini and tried to steady his nerves.
There was rough road up ahead.

Cardinal drove up the driveway of his Palm Beach estate.
The blonde from the polo match sat beside him in the
Mercedes. Her name was Jesse Somebody, and she was
nineteen years old and beautiful. It was the *only* combination Cardinal worked on these days. After three
failed marriages, he had realized he would never remain

faithful to any one woman. And recently he'd had a vasectomy to avoid any paternity suits. That afforded him infinite possibilities. It didn't mean that he couldn't have an heir, since he had stored some of his precious seed in a sperm bank. Someday he would seek out a prospective mother to bear his child, but that would come later. Right now he had too much to worry about. Like making money.

He pulled up in front of his splendid mansion and hopped out of the car. He opened the door for Jesse, and they walked arm in arm into the house. The maid took their things as they proceeded upstairs to his bedroom.

Jesse plopped down on the king-sized bed and looked at Cardinal seductively.

He smiled and joined her on the bed. "I have to take a bath, baby."

"Why?"

"I'm all sweaty and stink of horseshit," he said.

"So?" she asked as she nibbled his ear.

He laughed. "Give me a few minutes." He kissed her and went into the huge bathroom with sunken tub. He sat down on a cushioned bench and began to remove his boots and clothing.

Jesse came to the doorway. "Do you want company?" She began to unbutton her powder-blue blouse, her ample breasts spilling out.

He shook his head. "Not today, sweetheart."

She frowned and removed her shirt. "Are you feeling okay — you seem preoccupied or something."

"I'm fine," he assured her.

She undid her white shorts and let them drop to the tiled floor. She stepped out of them and stood before him in striped panties. "I'll be waiting for you," she said softly and left the room.

He got up and turned on the faucets in the tub. He had more than just a bath in mind. He was quite disturbed by Mandy Cronenberg's appearance. It had ruined his whole day. The polo match had gone extremely well, and Jesse was in heat. What else could he ask for?

How about some peace of mind?

He slipped into the tub and stretched out in the warm, soothing water. He gazed up at his reflection in the ceiling's mirrored tiles. His face was deeply creased with worry lines. *Jesus, you look so old and worn-out today.* It must be nerves. He could feel the anger eating away inside him. He had to do something about that.

He reached over and picked up the cordless phone. He made a long-distance call to Washington, D.C.

"Hello?" a strong voice answered.

"Pope?"

"Jon?"

"Yes."

"You know better than to call me at home," Pope said annoyedly.

"It's about Cronenberg."

"Yeah, Bava has been filling me in."

"She knows everything," Cardinal said nervously.

"Not really."

"She knows about Hammett, the murders, and that damn dioxin you used. And she knows that I'm involved. That's everything to *me!*" he shouted.

"Calm down," Pope said softly, trying to sound like he was still in complete control.

"I can't make a single move in this town without seeing her. She's pestering my friends. It's got to stop, Hank. *Now!*" Cardinal demanded.

"I'm working on it, Jon."

"You didn't prepare me for this, Hank. You said nobody would find out about my involvement. This goes beyond our original agreement."

"What are you talking about — cutting loose?" Pope asked with a sinister tinge to his voice.

"Maybe."

"I saved your ass. That goddamn airline would've been down the tubes if it weren't for me, Jon. Don't forget that. That was me and Bava, pal!" Pope raised his voice to emphasize his superiority.

"Yeah, yeah, yeah."

"Don't worry, Jon. I have one other thing to take care of. Then I'll focus my attention on our little reporter friend. Don't even think about her. She's gone."

"*Gone* . . . how come you people never use the proper word for *it.*"

"I'll be in touch, Jon."

"You certainly will. And it better happen *fast.*" Cardinal hung up.

Pope slammed down the phone. He was sick of all these spineless men he had to deal with. First Carpenter, now Cardinal. He had enough to worry about with Tommy Shepard. Sure he was behind bars accused of murder. But what if the authorities started listening to his accusations? It wouldn't take them too long before they stumbled onto the dioxin. Damn those jerks in the lab for coming up with that stuff. He'd told them he didn't want to use a dioxin like Agent Orange. It would have to be something else. Something less dangerous but just as effective. And what had they produced? EXP-44 — a dioxin that was even *more* powerful than Agent Orange! Of course, he was also to blame for rushing them along and going ahead with his plan without proper tests.

Fools rush in . . .

Now Pope saw that there were, indeed, snags in his plan. It would take weeks for him to trace them back and figure out how they went bad. He sat behind his desk with his head in his hands. He shouldn't waste his time thinking about past mistakes. He had to concern himself with covering them up. No one must find out the *whole* truth. That would be his downfall.

He had to finish off Tommy Shepard once and for all!

He pulled out a file folder and opened it up. It was a dossier on Harold Oates, Deputy Sheriff of Hammett.

It didn't take long for Pope to figure out what buttons he had to push in order to get Oates to do his bidding.

chapter 17

Oates pushed back his hat and nodded to Higgins. *Yeah, yeah, yeah — I'll be back in four hours to relieve you. No, I won't be late. NAG, NAG, NAG!*

Oates left the station house and got into the squad car and drove off. He was getting tired of old Higs giving him a hard time. There was no need for these four-hour, round-the-clock shifts to protect Tommy. The towns-people had ended their ritual. Everything was back to normal. That was one thing you could say about the residents of Hammett — they forgot real fast. Perhaps if Nick Hill wasn't so sick things would be different. He was always the renegade leader in this town. But he was home in bed suffering with some bug.

Oates spotted a blond-haired kid walking along the dark road. He didn't recognize him as a local. That was strange — you rarely saw strangers in Hammett.

The young man squinted into the glare of Oates' head-lights. He waved him down to stop.

Oates pulled up alongside him and reached across to

roll down the passenger's-side window. "Can I help you?"

"Yeah, my car broke down just up ahead. My buddy is stayin' with it. I was just hikin' into town for some help." The young man was missing his two front teeth, and Oates had difficulty understanding him.

"Well, you won't find any help in town — the gas stations are closed this time of night. I'm pretty handy with cars. Maybe I can patch her up for yer. Hop in."

The Kid got in, and they drove off. He put a small, dark nylon bag on the floor between his feet. He pulled out a pack of Marlboros and placed a cigarette between his lips. "Mind if I smoke?"

"Nope."

"Want one?" the Kid offered.

"Yeah, I could do with one."

Oates snatched a cigarette, and the Kid lit it for him.

"Damp night," Oates said.

"Yeah, feels like rain."

"Supposed to get some tonight." Oates exhaled a stream of smoke. "Where're you headed?"

"Just passin' through on our way to Jacksonville."

"Students?"

The Kid smirked. "You could say."

Oates saw the solid-green Firebird up ahead. "That it?"

"Yep."

Oates pulled up behind it. There was a redheaded man getting out of the car. He went up to the squad car with a broad smile on his face. He nodded to Oates and gazed over at the Kid. "Howdy. I was just comin' to get you. I fixed the car myself."

Oates took notice that the redhead's hands were not soiled with grease. "You must have yourself a clean engine."

"Huh?"

"Your hands are spotless."

"Oh!" The redhead laughed. "I just cleaned them up with some detergent and water I keep in the trunk."

"That's pretty smart — I'll have to remember to do that," Oates said.

"Well, false alarm — thanks anyway, Sheriff," the Kid said and got out of the car.

"Hell, I ain't no sher— " Oates paused. "No problem. Have a safe trip, now."

The Kid and his friend got back into their car and drove off.

Strange. Oates mused. *They had rental plates. Avis or any of those guys ain't about to supply you with a trunkload of detergent and water to scrub yourself up.* Oates shrugged. He was too tired to even try and figure those two guys out.

It only took him five minutes to reach his house. He parked the patrol car behind his red Mustang on the dirt-top driveway. He reached over to get a pack of cigarettes out of the glove compartment when he noticed the small nylon bag on the floor. "What the hell?"

He picked it up and held it on his lap. It was a zippered knapsack. *That kid must've left it behind.*

He got out of the car and carried the bag into his small, wood-framed house. It was actually a three-room bungalow. It was in bad shape and needed a lot of work. Oates was only renting it. He would never dream of buying this shitbox even if he could afford it. His wife, Jo, was giving him hell about buying a clean new house. How was he going to swing that? She wondered why they couldn't live in something like the Shepards had. *Yeah, right.* He wasn't getting any kickbacks like Higgins. That bastard was doing okay.

He went into his house and went through the small hall to the kitchen. He tried to be quiet because he knew Jo would be sleeping. He placed the bag on the table, took his hat off, and dropped into a chair. He twisted his neck around to work out the stiffness. His eyes never left the bag. Those two would know enough to go to the station house and pick up their bag, Oates reasoned. He sucked in air between his front teeth to try to dislodge a piece of meat gristle. The damn steaks they served in this town.

Maybe there was a name somewhere inside. Oates pulled the bag closer to him. He unzipped the smaller compartment on the front. It was empty. He undid the top zipper and spread open the flaps. It was filled with one-hundred-dollar bills.

Oates pushed his chair back and sprang up, his eyes popping out of their sockets. *Jesus H. Christ!*

The money was packed carelessly and smelled of mildew.

He knew there was something queer about those two. They must be bank robbers!

He sank down into the chair and began feeling through the money. It *felt* real. *God, there must be thousands and thousands here!*

Suddenly, the phone rang. Its shrill sound broke his excited trance. He raced to pick it up before the second ring. "Yeah?"

"Is that you, Sheriff?" It sounded like that kid he'd picked up.

"This is Deputy Oates."

"Oh, yeah," the Kid said. "It seems I left my sack with you."

Oates eyed the bag on the table. "Sack?"

The Kid laughed. "Yeah, you know the one."

Oates swallowed hard. "I don't understand."

"We got ourselves one hungry dude . . . huh?" the Kid joked. "I'm talkin' about the sack of cold cash, pal."

"Cash?"

"That's only half . . . I have another sack sittin' here with your name on it, Oates."

"Who are you?" Oates gulped loudly.

"I'm a friend of yours, Harry. I want to help you and the missus," the Kid said sweetly.

Oates leaned up against the wall. "Help us — what're
you goin' on about?"

"The cash."

"What about it?" Oates asked.

"It's all yours," the Kid said.

"Did you steal it?"

The Kid burst into laughter. "No, sir. That's just pay-
ment for services rendered."

"What services?"

"Well, you see, the dear late Mister Carpenter used
to work for us."

"Who's *us*?"

"Your friends, Harry," the Kid said. "It's okay. We're
the good guys. We'd like you to join our organization."

"Is this the Mafia or somethin'?"

The Kid could hardly contain himself. "Hell, no,
Harry. I told you — we're the good guys. We want to
make you happy. We think you deserve a promotion."

"A *promotion*?!"

"Yeah."

Oates rubbed his eyes. Maybe he was dreaming or
something. He beheld the cash on the table. *No, he wasn't
dreaming.* "Are you payin' me to do somethin' for you?"

The Kid said, "Now you're catchin' on . . ."

It was hot and sticky inside the house. Oates could hear
the rain pouring outside. He sat on the edge of the bed
looking at his wife as she slept soundlessly. She was all
curled up in the embryonic position. She was naked, the
sheet rolled up around her feet. She was bone-thin with
long, blonde hair. Her ribs stuck out, and she had tiny
breasts. Oates considered her childlike. And like a child,
she would have her tantrums. But for the most part she
was a good wife, and Oates adored her. He just wished
she would get off this money kick. She was never
satisfied. She always wanted *more.* How many designer
jeans can one girl wear? She didn't like working at the

diner. She wanted to have a big house and raise a family. Oates wanted a baby, too. But she refused to have one until he made more money. She wasn't going to live like colored folk. She had come from a poor Georgian family and wanted to better herself. Oates could understand that. Shit, he felt the same way. He was waiting impatiently for Higgins to retire so he could get the sheriff spot.

And now someone comes along with a bagful of cash and a way to *retire* Higgins. *Jesus, how could I do that?* Higgins wasn't a bad guy. Sure, he treated him like a shithead sometimes, but he wasn't really mean-spirited. He would also have to waste Tommy — his boyhood buddy! How could he do such a thing? What kind of man did they think he was? But all that cash . . . he'd never set his eyes on so much at one time.

Jo stirred in her sleep just as the thunder rolled across their roof. She turned onto her stomach, exposing her soft buttocks. Oates reached over and rubbed them. He stroked the long hair that poked out from her genitals. He cupped his hands on her bottom and laid his head down on them. *Oh, Jo, what should I do?* He wanted so much to ask her.

He kissed her and stood up. A flash of blue lightning lit up the room. Then the thunder roared and seemed to shake their little bungalow.

He returned to the kitchen, put the money back into the bag, and zippered it up. He put his holster back on. He hid the bag in the back of the living room closet and left the house.

The rain was coming down in a steady torrent. He hurried into the patrol car and sat there for a while as he smoked a cigarette. He thought a smoke might relieve the knots in his stomach.

He took off his hat and put it down on the seat next to him. Rainwater streamed down the windshield. He liked the sound of hard rain. There was a sereneness about it. It comforted him.

He thought about his wife as she lay just inside the house. Her warm, naked body. Oates imagined how she would look with a protruding belly if she ever got knocked up. Her breasts would swell. Her face would fill out. She probably would always have a smile on her face. Yeah, he would like to see her pregnant with *his* child growing inside her. She would be beautiful. And their baby. A son, of course — he would be beautiful, too. He would take after her in looks. Oates knew he wasn't a handsome man. With his face scarred with craters, he often wondered why his attractive wife ever married him. He tried to be real nice to her. He gave her everything he could afford. Maybe that was why.

He stamped out the cigarette in the ashtray and started the car.

He had a job to do before he could realize that dream.

The storm had awakened Tommy. He was standing by the barred window listening to the rain fall. Higgins was sitting behind his desk reading a newspaper. He would nod off from time to time, then catch himself and get up and walk around a bit. He appeared exhausted and anxious. The feds were coming tomorrow to pick up Tommy.

Tommy was tired of pleading his innocence. He hoped the federal authorities would listen to him. Maybe they would investigate and uncover the truth behind this mystery.

"I can't sleep, Higs," Tommy said as he leaned up against the bars.

Higgins put down his paper and squinted at him. "How could any man with a conscience be able to sleep after doin' what you did."

Tommy rolled his eyes. "How the hell can you seriously believe I killed Carpenter?"

"*And* his wife. She died this afternoon, y'know."

"You told me that *three* times already," Tommy complained.

"Sweet woman, she was. And Carpenter — he gave me this job."

"It's no use, is it? You'll never believe me," Tommy sighed.

Just then the door opened, and Oates came in with a shotgun in his hands. He shut the door and whipped off his wet hat.

Higgins scanned his watch. "You're early, Harry." Then he noticed the shotgun. "What's with the heavy artillery?"

Oates hung up his hat and swung around. They exchanged glances. Tommy saw the expression change on Higgins' face.

Oates pumped the shotgun and squeezed the trigger. The force of the blast pushed Higgins in his wheeled chair across the room where he collapsed against the wall, his charred shirt splattered with blood.

Tommy gazed, horrified, upon Higgins' body, then shot a glance to Oates as he approached the jail cell. He pumped the gun again. The look on Oates' face frightened Tommy.

"What the fuck are you doing?" Tommy asked as he backed away from the bars.

"Sorry, Tommy," Oates said as he pulled out his keys, the gun leveled at Tommy.

He unlocked the cell door. Tommy didn't have to be a genius to figure out what Oates had in mind.

"It's a shame old Higs was murdered while you tried to make a jailbreak," Oates said. "You tried to shoot me, but I managed to wrestle with you and retrieve the gun, killing you in the process." He spoke in a cool monotone as though he was a student reading aloud his homework assignment.

Oates gripped the latch and began to open the door.

That was when Tommy made his move.

He rushed to the door and pushed the barrel away just as Oates squeezed off another charge. Tommy forced all his weight against the door and whipped it open and back against the wall, trapping Oates in between. Tommy acted so swiftly Oates didn't have a chance to fight back. Tommy rammed the barred door against Oates again and again until he dropped the gun. Tommy kicked it away and continued to open and close the door against Oates.

Oates became dazed as blood dribbled from his broken nose and shattered teeth. He slowly melted down the wall to the floor where Tommy grabbed a handful of his hair and slammed his head against the wall. Oates fell forward, leaving a red stain on the wall.

Tommy stepped back, winded from the ordeal. He wandered over to Higgins' body. *Poor bastard.*

He went back to the jail cell and pulled out Oates' key ring that was stuck in the door. He sneaked quietly outside and got into Oates' patrol car and drove off into the rainy night.

When he arrived at the house, he saw *Murderer* scrawled on the front door in pig's blood. Tommy went inside and packed a bag with some of his things. He changed into his black jeans, white tee shirt, red nylon windbreaker, and Nike running shoes.

Then he went to Elmore's room. He took the bow and shotgun and jammed them into a canvas duffle bag with ammo and arrows. He slipped the Bowie knife sheath onto his belt. Then he loaded the pistol and put it in the back of his pants.

He put both bags by the front door.

He gave the house the once-over and remembered what Debra had told him. He went into her bedroom and pulled out the top drawer in the bureau. A thick envelope was taped to the back. Tommy ripped it off and stuffed it into his pocket. Debra had told him that was where she'd hid the last of the money Elmore had set aside for Tommy's living expenses. There was five thousand dollars in one-hundred-dollar bills left. That should be enough to keep Tommy going for a while.

But where was he going?

He went back outside where the rain had stopped. He loaded up the car with his things and locked up the house.

He wondered if he would ever see it again.

He started the car and drove off. He would "borrow" a neighbor's car or truck and drive down to Jacksonville where he would steal another vehicle and head for . . . *where*?

He was back to square one. Where could he go? Who could he trust? Should he drive up north and hide out with Deb and Sage?

No, he didn't want to endanger their lives.

He had to get to the bottom of this. Mandy seemed to think Cardinal was involved. Maybe that was where he should head — to Miami.

And *Mandy*.

He had to trust her. She was the only person he had left. . . She knew what he had gone through. He would not have to waste his time explaining things to her, as he would with the authorities.

The *authorities*? Tommy laughed at the thought. There were two lawmen back in town who had some strange ideas about law and order.

There was nobody he could trust except for Mandy.

It was them against the world.

part three
IN BLOOM

chapter 18

Frank Bigelow stood by the fallen chair and blood-streaked wall. There was a white chalk outline of where Higgins' body had been found. He eyed his partner, Pete McGuane. He was just a rookie. He had light-brown hair and mustache, small but stout frame, and took his work very seriously.

Bigelow said, "What a mess."

McGuane nodded. "The doctor is patching up the deputy."

Bigelow, dressed in a light gray suit, blue shirt, and print silk tie, sighed heavily. He undid the top button of his shirt because the collar was too tight. He could never find himself a large enough neck size. He wondered if he was the only man with that problem. Or did everyone have a turkey neck like McGuane, whose only hindrance was a huge Adam's apple?

"Whaddaya think, Frank?" McGuane asked.

"I don't like it," Bigelow said.

"Oates' story?"

"It stinks."

"He's busted up pretty bad."

"Yeah." Bigelow wandered over to the jail cell. He squatted down by the bloodstained wall. "A broken nose, ten stitches in his head . . ."

"A few missing teeth," McGuane added.

"And a helluva tale."

"You don't believe him?"

"That doctor said he found him right here." Bigelow pointed to the wall beside the cell. "And judging from his wounds, I'd say Shepard used the cell door on him."

"Yeah?"

Bigelow stood up. "That means Shepard was most likely *inside* the cell when he started beating on Oates."

"Why?"

"Shepard must've pushed the door open on Oates, pressing him between the door and the wall. It's the only way that it makes sense."

"Yeah — so?" McGuane had trouble following him.

"Oates said he came into the station house and found Shepard *out* of his cell standing over by Higgins' body."

"But why do you think he used the cell door on Oates?"

"Didn't you see the horizontal gashes and bruises across his face? Only this barred door could do something like that, Pete," Bigelow explained.

"Oates says he rushed up to Tommy and they started to struggle. Tommy beat him up. Banged his head against that wall."

"Yeah, but he didn't say anything about the cell door."

"That's why I don't get your scenario about the door," McGuane said. "Sure, Shepard might've used the door on Oates. But he didn't have to be *inside* the cell for that. During the struggle, Shepard throws him up against the wall and then slams the door on him."

"Maybe," Bigelow mused. "But why didn't Shepard blow Oates away as soon as he set eyes on him?"

"He *sneaked* up on him, remember?"

"I don't believe that asshole deputy could sneak up on anybody."

"You really dislike him, don't you?"

"I dislike this whole fucking town," Bigelow snarled.

"Why?"

"I told you what went on here. The mayor. The sheriff. *Oates.* They were all involved. I tried cleaning up this town not too long ago. Then Bishop pulled me out. Said Washington had their own plans for this town. Something smelled fishy to me. I figured the kickbacks stretched all the way to D.C."

McGuane smirked.

"You don't believe that, do you? You think I'm jerking off, right? You're new to this game, Pete. You'll see a lot of firsts on this job. The corruption used to make me physically ill. But I've seen so much of it through the years now I realize I'm part of a minority in this world. The majority is on the take. I know the boys back at the office laugh at me behind my back. They think I'm some kind of sicko righteous crusader." Bigelow smiled. "Maybe I am. If that's what they call honest people these days."

"You're preaching again, Frank." McGuane chuckled.

Bigelow laughed. "You're right, kid." He walked up to him. "I want you to go through *everything* in this town. Don't leave a single stone unturned. I want to know what has been going on. The shootout. Tommy Shepard's movements since he came to this town — the whole number. I'm calling in for additional help. I think we're onto something very big in this town."

"This really turns you on, doesn't it?" McGuane noticed the gleam in Bigelow's eyes.

"I don't know if I would phrase it quite like that, Pete. But, yeah, a case like this doesn't come along too often. And when it does, it starts the adrenalin flowing. It's the reason why I got into this business."

McGuane said, "Gee, I wonder if this town knows that *Underdog is here!*"

Bigelow glared at him.

Pope sat behind the desk in his office. He was very unhappy about what had transpired. He could not get hold of Alexis. An afternoon with her usually cheered him up. He had a feeling she was avoiding him. He had also heard an unconfirmed rumor that she was seen in the company of Barry Nulls. That bugged the hell out of him. He would crack his skull open if it turned out to be true. He had to forget about that for now. He had *real* problems to worry about.

He had just heard from Karb. There was a manhunt for Tommy. He was accused of breaking out of jail, killing Higgins, and wounding Oates. That meant Tommy was out of their sight. But it wouldn't be long before the authorities tracked him down. Pope would have to make sure that he got to him before they did. If they ever started investigating his allegations . . .

It was bad enough that Federal agent Frank Bigelow was involved. Pope knew him well. He had gotten very close to Hammett with his drug-enforcement investigation. *Too* close. Pope had sent orders to the Jacksonville office to pull Bigelow off the case. That had been months ago. He hoped that wasn't a mistake. He didn't want Bigelow to trace it all the way back to Pope.

Yes, he definitely had to find Tommy Shepard. But how was he going to do it? He only had Karb and the two boys helping out. He couldn't call his real agents in to do the job. No, there was only one thing he could do. He had to make Tommy come to him.

But how?

Mandy Cronenberg.

He had underestimated her. She had followed the trail all the way back to Cardinal. How far behind was she from discovering Pope's own involvement?

She was the only friend Tommy had left, Pope

reasoned. And she would lead him to Cardinal and Bava. Tommy would go to them for answers. Then Pope would have Karb terminate the two pests. That would clear up everything.

He picked up the telephone and dialed Cardinal's number.

Pope had a favor to ask of him.

Cardinal hung up the phone. He'd just gotten through talking with Pope and was more confused than ever. Pope had wanted him to be *nice* to Mandy now. "Charm the pants off her!" was the way Pope had put it. When Cardinal had asked why, he heard Pope snickering on the line. "I have my reasons . . ." had been his reply.

Cardinal picked up the phone again and called a florist. If anyone knew how to charm a woman — it was Jonathan Cardinal!

Mandy was watching the news on television when the one dozen long-stemmed red roses arrived. The note card read:

Let's be friends. . .

— Jonathan Cardinal

The flowers didn't cheer her up. She had been watching the news report on Tommy. He was accused of three murders and a jailbreak. She didn't believe it for a second. They must have framed him. She was worried about his welfare. If he ever got killed . . . where would she be? No one would believe her then.

The phone rang.

Mandy answered it.

"Mandy?" a sexy man's voice asked.

"Yes?"

"Jon Cardinal here."

"Oh, Mr. Cardinal. I thought you were going to have me arrested or something."

He laughed. "I apologize for that. I was very rude.

Did you get the flowers I sent you?"

"Oh, yes — thank you. They're lovely," Mandy said. "I just don't understand, Mr. Cardinal."

"Please call me Jon."

"Jon," she said. "I thought you said I was a lunatic."

He laughed uneasily. "I was just upset . . . please forgive me. I really would like to make it up to you, Mandy."

Now Mandy was really confounded. *"Make it up to me? Is this the Jonathan Cardinal?"* she asked.

"You have a great sense of humor, Mandy," he chuckled.

"Uh-huh. Which is surprising after the way you treated me."

"Please, I would like to see you again," he said. "How about flying down to Key West with me? We'll have a nice relaxing day down there. Just the two of us."

Mandy sat down on the edge of the bed. "You're serious, aren't you?"

"Of course."

"Why the sudden come around?" she asked.

"Well, to be honest, Mandy, I got a bad case of the guilts."

"Ahh!" Mandy laughed. "You should have."

"So how about it?"

"When?"

"First thing in the morning," he said.

"Sounds good to me."

"I'll pick you up," Cardinal said. "Good night."

Mandy hung up. Her mouth was wide open.

It was dark. There were few people inside. Mainly local old-timers who had spent their whole lives there. It had a musty smell, as if it had been sealed up for many years. A tomb for unfortunate souls.

It was perfect.

Tommy sat on the bar stool eating a cheeseburger,

washing it down with cold draft beer. The jukebox played C-and-W hits of yesteryear. The place had atmosphere, Tommy joked to himself.

He was reading one of the daily Jacksonville papers. His face was on the front page. The headline above:

KILLER ON THE LOOSE

It was his old high-school graduation photograph. Back then he had long stringy hair on his shoulders and was clean-shaven. Now he had shorter hair and a beard. No one was about to recognize him, especially in this rattrap.

He had ditched the pickup truck he stole from a neighbor on a road just outside of the city. Then he'd hitched a ride into town. He had walked around for a while before he found this secluded bar.

He finished his lunch, paid, and went outside. It took a few minutes for his eyes to adjust to the midday sunshine. He wandered around the corner and into a supermarket parking lot.

He had to find himself a new set of wheels.

The two bags he carried weighed a ton and made his shoulders ache. He set them down and stood before the storefront. He observed the people as they left their autos and went in to do their grocery shopping. Sometimes he would venture over to an empty car and check to see if the doors were unlocked.

Tommy was out there in the hot sun for close to an hour before he spotted a potential vehicle. A Honda Accord. A man was sitting behind the wheel reading a newspaper. His wife and kid were inside the store. When they came out with a huge wagon filled with groceries, the man got out of the car and walked around to the back and opened the hatchback. The three of them began loading up the car.

Tommy made his move.

He sneaked around the front, threw in his bags, and slid in on the driver's side where the man left the door open. While lying on the floor, he quickly worked on the wires beneath the dashboard. He hoped he could pull it off faster than he had taken trying to hot-wire the pickup truck. He was out of practice. It had been years since old Higs had picked him up for car theft.

He succeeded just in the nick of time as the driver shut the hatchback. Tommy slammed the door closed and gunned the car. He sped through the parking lot and out of the exit, the owner running after him waving his fists.

Tommy got on 95 South and headed for Miami.

Not only did he manage to steal a car, but he got enough food to feed a family for a week!

As he cruised down the highway going the legal speed limit, he began to think about Mandy. Did she know about his predicament? How could she not with his face blown up on the front pages of newspapers! Now he was famous . . . for being a murderer.

Jesus, how am I going to get out of this one?

Mandy would help him.

Or would she? If not, there was always Gator Stanton. If Mandy backed off, he would head for the Everglades and look up Gator.

He had to uncover the truth before he was captured. How could one man alone take on such a challenge? He was dealing with superpowers here.

Tommy sighed. He couldn't get despondent now. He had to fight back. Keep up his strength. He gritted his teeth and gripped the steering wheel. He would get to the bottom of this even if it meant getting killed in the process.

He was doing this for Elmore.

And he would never forget that.

chapter 19

Mandy was roused by her seven o'clock wake-up call. She dragged herself out of bed and shuffled into the bathroom. Pulling her cotton nightie over her head, she observed herself in the mirror. She pinched the fat on her hips. It was that annoying extra layer she could never lose. It must have been baby fat, Mandy reasoned. She wasn't overindulgent. Stayed away from bread and pasta. Drank diet soda. Took a diet pill every morning. Unhealthy though it was, she liked the buzz it gave her. She also drank too much coffee and smoked too many cigarettes. That went with the job.

Her *shitty* job.

She felt relieved that she had sent off a short Marlowe piece to Manville so he would get off her back. She hadn't heard anything yet.

Turning on the water, she adjusted the temperature and stood under the shower. She soaped herself up, spending extra time on her large breasts — checking for dreaded lumps. She knew the chances were bad for women who didn't go through a pregnancy.

Howard and she had talked about having a child once upon a time. She wasn't getting any younger. She really was afraid. Not so much of the actual physical aspects involved, but the later years. Would her child come to dislike her as much as she did her own parents? Jesus, did that scare her. Now she didn't have to worry about that since Howard was gone.

She had to get her head in gear to prepare herself for Cardinal. Obviously, he was up to no good. Maybe he wanted to find out exactly how much she really knew or to convince her that he was not involved at all.

She rinsed the soap from her hair until it squeaked. Shutting off the water, she stepped out of the tub and began to dry herself. She had to get a move on; she expected Cardinal at eight. She hurried out into the room and slipped on her panties. Then returned to the bathroom to pop in her contacts and put on some makeup.

She just finished dressing when there was a knock on her door. She tucked her pink shirttail into her white pants and answered the door.

A blond-haired young man dressed in a black suit stood before her. "I'm here to collect you, Ms. Cronenberg." His smile revealed two missing front teeth.

Mandy felt her heart pounding in her chest. *Blond hair. Two missing teeth. A lisp.* Wasn't that the description Peter Powell had given her of one of the two strangers at the scene of Howard's accident?

"Are you from Cardinal?" she asked breathlessly.

"I'm his chauffeur," he said.

She swallowed hard. What should she do? Go along with this . . . this killer? She couldn't believe Cardinal would be foolish enough to do away with her. She had called King last night and told him that she was spending the day with Cardinal. If anything should happen to her, David would investigate.

"Let me get my jacket."

He nodded.

She whisked the linen jacket off the back of a chair and put it on her shoulders. She locked the door and followed the driver down the hall.

"Beautiful day out there," he said as they waited for the elevator. "Should be *really* nice in the Keys."

"Are we driving down there?"

The Kid put on a pair of dark sunglasses. "Naw — ya takin' the chopper."

The door opened, and they entered the elevator. There was Muzak playing. Mandy tried to act as coolly as possible, though she felt the nervous perspiration dribbling down her forehead.

They got off on the lobby floor and walked out into the glaring sunshine. The Kid opened the back door of the navy stretch limo for her. She got in and was met by the gleaming white teeth of Jonathan Cardinal.

"Good morning, Mandy." He was dressed in a pair of white cotton shorts and a polo shirt.

"Morning." She made herself comfortable in the black-leather seat as the car took off.

He offered her a cup of freshly brewed coffee and a croissant from the bar.

She sipped her coffee from a bone china cup and nibbled on the flaky croissant. The air conditioner evaporated the sweat from her brow, and she felt less tense in Cardinal's company.

"We'll be flying down to Key West. I know the manager of a nice resort there. There aren't too many tourists there this time of year. I hope you brought along your suit."

"My suit?"

"Yes," Cardinal smiled, "your bathing suit."

Mandy brought a hand to her mouth, "Shit!"

Cardinal threw his head back and laughed. "That's no problem. Actually this hotel allows topless bathing — a pair of panties should suffice."

Mandy smiled and noticed the glint in his eye. She

wondered if this guy had something else in mind other than what she'd originally thought. Now that would be interesting. Maybe he was going to try and charm his way into her pants. *Good luck, pal.*

She watched him sip his herbal tea, his blue eyes avoiding her gaze. If he couldn't deal with her in one way, why not try a different approach? Too bad she didn't think of it first. But then again, he had a lot more to work with than she did. He was definitely up to something.

But *what*?

They pulled into a small airstrip where a helicopter was waiting for them. Mandy and Cardinal exited the car and briskly walked to the chopper. A tall redhead was standing by. He helped Mandy get on board the small craft. The pilot, a haggard-looking man with cropped white hair, nodded to her. Cardinal sat next to her.

"Okay, Karb," he said to the pilot.

The copter took off, leaving the driver and redhead below. Mandy felt even more relieved when they left the chauffeur behind.

The flight was short and exciting. Cardinal pointed out many of the landmarks as they flew over them.

"That's Highway 1 down there," Cardinal said. "It goes through thirty-two islands, connected by forty-two bridges. It's the *only* road to Key West."

Mandy took notice of the ugly billboards and fast-food restaurants along the strip.

"Is this your first trip to Key West?" he shouted above the engine noise.

Mandy nodded. "First time in Florida, in fact."

"There's still some beauty left. Not much. It's become too commerical," Cardinal explained. "It's a shame."

They landed right on the surf before the hotel. The chopper floated on top of the water. The pilot steered it closer to the shore as a small speedboat came to pick them up.

A young, dark-skinned man helped her board the boat.

He wore a "Save the Bales" tee shirt.

After Cardinal got on, the boat sped off to the dock.

On shore, Cardinal introduced her to the owner, and they settled down on the beach. Cardinal stripped down to a pair of microbriefs that barely contained his bulging manhood.

Mandy looked around and saw the other women with bared tops, their flat chests glistening with suntan oil. *I don't know if I'm ready for this.*

She removed her blouse and pants and was down to her underwear.

Cardinal was already stretched out on the lounge chair sipping ice water. His eyes were closed as he took in the sun.

What the hell!

She undid her bra and her breasts were exposed. They looked like two huge white melons smothered with brown dots. She quickly sat down on the chaise lounge and put on some lotion.

"Do you want me to help you with that?" Cardinal asked as he looked at her with one eye open.

"Eh." Mandy, her hands filled with lotion, looked down at her nakedness and then up at him. "I think I can manage."

Doc Crichton clutched his crinkled, black-leather bag close to him. His fluid eyes were darting nervously about the station house as he spoke to Frank Bigelow.

Bigelow sat behind Higgins' desk with his feet up. He nodded from time to time, but he was too preoccupied to be listening. He had too much on his mind. He wanted to grill Oates once again. He knew he was lying. He was holding something back. Bigelow had interrogated enough men in his time to know that.

"You'll have to see it for yourself, Bigelow." Doc Crichton dropped his medical satchel on the desk loudly.

Bigelow snapped out of it. "What?"

"Have you been listening to me?"

"I'm sorry . . . what were you saying?"

Crichton sighed disapprovingly. "I'm not going to repeat myself, Bigelow."

"He's talking about a bad virus," McGuane, who stood off by the jail cell, said.

Bigelow eyed his partner. "A virus?"

"I'm not sure what it is," Crichton said. "But it's spreading quickly, and I can't seem to stifle it."

"What has this virus got to do with *me*?"

Crichton looked over at McGuane, then back at Bigelow. "I saw the same oozing sores on Elmore Shepard's body."

"So?" McGuane asked. "Maybe he was sick, too."

"Tommy Shepard was going on about something."

"Whaddaya mean?" Bigelow asked.

"Tommy suspected this virus had something to do with the killings. That's what he was investigating here in town."

"He linked this virus with his brother's murder?"

Crichton nodded. "I don't know the whole story."

"What did the autopsy reveal?" McGuane asked.

"That was the *other* thing," Crichton said. "I looked up the files. There was no autopsy performed on Elmore's body. The others — yes. But not Elmore's."

Bigelow stood up. "Why not?"

"I didn't handle it — Carpenter called in a Jacksonville coroner."

Bigelow gazed at McGuane. "Whaddaya think?"

"I think the Doc is onto something."

"A *virus*?" Bigelow asked.

"I don't know that for certain . . . it's something I've never confronted before," Crichton said.

"Who has it?" Bigelow asked.

"The Hills."

"I want to see them," Bigelow said.

Crichton drove him to the Hills' place in his late-model

Chevy. They lived off on a dirt road deep in the woods. When they approached the house, Bigelow saw a man standing on the roof with a shotgun.

"What the hell?"

"I should've warned you," Crichton smirked. "Our friends have several marijuana patches growing here."

"On their *own* property?" Bigelow asked wide-eyed with amazement.

"Yep."

"I don't believe these guys," Bigelow said, shaking his head. "Whatever happened to good old stills?"

"I think you already know the answer to that, Bigelow."

"How could they get away with this?"

"I think you already have the answer for that one, too," Crichton said, smiling.

Bigelow said, "I *just* knew it."

They pulled up in front of the house. "Now, the old man and his eldest have it. The rest of the family seem fine." The Doc handed him a medical face mask. "You better wear this."

The two men put on their masks and went inside the house. Mrs. Hill greeted them at the door. She was a broad woman with a big bust, her gray hair tied up in a bun. She appeared solemn and spoke in a hushed tone.

She escorted them to the bedroom where her husband lay on the bed. His breathing was heavy. Tubes were feeding him oxygen through his nose. His face was totally covered with red sores. His eyes were cloudy and lifeless.

Bigelow gasped. "My God."

Crichton took Hill's pulse. He eyed Bigelow and shook his head. "He's fading fast."

"Why don't you put him in the hospital?"

"My husband won't have anythin' to do with them hospitals," Mrs. Hill said.

"But he's . . . *dying*." Bigelow said.

Crichton shrugged. "That's the way these people are, Bigelow."

Bigelow stood at the foot of the bed, his eyes on the swollen body before him. "This is no virus."

Crichton nodded.

"What the hell is going on in this town?" Bigelow asked.

Crichton brought him to the other sickroom, where Sam was sitting up in bed watching cartoons on television. His face and arms were covered with the same pimples. His skin tone was almost green.

"Howdy, Sam." The Doc took his pulse. "How ya feeling?"

"Weak," Sam said. "I ain't got no energy." He beheld Bigelow with his one good eye, a patch covering the other. "Who're you — 'nother doctor?"

"Sort of," Bigelow said. In a way, he was a doctor. He was here to help an ailing town.

"I think you should go into the hospital for some tests, Sam. You don't wanna end up like your daddy," Crichton said.

Sam shut off the set with the remote control. "I ain't gettin' any better, am I?"

Crichton shook his head.

Sam eyed his mother who stood by the doorway. She nodded.

"Guess you're right, Doc."

"Good boy," Crichton said gleefully. "I'll make the arrangements."

The two men left the house and got into the car. "Well?" Crichton asked.

"I think Tommy Shepard is right," Bigelow said. "Tell me something, Doc."

"Yes?"

"Did you know Tommy?"

Crichton nodded.

"Was he the killer type?"

Crichton shook his head. "He's a bright young man. Sensitive. I don't believe he killed those people."

"And what about Oates?"

"I dressed his wounds — he was pretty busted up."

"But would *he* have killed Higgins?" Bigelow asked.

"He's just a dumb farm boy," Crichton said.

"I don't believe his story," Bigelow said frankly.

"I don't know what to believe anymore. Whole town's gone crazy."

"Who else has this *disease*?"

"A few of the farmers . . ." Crichton said.

"Farmers?"

"Yeah," Crichton said, "which makes it real interesting."

"Why's that?"

"They all grow marijuana," Crichton said.

Bigelow thought that over. "The state hasn't sprayed anything up here in years. If they did, I would've known about it."

"Something is causing it," Crichton said.

Bigelow's face lit up. "There's only one way to find out."

"How?"

"Perform an autopsy on Elmore's body," Bigelow suggested.

Crichton looked at Bigelow confoundedly. "He's buried."

"So?"

"You need permission from the immediate family."

"Tommy?"

"Or his wife."

"Where is she?"

Crichton shrugged. "Tommy sent them off somewhere," he related. "He was worried about them."

"Worried about them catching this sickness?"

"Maybe." Crichton started the car. "Maybe."

Bigelow thought it over as they drove off. Finally he said, "The tests on Sam Hill should show something."

"I'm sure they will."

"I want to know as soon as you hear anything."

"I don't envy you, Bigelow."

"How's that?"

"I wonder how deep this whole thing goes."

Bigelow didn't answer him. He just stared straight ahead. He had to crack Oates before he could delve any deeper into this case. Then he wondered if Barry Nulls knew anything about this virus . . .

Mandy and Cardinal were eating a seafood lunch at Captain Tony's saloon, formerly the old Sloppy Joe's where Hemingway had done most of his drinking. Cardinal, his face and body deeply tanned, sipped his chilled water as he eyed Mandy. She took a drink of her white wine.

"You don't drink or smoke?" Mandy asked.

"I'm also a vegetarian."

"Oh, I wasn't aware of that," Mandy said.

"Still writing your article on me?"

Mandy smiled. "I'm just wondering what you're up to."

"I'm not up to anything," Cardinal smirked.

"I don't buy that line about you having the guilts. No maverick businessman has a conscience."

Cardinal chuckled. "Your sense of humor." He shook his head.

Mandy became serious. "What is it, Cardinal?"

"Call me Jon." He poured her another glass of wine from the bottle. "I just want to play nice, Mandy."

"Uh-huh."

"You don't believe me?"

"Not for a second."

Cardinal blinked his baby blues. "You're hurting my feelings."

"You don't have any feelings."

"You have the wrong picture of me, Mandy," he said. "I'm not a skinless capitalist. I didn't come from money. I know the type of man you're referring to. That's not me."

"What about Hammett?" she asked.

"I don't know anything about that," he said.

"Dioxins and living things don't mix," she stated.

Cardinal swallowed loudly. He lost that twinkle in his eye. "If you're so certain of my guilt, why don't you inform the authorities?"

"I'm working on it."

"You don't have any proof," Cardinal said. "Why don't you stop this little mindless crusade and relax, huh? I'm trying to make peace with you. I know it must be upsetting to lose a loved one. But chasing after phantoms or *windmills* will get you nowhere." He put his hand on hers. "I'm trying to understand you, Mandy. I think I like you. You have a lot of courage. You could go far with a passion like yours. You lack only direction."

"Are you trying to bribe me?" Mandy asked nastily.

Cardinal rolled his eyes. "Why do you choose to be so difficult? I'm only trying to help you. I think we could be good together." He squeezed her hand.

She laughed. "You're really something else."

"I fail to see the humor . . ."

"You're probably responsible for the death of my husband and now you expect me to fall into bed with you?"

"Bed?" Now Cardinal snickered. "Your sense of humor . . ."

"Don't patronize me, Cardinal," she said through clenched teeth.

Cardinal backed off. "I'm sorry. Obviously, you're reading me all wrong. Why do you suspect me of being involved in this . . . this conspiracy of yours?"

"Bava."

Cardinal pursed his lips and nodded. "And because he works for me, therefore I'm implicated."

"That's correct," Mandy acknowledged.

Cardinal sat back in his chair and thought it over silently for a few minutes. "You really believe Bava is involved in all this?"

"Yes . . . his name was dropped by a reliable source," she informed him.

Cardinal now knew what to do. It might just work. He studied Mandy carefully. He liked her eyes. They were intelligent. Shrewd. It would be difficult to convince her of what he had in mind. But if she fell for it, it could clear his name. He might be able to get himself off the hook. "I think I can trust you, Mandy."

"Well, that makes one of us."

He raised his eyebrows. "You don't trust me?"

"Not as far as I can throw you."

"How can I convince you that I'm telling the truth?"

"When you start telling the truth," Mandy smirked.

"Very good." Cardinal was amused. "Would you believe that I'm not involved in this whole thing? That perhaps Bava is. I could check that out. We could work together on this."

"Work together?" Mandy wasn't buying it.

"Yes. Perhaps you're right above Bava. I surely hope not. But if you are, I will personally hand him over to the authorities."

Mandy cocked her head to one side. "Are you being straight with me?"

He took her hand. "Please believe me, Mandy. I'm a public figure. Do you think I could get away with a scheme like you have in mind? I'd be crucified by the media. My face has been on every national magazine cover. I'm no criminal. People . . . the *common* people have respect for me. I could never let them down. I'm an honest businessman who has worked his way up from the street. You act as though I have no ethics. That I'm immoral. Well, believe me, Mandy, those people out there are the greatest judge of character. They can't be easily duped any longer. They've grown more cynical through the years because of Watergate, the Iranian arms deal, and the dozens of other scandals constantly exposed by the media."

She nodded in agreement.

"I'm in the position to do something about this inquiry of yours. I must admit I have my doubts. I distrusted you completely from the start . . . the way you approached me. You had me guilty before I even stated my case."

Mandy sat there silently for a spell listening to Cardinal. He was so animated. Every part of his body seemed to be in motion. He was a bundle of energy. And though he was so strong and direct, his tone was soft and sincere. After he was through, she decided to see just how sincere he was. "What about your chauffeur?"

"My chauffeur?"

"He was seen at my husband's *accident*," she said accusingly. "I have a witness."

Cardinal took a sip of water. "Hmmm . . . that disturbs me. He's Bava's driver. Perhaps you are right about Bava."

"Why should I believe you?"

Cardinal shrugged. "I don't know how I can convince you, Mandy. But go along with me. I promise I will investigate this matter and keep you informed."

She gave him a crooked grin. "You're a real charmer, aren't you?"

He smiled radiantly. "I only want to be friends."

"Why?"

"I find you attractive. Intelligent. Very direct. I like that in a woman. I'm also concerned about your welfare. If Bava is involved in this, he might want to *silence* you." Cardinal's eyes looked directly into hers. "I *wouldn't* want that to happen."

She tried to pull herself away from their trance but there was no use. He had her hooked. His hand felt warm in hers. It was not a killer's hand, she decided.

"Did you enjoy your lunch?" he asked.

"Very much so."

"How about some time in the sauna back at the resort for dessert?" he offered.

She smiled. "Sounds delicious."

chapter 20

Oates sat in a chair pushed up against the white wall in the station house. He had a bandage around his head. His ribs were taped up. His face bruised beyond recognition. He didn't like the way Bigelow was tearing into him. Couldn't he see how much pain he was in? Bastard. His partner, McGuane, he was nice. He had given Oates a cup of coffee and a cigarette. But this Bigelow — he was a hard ass. He reminded Oates of Higgins.

Bigelow paced before Oates, stripped down to his white shirt and pants. The fans gave little relief in the intense, muggy heat of Indian summer. Bigelow stuck his sweaty mug into Oates' face. "I think you're full of shit, baby."

"Go easy, Frank," McGuane said as he sat behind Higgins' desk.

Bigelow straightened up, eyeing his friend. "I've *been* going easy with this clown."

"He's hurting."

"Yeah, he sure is." Bigelow examined the bruises in front of him. "You don't look so good, son. Tommy Shepard remade your puss something fierce."

Oates glared into Bigelow's hazel eyes. He didn't like the look on his face. He knew Bigelow wouldn't give up until he found out what he wanted to know. They had been at it for over two hours now.

"I think we could all use a break, Frank." McGuane stood up to stretch.

"Good idea," Bigelow said. "Get lost."

"Frank."

"*Out!*" Bigelow ordered. "Call the hospital — I want the word on Hill. Also get me the file on Tommy Shepard. I think our boys should be through with it by now."

"What about him?" McGuane thrust his chin out at Oates.

"I'll handle him."

"Take it easy, Frank."

"Don't tell me how to do my job," Bigelow snapped. McGuane left the office.

Bigelow grabbed a chair and straddled it backwards. "Now, Harry, we're all by our lonesome."

"I told you everythin' I know," Oates said. "I'm tired . . . I'm achin' . . . I'm hot."

"Poor baby."

"You don't have any right doin' this to me. I'm on *your* side."

"Don't ever say that, Oates. I know exactly *what* you are. You're scum. You're like Higgins and Carpenter — just white fuckin' trash. You can be bought just like that." He snapped his fingers. "No, I'm not on your side."

"Why're you doin' this to me?"

"Because I don't like you. I think your story stinks. Whaddaya think about that?"

"I want my lawyer."

"There aren't any *real* lawyers in this town. No more than there is any law in this town. How much did you make in kickbacks, boy?" Bigelow asked.

"I never got none," Oates mumbled.

"Bullshit," Bigelow snapped.

"Higgins . . . he hogged it all."

"Tsk-tsk — poor deputy didn't get shit." Bigelow shook his head. "Just wasn't fair. Another man might've done something about that."

"Whaddaya mean?"

"He might've changed things . . . turned the tables, so to speak. Maybe even blow the poor fucker away. Is that how it was, Oates?"

"I told you what happened," Oates said, his eyes downcast.

"And I don't believe a word of it. Tommy Shepard didn't shoot old Higs — you did. Why? Because you wanted his job."

Oates shook his head. "This is illegal."

"Ha!" Bigelow laughed. "That's funny coming from you, sport."

"I refuse to answer any more of your questions."

"Then you'll sit here all day and night until you do," Bigelow said firmly.

Oates sighed heavily. Tears began to well in his eyes. He wished this prick would leave him alone. It just wasn't fair. He would never tell him about the money. That was for Jo.

Bigelow gazed at him, his eyes burning a path through him. "Crying isn't going to help. All I want from you is the truth, Oates. You blew it. Your plan backfired. I can see that. A judge in a court of law could see that."

"You're lyin'!" Oates sobbed. "Lay off me."

"Come on, son. I'll make it easier on you. All I want is the truth."

"You just want to hear what *you* want to hear — not the truth."

Bigelow smirked. "You want me to bust you up some more?"

"I'll sue you if you lay a hand on me!" Oates' Adam's apple bobbled excitedly.

"Who's going to know? You're so broken up, nobody'll notice."

"Where's McGuane?" Oates knew he would protect him.

"He's not going to save you, Oates."

Oates hung his head and began to sob loudly. "Ain't fair."

Bigelow kicked him in the shin. "I want the truth, Oates — *now!*"

Oates rubbed his shin. "You can't do this . . . I have rights."

"You blew Higs away. Then you opened the cell door. You were going to blast Shepard when he jumped you. He beat you up. Bashed you with the cell door. Those horizontal gashes across your face . . . the broken ribs. He took your stupid head and banged it against the wall. Sound like it, buddy?"

"I don't remember . . . I told you what I saw. He was standin' over Higs' body. Shotgun in his hands. It was still smokin'. I crept in and took him from behind."

"Crept in?" Bigelow asked. "I don't believe it for a second. You're too stupid to sneak up on anybody. He would've heard you and blown you away. Come off it, Oates, you better change your story. It will never hold up in a courtroom."   ·

"I'm telling you what happened, man," Oates said in a cracked voice.

"You're falling apart, sonny. Do you have any idea what a DA would do to you? He'd eat you alive. Bones and all. It'll be easier on you if you confess."

"Confess?" Oates said. "I've had it. I ain't sayin' nothin'. I have a right to a lawyer."

Bigelow rubbed his face. "Okay, Harry." He stood up and leaned against the wall. "I was trying to do you a favor, sonny."

"Stop callin' me sonny."

"You're just a dumb boy."

"I ain't dumb," Oates said. "And I'm a man. I'm thirty years old just like Tommy Shepard."

Bigelow shook his head. "Sad excuse for a man . . . "

"Why're you doin' this?"

"Because I'm pissed the fuck off. I have a helluva case here and no clues. Just a dumb retard deputy who doesn't have a pot to pee in."

That did it.

Oates shot up and gripped his hands around Bigelow's throat. Bigelow punched him in the ribs and he collapsed onto the floor like a rag doll.

"Jeezus Christ!" He squirmed on the floor, screaming in agony, as he hugged his ribs.

Bigelow stepped over him and went outside for some air. McGuane was just coming back

"How's it going?"

Bigelow shook his head. "It got out of hand. The bad guy approach isn't working. The bastard's tougher than I thought he was."

"Maybe he *is* telling the truth."

Bigelow eyed McGuane. "No way."

"I'll talk to him." McGuane was about to enter the office when Bigelow grabbed the file folder out of his hand. "This Shepard's file?"

"Yep. He was clean up until now. He made some long-distance phone calls."

"Where to?"

"Miami."

Bigelow nodded. "And Hill?"

"We should know something by morning." McGuane said. " I also called Bishop and filled him in. It seems Nulls has set up a command post in Jacksonville."

"A command post?"

"That's right."

Bigelow wondered what that guy was up to. He had a feeling Nulls knew more about what was going on in Hammett than Bigelow did. "Thanks."

McGuane went inside and helped Oates back onto the chair. "Are you okay?"

"I'm goin' to press charges against that asshole," Oates threatened.

McGuane squatted down. "Take it easy."

Oates was sweating from the pain. "I'm hurtin' bad."

"I'm sorry about Bigelow's temper. He just knows you're lying and he's not about to give up until you admit to it."

"I ain't lyin'."

"Well, to tell you the truth, Harry, I kinda believe you. But I don't think a judge would. Bigelow has this case pretty sewed up. He's a pro. He can smell when something is wrong. All you have to do is tell us what *really* happened. That's all. It'll make it easier on you."

"I've been tellin' the truth," Oates said. "I'm hurtin' and I'm tired."

McGuane stood up, his hands on his hips. "The sooner you tell us the truth, the better off you'll be."

Oates sighed. He scanned the ceiling. *God help me.* He'd known it was the wrong thing to do. He hadn't wanted to kill Higs. But *that* money. It was in his hands. He couldn't part with it. They said it would go okay. There would be no hitch. He covered his face with his hands and cried some more. He didn't want to go to jail. It just wasn't fair. It was the first time he had ever made a mistake. Maybe the judge would understand that. No, he killed a sheriff. They would throw the book at him.

Oates felt McGuane's hand on his shoulder. "It'll be okay, Harry."

Oates shook his head.

"He was a bad sheriff . . . he was on the take. The judge will take that into consideration . . ." McGuane spoke softly. "A smart lawyer might be able to get the charge reduced to manslaughter."

Oates looked up at McGuane with his wet, sloppy eyes. "You think so?"

"Sure."

"It just ain't fair," he sobbed.

"It never is, Harry." McGuane went behind the desk and switched on the tape recorder. He returned to Oates and squatted down in front of him. "Do you have something to tell me, Harry?"

Oates nodded.

McGuane said, "Okay, go on and tell me."

Nulls stood before Bishop's desk with his hands on his hips. Bishop had just gotten off the phone with McGuane and was informing Nulls of the latest news from Hammett.

"A virus?" Nulls interrupted him.

"That's what McGuane said. The local doctor claims this disease is spreading like wildfire down there."

"What're the symptoms?"

"Open sores . . . chills . . . rapid weight loss."

Nulls shut his eyes. He didn't have to hear any more. "Oh my God. He did it. He *really* did it!"

Bishop was perplexed. "What are you going on about? You know what this virus is?"

"I know it's no virus," Nulls declared.

"Then what is it?"

"Dioxin poisoning," Nulls said.

Bishop's mouth dropped open. He stood up, leaning heavily on top of the desk, his eyes never leaving the Assistant Attorney General. "You mean like Agent Orange?"

"EXP-44 to be exact."

Bishop collapsed in his chair. "What does this mean?"

"It means we have a major catastrophe on our hands. We'll have to call in the National Guard and seal off that town. I'll send in some scientists who will help us cope with this . . . *nightmare.*"

"Did you know about this all along?" Bishop asked agitatedly. "I have two good men in that town right now!"

"I suspected it . . . I had no way of knowing for sure."

"You could have warned me!" Bishop snapped.

Nulls inhaled deeply. "I apologize, Mike. But this is a highly confidential matter. I'm here without government sanction. In fact, I believe it's one of our own who's responsible for this."

Bishop nodded. "It's Pope, isn't it? He's the one."

"I have no positive evidence at this time . . ."

Bishop shot up. "Fuck evidence! What the hell do you plan on doing about those poor people in Hammett?!"

Nulls put a hand to his brow. "Jesus Christ."

He stood before her in the doorway. There were two bags by his feet. He had a full beard. His hair was greasy and untamed. There were dark rings under his eyes. She hardly recognized him.

"Tommy?" Mandy asked.

"Mandy," he said tiredly.

"Jesus Christ, am I glad to see you." Mandy beamed as she let him inside.

Tommy stood awkwardly next to her. "I didn't know where else to go . . ."

"You came to the right place."

"Did you hear about me?"

"You're all over the media."

"I didn't do it," Tommy said in a cracked, exhausted voice.

"You don't have to tell me that. I know." Mandy smiled. "You look beat."

"Been on the road for a long time."

"Did you drive?" she asked.

"Picked up a car in Jacksonville," he said. "I ditched it in some parking lot on the other side of town."

She went up to him. She was dressed in a pink terry cloth robe. "You could use a bath."

"Probably stink like a hog." He smelled his clothes. "A bath sounds great."

"I'll get it going." Mandy went into the bathroom and turned on the faucets.

Tommy plopped down on the edge of the bed and pulled his sneakers off. His body ached all over. His legs were stiff from all the driving.

Mandy returned a few minutes later. "I hope you like bubbles in your bath."

"I don't care as long as it's wet and hot."

He stood up. They exchanged glances. Mandy averted her eyes. "There're towels in the bathroom."

"I want to thank you, Mandy."

She nodded.

"I'm sorry I dragged you into this . . . so *very* sorry."

"It's okay."

He reached out and touched her cheek. They smiled at one another. Tommy went into the bathroom and shut the door. He peeled off his clothes and slipped into the tub. It was good and hot, the steam rising off the top.

He pushed his head back and put a wet washcloth across his face. So far so good, he thought. She seemed genuinely concerned about him. That made him feel better . . . *safer.*

Mandy sat on the foot of the bed and wondered if she was doing the right thing. Here she was taking a fugitive in. A stranger. But he seemed so desperate standing there. So dead tired. He looked like a stray cat. How was she going to take care of him? Where could he hide out? He could not stay in her hotel room without someone getting suspicious. Maybe Dave would have a suggestion . . . or even Cardinal.

Could she trust Cardinal?

He seemed sincere. Maybe he really was unaware of Bava's illegal activities. It would mean risking Tommy's life to find out.

She heard Tommy splashing around in the tub. She felt so confused. Who could she trust?

She remembered the way Cardinal had touched her in the sauna. He had run his fingers all along her body . . . massaging her. Her towel had fallen aside. His hands had been on her breasts as he worked the oil into them. His towel had dropped, his manhood at attention. Their lips together . . . kissing.

He'd cupped her buttocks with his strong hands as he brought her closer to him. The heat of the sauna had been swirling all around them. The smell of the burning coals mixed with their sweaty, sexy musk as they made love.

It had been a long time for Mandy. She needed it. Something . . . *anything* to relieve the tension that pulsed inside her. And it had all flowed out of her at once. The pressure . . . the pain . . . the uncertainty . . . like a gusher exploding. And her body had trembled as tears swelled in her eyes. She'd felt good again. Like a real person. But now all that had changed with Tommy's arrival. The doubts returned. Reality wagged its ugly head once again and brought her down to earth.

Just then the bathroom door opened and Tommy appeared, dressed in a pair of clean Levi's and a fresh, white tee shirt. "Feel like a new man." He smiled wryly.

"You look a whole lot better." Mandy stood up.

"Has anything happened since the last time we spoke?" Tommy asked.

"Some," she said cautiously, not knowing how much to reveal. "It seems that Bava is running the show all right."

"What about this Cardinal guy you told me about?"

She shrugged. "He seems clean. He says he doesn't know anything about it."

"This Cardinal . . . are we talking about the same man?" Tommy asked.

"Mister *Time* magazine cover himself."

"And you trust him?"

Mandy looked away and nodded.

Tommy noticed her lack of conviction. "But this Bava works for him — right?"

"Yes — but Cardinal says he's not aware of any wrongdoing on Bava's behalf. He's agreed to look into the matter." Her voice was a bit wobbly.

"Uh-huh." Tommy didn't sound very convinced.

"I think he's telling the truth," she said.

"Is there something the matter?" Tommy asked.

"What do you mean?"

"You seem to have difficulty talking about Cardinal."

She sat down on the bed and crossed her legs, her lips sealed.

"Is it me?" Tommy asked. "I could go . . ."

"Don't be silly."

Tommy squatted down. "You sure?"

"Yes," Mandy said. "I just don't know how long you should stay here . . ."

"I plan on staying only for the night." Tommy stood up. "Remember I'm on the lam — I don't want you to get into trouble. I would just like to be able to stay in touch with you, Mandy. You're my *only* contact with the outside world."

"Where are you going to hide out?"

Tommy shrugged.

"Hmmm," Mandy moaned in thought. "I might have an idea."

"I'm all ears."

"Jonathan Cardinal."

"What about him?" Tommy asked.

"He might help. A man with his kind of power could be an asset for you," Mandy explained.

Tommy had a bad feeling about her suggestion. "You're not telling me something, Mandy."

She laughed insincerely. "What are you talking about?"

"Come clean with me. What's going on?" he asked suspiciously.

She sobered up. "There's nothing going on . . ."

Tommy grabbed her by the shoulders, lifting her to her feet forcefully. "We're talking about my life here, Mandy! You're holding something back — I can tell. You've been acting strangely ever since I got here . . ."

"TAKE YOUR HANDS OFF OF ME!" Mandy demanded.

Mandy rubbed her sore arms from Tommy's assault. "Why are you treating me like this?"

"Because you're a bad liar, Mandy," Tommy said. "I've learned some things these past weeks about human nature. Now I have an automatic bullshit detector inside me that sounds off whenever somebody is holding out on me."

Mandy collapsed onto the bed and rubbed her eyes. "I wish I had one of those gizmos built inside of me."

"It's Cardinal — isn't it?"

She nodded.

"He got to you."

She dropped her hands and Tommy saw the tears in her eyes. "Crying is bad for contact lenses," she sobbed.

"What happened?"

"He's a real charmer," she said.

Tommy sighed. She didn't have to spell it out for him. He knew how she felt. She was hurting as much as Deb was. "Things happen."

"I'm a fuckin' journalist and I let some rich bastard sweep me off my feet," she said. "He really had me going there . . . shit — I still believe him."

"He might be telling the truth," Tommy said.

"How could we be sure?"

Tommy gulped loudly. "By testing him."

Mandy wiped her eyes. *"Testing him?"*

"That's right. Call him. Tell him I need a hideout. Let's see if he delivers."

"But what if he *is* involved?"

"I can handle myself," Tommy said boldly.

Mandy scrutinized him. "What is that supposed to mean?"

"It means I'm playing for keeps," Tommy declared. "It's me against the machine. And I plan on winning."

"You frighten me," Mandy said. "You're turning into *them.*"

"Turning into *Cardinal,* you mean?" Tommy emphasized as the anger continued to swell inside him.

"I'm sorry I'm not as strong as you, Tommy Shepard," Mandy sneered.

Tommy walked to the bedside table, picked up the phone, and brought it to her. "Call him. Tell him I'm dying to meet him."

Mandy shifted her gaze from the phone to him. "He just might be able to accommodate you."

chapter 21

Nulls sat behind Bishop's desk with a team of men gathered around him. There was a government scientist, Professor Ellison, an expert on dioxins who cut his teeth studying the effects of Agent Orange on Viet Nam veterans. Next to him sat Lieutenant Dunne, Commanding Officer of the local National Guard. Behind them stood James Serling, a representative of the pharmaceutical firm that created EXP-44. Mike Bishop held up the rear, cigar in mouth, his haggard face showing the strains of the past twenty-four hours.

Dunne said, "So we go in, seal it up, gather the townspeople together . . ."

Ellison added, "And I start the testing procedures."

Nulls nodded, then eyed Serling who had been silent during most of the briefing. "I haven't heard any feedback from you, Mr. Serling."

He snapped out of his trance and cleared his throat. "I was just thinking about how much this could cost us."

Nulls cocked his head to one side. "You mean in damages . . . lawsuits?"

Serling replied quietly. "It could put us into Chapter Eleven."

"You should have thought of that *before* you sold that shit to Pope," Bishop said sharply.

"We didn't know what he was going to use it for!" Serling snapped.

"Bullshit," Bishop said under his breath.

"That'll be enough," Nulls ordered. "We have more important matters to deal with before we start pointing fingers at one another."

"What about my men?" Bishop asked. "What are the chances they have been affected?"

Ellison shrugged his shoulders. "I can't say at this time. I don't know how extensive the spraying was." He addressed Nulls. "Can we get any accurate information out of the Operation Grim Reaper office?"

Nulls shook his head in annoyance. "We have not informed Pope of our little discovery *yet*. I've briefed the Attorney General on the matter and he'll have to discuss it with the President. My orders are just to seal off Hammett and evaluate the situation. And remember, gentlemen, this is a highly confidential matter. Nothing — and I mean absolutely *nothing* — should be said to anyone outside of this group. Is that understood?"

All the men nodded.

Nulls continued, "I will not tolerate any leaks. Any breach of security will be dealt with harshly."

Nulls eyed each man intently. "Are there any questions?"

Silence fell over the room.

"Then let's get to it," Nulls commanded.

Tommy was sitting on the floor reading the file on Jonathan Cardinal as Mandy lay sleeping in bed. The room was gray-dark, dawn still some hours away.

Tommy wanted to learn as much as he could about Cardinal. Where he lived. His business. How the whole country had come to know and respect him. Hero worship was rare for Tommy. Except as a boy with Clint Eastwood/Bruce Lee/Charles Bronson movies. But all kids went through that stage. Americans, however, seemed preoccupied with heroes. Conjuring them up was a favorite American pastime. Too bad there weren't many worthy of the title.

Tommy examined the black-and-white glossy of Cardinal. It was a recent shot. Even the crow's feet and gray hair added to his persona. Rugged. Determined. A real Marlboro Man.

Why would such a man be involved with drugs and dioxins? Is that how he made it to the top? Or did he do it to *stay* on top?

It was time for Tommy to confront Cardinal. He had to find out the truth. If he had to die, he wanted to go knowing why.

The only way Cardinal could prove his innocence or guilt was by helping Tommy find a hideout. When Mandy had made the call, Cardinal assured her he would do his best and would get back to her. Twenty minutes later he'd called and told them that Tommy could hole up in his small cabin located in the Everglades. Tommy was prepared to set out that morning to get there.

But could he trust Cardinal? Mandy seemed confident enough . . . but she was biased. For all that Tommy knew she could have switched sides and was now working with them to snow job him. He could be walking straight into a trap.

Tommy prepared himself for the worst. His gaze drifted over to his duffel bag. Inside was a small arsenal.

He eyed Mandy as she stirred in her sleep. He would leave before she woke up. He didn't want to confront her. She would want to come along. He had enough things to worry about.No, this was his battle — his *alone*. He planned on getting some help from old Gator — he knew the Everglades better than anyone in the state.

He stood up and stretched, his bones cracking loudly. His eyes never left Mandy. He tried real hard to trust her. She seemed sincere. She had even come clean about making it with Cardinal. She did not have to reveal that.

He put on some clothes and quietly got his things together.

He watched her sleep for a while and then left.

It was time to see the whites of his enemies' eyes. . .

The horizon glowed from the pre-dawn sun. There was a pink light in the air. Not a breeze stirred. Two two-lane blacktop was wet from dampness. The foliage was bright green. No sound disturbed the sereneness.

Until *they* came.

The first truckload arrived just as a sliver of yellow sun appeared. The soft rays of light, filtered through the thick trees, fell onto the road. Two men, dressed in white POTMC suits and masks, hopped off the back of the truck. Their POTMC gear — Protective Outfit, Toxicological, Microclimated Controlled uniform — protected its wearer in the event of chemical warfare. They also carried M-16s over their shoulders. One man waved the truck on.

The two National Guardsmen set up a barrier across the road at the signpost that read:

Welcome to
HAMMETT

They permitted a jeep and a truck loaded with scientific and medical equipment through. Those were the only vehicles that had clearance. Any other admittance would require special authorization. Both stood before the roadblock, one standing in each lane, their weapons at the ready.

The first truck arrived in town a few minutes later. The National Guardsmen were all dressed in protective gear and carried M-16s. They were divided into two four-men platoons by Dunne who arrived by jeep. One group started off down Main Street on foot. The others returned to the truck and drove off.

Dunne went inside the station house where he found Bigelow asleep on the cell bed.

Bigelow lay on his back, an arm draped across his face. He was wearing trousers and a wrinkled white shirt opened at the neck, black hairs curling out.

Lieutenant Dunne leaned over him. He sounded like Darth Vader breathing beneath his mask.

Bigelow moved his arm away, opened his eyes, and shot up. His heart pounded in his chest. "What the fuck?!"

Dunne cracked a smile beneath the clear dome of his helmet. "You Bigelow?" he asked beneath his mask.

Bigelow wiped the sleep from his eyes. "Yeah . . . Jesus I thought I was having a nightmare or something."

"I'm Lt. Dunne." He offered his gloved hand.

Bigelow beheld the hand. "What's with the spacesuit?"

"We were summoned as soon as the tests were completed on Sam Hill."

"Why wasn't I notified?"

"We had to act quickly."

"What's the verdict?" Bigelow asked.

"Dioxin poisoning," Dunne said.

Bigelow stared at Dunne's eyes through the space helmet. *"Dioxin?"*

"That's right," Dunne said. "We're sealing off the town. No one enters or leaves. Everybody and everything will be tested."

Bigelow stood up and wandered out of the cell and into the office. His hand gripped the back of his neck as he pondered. He swung around and gazed at Dunne. "That means I . . . we all could be infected?" He flashed on his wife and kids. He felt the gears beginning to churn in his stomach.

Dunne said, "We have to figure out where the contamination lies."

"How?" Bigelow asked. "Who would've . . . ?"

"We're checking into everything. It seems to be a her-bicide . . . an offspring of Agent Orange."

"*Agent Orange?* I thought that was outlawed stateside?"

"I said it was an offspring. This stuff is more power-ful . . . faster acting."

Just then McGuane barged into the office. "What the hell is going on here, Frank?"

"The cavalry has arrived," Bigelow said.

McGuane beheld Dunne. "I thought it was an alien invasion."

"What's going on out there?" Bigelow asked.

"They're rounding up everybody . . . the whole town . . . scaring people to death."

Bigelow looked at Dunne for an explanation. "It can't be helped." Dunne shrugged beneath his heavy uniform. "We must act quickly."

"What is it, Frank?"

"Dioxin."

McGuane mouthed the word but no sound came out. The color drained from his face.

"We'll all have to be tested." Bigelow's eyes never left Dunne.

Dunne said, "I'm sorry, guys."

Bigelow said, "Not as much as we are."

Screams were heard coming from the street.

Bigelow rushed to the window. Outside several pajama-clad people were running from the National Guardsmen. "You're scaring those poor people to death!"

"We have a job to do," Dunne said apathetically.

Bigelow faced the CO. "Well, there are ways of handl-ing situations delicately, Lieutenant."

"I'm in charge here, Bigelow," Dunne said arrogantly.

Shots rang out.

Bigelow raced up to Dunne and gripped him violently with his two hands. "If any innocent people get killed out there I'll make damn sure it comes out of your hide, Dunne!"

"HANDS OFF!" A National Guardsman shouted from the doorway as he took aim with his M-16.

Bigelow backed off, his eyes burning into the mask.

McGuane put his arm around Bigelow. "It's their show now, Frank."

"Start searching the outskirts. I want the whole town rounded up," Dunne said to the man at the doorway.

"Yes, sir." The man saluted and left.

Then Dunne beheld Bigelow and McGuane. "I trust I will have only your fullest cooperation, gentlemen?"

Bigelow saluted him mockingly. "Aye-aye."

The truck pulled up in front of the Hills' home. The four men jumped out and started walking towards the front door.

Suddenly, shots rang out. The top of the domed helmet the first man wore shattered as his body dropped to the ground. The other men scattered in every direction.

The gunshots stirred Mrs. Hill as she sat by her husband's bed. She stood up and went to the window. She saw the truck and the men dressed in white outfits, automatic rifles in their hands. Then the window disintegrated and Mrs. Hill was hurled to the floor, her housecoat riddled with bullet holes.

Nick Hill could barely open his eyes. He was paralyzed, his body rotting away with disease. He heard the racket outside. Gunfire. Voices. It sounded like a scene from a war movie. He opened his mouth to speak, but nothing came out.

Outside, one National Guardsman spotted the man on the roof with a 12-gauge shotgun. "He's on the roof!"

The three men sprayed the roof with gunfire. The gutter pipe fell to the ground as shingles vaporized into black dust.

Then silence filled the air.

The troop leader picked up a megaphone. "Please surrender. We are the National Guard! Drop your weapon!"

The barrel of the shotgun appeared at the edge of the roof.

"Throw the gun down!"

Sam Hill stood up and managed to squeeze off another round before his body exploded as the three guardsmen emptied their M-16s into him.

Smoke and silence fell over them. They stayed put for a while in case there was another sniper on the loose. The sergeant said, "Do you *believe* this?"

"Fuckin' scary, man," another man said.

"We better check the house," the sergeant said.

"Who goes first?" a black guardsman asked.

The sergeant smiled. "Don't worry — I will."

The black guardsman said, "You *know* it."

The sergeant walked slowly to the front door, his 9MM pistol drawn. He had difficulty maneuvering within the POTMC suit. He didn't hear anything except his own pounding heart. He knocked with the barrel of his gun. "Anyone home?"

"Nice question, Sarge," one soldier laughed.

"Shhh!" the sergeant hissed. He stepped back and kicked open the door. He waved his men in. They reloaded their weapons and hurried into the house.

"You — check down here," he ordered one guardsman. "*You* come with me." The sergeant started up the stairway. He inched his way up, step by step, his back against the railing. When he arrived on the top landing, he was confronted by a hall with four closed doors. "Beautiful," he sighed.

"You check out those two rooms . . . I'll hit the front rooms." The sergeant went up to the closest door and kicked it open. It was the bathroom. The toilet was hissing. He beheld the next door. He inhaled deeply. "Well, here goes nothin'." He twisted the doorknob slowly, then whipped it open, hitting the floor with the gun in his gloved fist.

He took in the woman's body on the floor. Her bulging

eyes stared at him. Her floral housecoat soaked with bright red blood. *"Jesus!"* He gazed up at the man reclining on the bed. There were oxygen tanks close by. He stood up.

And then he saw him.

His face was a mass of oozing sores. His eyes were fluid and yellow. He was breathing irregularly, tubes riding up his nose. His body was all bloated beneath his white hospital gown.

The sergeant came closer to the bed. He saw that the man was aware of his presence. He moved his fingers. Then his eyes widened. His mouth dropped open. He began to moan . . . working his mouth . . . trying to speak.

The sergeant stood motionlessly, still stunned from the man's appearance. The black guardsman came up behind him. "Did you find . . . ?"

Hill managed to raise his arm, groping for them.

"What's wrong with him?" the guardsman asked.

Hill cried out and fell back onto the bed. His body quivering as his skin began to tear, blood seeping from the openings. His white gown turned a purplish red as it began to grow.

The two men stepped back as they watched in horror.

Bloody organs spilled out from the gown; steam hit the air like a crimson mist.

And then it all stopped. The carnage covered the bed.

The two men eyed one another.

The black guardsman said, "Far-*fuckin'*-out!"

part four
THE HARVEST

chapter 22

Karb sat down on the desk chair next to Red, who was operating the ham radio. He was patching in with Cardinal's communication terminal back in Miami to place a call to Pope in Washington. The Everglades shack was just that — a shack. No electricity. No running water. Nothing. One large room with a few chairs and tables, set up simply as a drop-off point for drug smuggling via air. A noisy generator worked the ham radio, lights, and a small fridge.

Karb snapped in an eight-shot cartridge in his Walther P-38 9MM Luger. He stuffed it in the back of his pants.

Red said, "You expectin' trouble?"

Karb faced Red and smiled. "I *always* expect trouble, son."

Red managed to place the call. "Here ya go, Karb."

Karb took the mike. "Split."

"Where to? There's nothing but swamp out there."

"Go join your friend outside and feed the alligators," Karb ordered.

Red shook his head and took his time leaving. He slammed the door behind him.

Karb said into the microphone, "Pope? — over."

"This is Pope. What's up?"

"I'm at Bava's shack. I got the two numbskulls with me. When should I expect Shepard?"

"Any time now. Be on the alert. He was last seen leaving Cronenberg's hotel. Bava's boys lost him after that. If I know that guy as well as I think I do, he'll be heading your way. I want you to finish this one off once and for all."

"Right," Karb said. "What about the girl?"

"She's next. I have Bava cooking something up for her."

"Oh, that's too bad. *I* was looking forward to whacking her," Karb said with remorse.

"What did you have in mind?"

"How's a boating accident sound?" Karb asked gleefully.

"Ummmm. Could work. Okay, I'll save her for you."

"I'll throw her in as a freebie," Karb offered generously.

Pope laughed. "I like the way you work, Karb."

"Over and out."

Karb stood up and walked to the door. He opened it and saw the two boys standing against the dock's railing. An airboat was tied up alongside the shack. The Kid held a Browning BPS pump shotgun in his hands.

"You're supposed to be on guard, Kid."

"That's what I'm doin', Karb."

"You wouldn't last a second if somebody was out there."

"Sez you."

Karb shook his head. "Red, come inside now."

Red made a face and followed Karb into the cabin.

Karb went to the aluminum suitcase on the table and took out an Uzi. "You know how to work this thing?"

"Sure do."

"You relieve the Kid in a few hours."

Red took the submachine gun.

"It'll be dark by that time. He might strike then. Can you handle that?"

"Uh-huh," Red said, his head leaning to one side defiantly. "There's only one of him, Karb."

Karb nodded. "That's what worries me."

Red squinted at him.

"You better get some rest now so you'll be fresh for later," Karb ordered.

"You dig bein' the bossman, don't ya?" Red asked.

"Sure beats the hell outta being a gopher."

"I'm *no*body's gopher, man," Red snapped angrily.

"Why don't you relax?"

"I will as soon as this gig is over with. Then I'm comin' after you, Karb." Red narrowed his eyes threateningly.

"I'm looking forward to it." Karb smiled sardonically.

Bigelow, dressed in a navy suit and tie, entered the elevator. He undid his collar button. His forehead was beaded with perspiration. He leaned up against the back wall as the other passengers crowded around him.

Although it had been determined that he wasn't infected with dioxin poisoning, he wasn't feeling very well. He was fatigued. It had been a long day since the crack of dawn, when the National Guard swooped down on Hammett. He was the first person tested. He was in the middle of a case and had to fly down to Miami to follow up on a lead, he had told them. That was only a small part of the truth. He was actually worried about being poisoned. The thought of turning into something like Nick Hill really disturbed him. He had seen his remains. The doctors at the scene had never seen anything like it. This went beyond their experience. But one government scientist, Professor Ellison, hadn't seemed particularly perturbed by the sight. That had bugged the hell out of Bigelow. He wondered who was behind this whole mess — maybe his own employer!

The doors opened on the twenty-first floor, and
Bigelow pushed his way out. He walked down the long
corridor, the room numbers flashing by. Turning the
corner he saw the room he wanted. When he put his ear
to the door, he heard a woman's voice. Was it the radio
or television? No, it sounded like she was on the phone.
He knocked firmly on the door.

"Who's there?" the woman's voice asked from inside
the room.

Bigelow knocked again.

A few moments later, the door cracked open. He saw
a blue eye and freckled nose and then heard her husky
voice: "Can I help you?"

Bigelow flashed his I.D. "Frank Bigelow — I have a
few questions to ask you, Mrs. Cronenberg."

She opened the door. "I'm on the phone." She ran
back to the phone. "Rob, I gotta go. You don't understand . . . there's a Federal agent here. I don't know. Yes,
Rob. I'll rewrite the article. Okay." She slammed down
the phone and rubbed her forehead. She was wearing a
terry bathrobe, a smoking cigarette dangling from her
lips. She puffed away angrily. She yanked it out of her
mouth, exhaled smoke through her nostrils like a fiery
dragon, and took in Bigelow. "It hasn't been one of my
better days."

Bigelow smirked. "I know what you mean."

"What can I do for you?"

"I've just come from Hammett."

A concerned look came over Mandy's face. "Oh?"

"You placed several calls there recently, I understand."
Bigelow shifted his weight from one foot to the other.
"You spoke with Tommy Shepard."

Mandy nodded, puffing nervously on her cigarette.
"That's right."

"Have you seen Tommy?"

She paused a few moments, then shook her head.
"No."

"Are you sure?"

"I'm a little confused."

"Can I sit down?"

"Sure — can I order up something for you from room service?"

Bigelow plopped down on the vanity chair. "I could use a cup of coffee."

"I have some left here." She wandered over to the silver insulated coffee pitcher on the vanity and poured him a cup. He observed her as she worked. Her hands were trembling. She steadied them.

"You alright, Mrs. Cronenberg?"

"Fine," she snapped.

He sipped the coffee. "Thank you — that should do it."

She went to the edge of the bed and sat down. She lit up another cigarette and wrapped her arms around herself. "Pretty chilly in here with the air conditioner." She stood up and went to the terrace door and slid it open. A warm breeze blew her hair. She returned to the bed.

"You appear very nervous, Mrs. Cronenberg," Bigelow said.

"I'm okay."

"I want to know about your involvement with Tommy Shepard."

"We were acquaintances," she said.

Bigelow smirked. "How would a New York rock journalist be friends with a reputed grower of illegal substances?"

"I was working on a story about the new moonshiners — marijuana growers," Mandy explained, her nerves settling down.

"How did you hook up with him?"

"He came to me . . . in my Brooklyn office."

"A hick from a small town in Florida. . . ?" Bigelow asked in disbelief.

"He was going to school in New York," she informed him.

"Why did he come to you?" Bigelow was intrigued by her story.

Mandy shrugged. "Make a buck. I write the story, he supplies the facts — we both split the profits."

Bigelow laughed. "You must take me for a fool, Mrs. Cronenberg. My men did their homework on you. Your husband died recently in a traffic accident — "

"It was *no* accident," Mandy interjected.

"I'm coming to that," Bigelow continued. "Your employer sent you down here to do a story on Rick Marlowe. Instead you pursued a wild fantasy about drugs and Jonathan Cardinal and these new moonshiners, as you call them."

"Don't forget about the dioxin," Mandy added.

Bigelow put the coffee cup down, the color fading from his face. "Now, how would you know about *that*?"

She smirked. "Man, do I have a story to tell you."

Bigelow smiled and said, "I'm all ears."

Tommy pulled off the Tamiami Trail and into the parking lot of a Miccosukee Indian souvenir shop. There was only one other car parked outside the small wooden structure.

Tommy had stolen a car just down the street from Mandy's hotel. He would have to ditch it.

He entered the shop and saw Betty Stanton standing behind the counter selling a handmade bracelet to a young couple. Their little girl was hugging a palmetto-fiber doll.

Betty looked up at Tommy. She motioned to the back with her black eyes. Tommy went behind the counter and slipped into the back room. He found Gator hunched over a worktable painting a tiny wooden tomahawk.

Gator was too preoccupied to notice him. Tommy came up behind him and grabbed him by his midsection. Gator jumped out of his chair. "JESUS CHRIST!"

He swung around, lashing the tomahawk menacingly before realizing that it was Tommy.

"How's it going, Gator?" Tommy smirked.

"You sumbitch. . ." Gator roared and hugged Tommy. "You've made it on the tube, boy."

"Yeah," Tommy said without much enthusiasm. "I'm on the Ten-Most-Wanted list."

"How did you get here?"

"I picked up some dude's wheels — you gotta help me lose it."

Gator nodded. "No problem. What brings you down here?"

"I have to get to a cabin out in the swamp. It belongs to a man named Cardinal. Do you know it?" he asked.

Gator squinted in deep thought. "Cardinal, you say?"

"Yeah that airline owner — Jonathan Cardinal."

Gator shook his head. "Can't say . . . "

"Here." Tommy gave him the written instructions Mandy had transcribed from Cardinal's phone call.

Gator studied the map. "This here doesn't belong to nobody named Cardinal. It's Bava's shack. Yeah. He has a place out in the uncharted sector. He don't use it no more."

"Why's that?" Tommy asked.

"The place been busted a few times. You see, it's the drop-off spot for a dope operation. A plane flies low and unloads a few bales. An airboat picks them up and brings 'em to the cabin. There they bag it and bring it on in. But they haven't used the place in over a year," Gator related.

"Ummmm . . . probably since Bava turned supposedly legit."

"It still goes on . . . but not *there*."

"Can you take me there?" Tommy asked.

Gator nodded.

"Tonight?"

"What's goin' on?" Gator became concerned.

"It could be dangerous," Tommy said seriously.

"Danger is my middle name."

Tommy laughed. "Gator, you're too much."

"We talkin' firearms, Tommy?"

"I have a sackful out in the car."

"Y'know I'm well equipped because of my line of work," Gator said.

"Yeah," Tommy smirked as he picked up the toy tomahawk. "I can see that."

Bigelow sat there shaking his head as Mandy told him her story. She filled him in on everything — *except* that she had seen Tommy. Afterwards, Bigelow stood up and walked to the terrace window. He pulled the drapes aside to peer out. He swung around and eyed her.

"Why didn't you come in and tell the police your story?"

"Would they have believe me? They didn't believe me about my husband's death. Why should they believe this . . . *this* sci-fi tale?"

"It's no science-fiction tale . . . what's going on in Hammett is all too real," he said gravely.

"You know that now . . . but not a few days ago. They would've locked me up for being crazy."

"And Tommy — he knew this all the time?" Bigelow asked.

"He tried telling them in Hammett."

"In Hammett?!" Bigelow laughed. "They were probably all in on it, for chrissakes. I just knew it. I was working on a drug bust in Hammett a little while back. Elmore Shepard, Al Romero . . . the whole bunch of them. I knew if I nailed Romero he would lead me to Bava. We've been trying to get him for years."

"What happened to your drug bust?"

Bigelow sighed. "I was yanked off the case."

"Why?"

"I was told the order came from Washington. That they were conducting their own investigation in that region."

"Who's *they*?"

Bigelow shrugged.

"Weren't you suspicious?"

"Yep," he said. "But I had my orders."

"Then it's possible that whoever gave you the orders to pull out of Hammett might be the one behind the dioxin."

"You got my drift," he said, winking.

Mandy's reporter's feathers were ruffled. If the government was behind it, this could be the biggest caper since the Iranian-Contra arms deal. And she had more facts than anyone out there. The complete story would be hers. This could break her out into the limelight. Maybe she would get more respect as a serious journalist.

"You better come with me." Bigelow disturbed her musings.

"Huh?"

"We better get your story down officially," he said.

"Oh." Mandy didn't like that idea. They would probably have her swear not to reveal anything until the trial. *No way, buster.* "I have to get dressed."

Bigelow nodded. "I'll go out on the terrace. It's a beautiful day out there," he said and stepped outside and leaned up against the railing. She could see his shadow through the drapes. She swiftly ripped off her robe and got dressed. She put on her shoes and grabbed hold of her pocketbook. "I'll only be a few more minutes,"she cried out.

"Fine, take your time."

She smiled, then quietly opened the door and slipped out.

Bigelow watched the orange setting sun disappear behind the high-rise buildings across the street. He faced the window. "You okay, Mrs. Cronenberg?"

He took a few steps to the door. "Mrs. Cronenberg?"

He entered the room and saw that it was empty. He checked the bathroom. She was gone. "Son of a bitch!" Bigelow shouted as he rushed out of the room and ran to the elevator. He pressed the button. "Come on, come on!"

The doors opened and he got on. It made two additional stops before hitting the lobby floor. He scanned the crowds and hurried out into the street. She was nowhere in sight.

He stamped his foot and said, "SHIT!"

chapter 23

There was a full moon high in the starry sky. A thick, pungent odor hovered above the brown, stagnant water. Gator was perched in the airboat seat, his hand gripping the rudder stick. Tommy sat down below in the flat-bottom skiff. The wind pushed back his hair. He put more Cutter's insect repellent on his arms and face. The mosquitoes were fierce this time of year.

Tommy prepared his gear. He loaded arrows onto Elmore's bow, then checked his shotgun and automatic pistol.

Gator shut off the engine, and the fan revolved slower and slower until it came to a halt. The boat eased through the vines and bumped up against a *head* — a small island. Tommy cut some vegetation away and tied up the boat.

Gator eased down from the chair and picked up his high-powered rifle with scope. "The cabin's a few yards up ahead."

Tommy nodded. He inhaled deeply, then exhaled slowly. He hoped that would settle his nerves.

Gator patted him on his back. "You okay, Tommy?"

"Yeah."

"Just remember what these animals did to Elmore."

"Yeah."

"Come on." Gator went onto the land and stuck low to the ground. Tommy trailed after him, the shotgun and bow in his hands.

They hid behind some reeds. A faint light coming from the window of the cabin showed a man sitting on the edge of the dock, his feet dangling in the air. The cabin was fixed on stilts and built onto a hardwood hammock. A wooden dock and walkway surrounded the front and sides of the structure.

"He's packin' an *Oouzie,*" Gator whispered. "Looks like they're expectin' you, Tommy."

"Like I said."

"I could tag him with this." He picked up his rifle. "But it'll make an awful racket."

"I'll use the bow." Tommy put down the shotgun and loaded an arrow into the bow. He took aim. The sweat from his brow burned his eyes. He wiped them with his shirt sleeve. He swallowed hard.

"You want me to do it, boy?" Gator asked.

Tommy shook his head.

"If you're half as good as Elmore was with a bow, you're still a helluva lot better than me."

Tommy flashed on Elmore. The last time he had seen him alive. Bloated and pimpled. Then later, his face shot away, his body up on the table. He thought about Matt. And then Mandy's husband.

He held his breath. Stood up. And released the arrow.

It whizzed through the air and struck the man dead center of his chest. Without a sound, he fell back onto the dock. The arrow protruded from his chest, glistening in the moonlight.

Tommy shut his eyes.

"*Beautiful!*" Gator hissed and put his arm around Tommy's shoulders. "Now let's go finish it."

The two men waded through the waist-deep water holding their weapons above their heads.

Tommy climbed up the ladder and crawled onto the dock. He checked on the body. He was a redhead. Young and very dead.

Gator came up behind him. They squatted down and crept towards the cabin. Gator arrived at the door and waited for Tommy to get to the window. Tommy stayed below, out of the glare of the light. He slowly eased up to peek through the window. Gator saw the top of Tommy's head in the illumination.

Then the window shattered, the glass showering down on Tommy as he hit the ground, the jagged particles cutting his hands and face.

Gator gritted his teeth and kicked open the front door.

The Kid stood before him with a shotgun. He squeezed the trigger and the blast knocked Gator to the floor.

Tommy saw Gator writhing in the doorway, the front of his shredded shirt bloodied. Tommy rolled a few times until he hit the doorway and then squeezed off a charge. The Kid's face came apart as his body was thrown up against the wall. He slid down to the floor, the life drained from him.

Tommy heard an airboat starting up behind him. He shot up and ran to the edge of the dock. A white-haired man sat in the seat of the boat. He aimed his pistol and fired a round at Tommy.

Tommy jumped out of sight and watched the boat ride off. He ran back to Gator. He was holding his stomach, his eyes bulging with pain.

"Gator!" Tommy cradled Gator's head in his arms. *"Gator. . ."*

"Go after him, man." He swallowed hard. "There's nothin' you can do for me." He coughed.

"I can't leave you like *this*," Tommy said in distress.

Gator smiled. "We did okay . . . didn't we?" He

closed his eyes and moaned. Then he loosened up. His body became a rag doll in Tommy's arms.

Tommy felt the rage building inside him. He tasted blood in his mouth. He stood up, pumped the shotgun and started off.

He waded through the water, ran across the head, and got on board the airboat. He started it up and took off.

He cut through the grass as fast as the boat could go. The wind whipped at him, his knuckles turning white as he gripped the stick. The noise from the fan vibrated in his eardrums. Blood seeped from the cuts on his face. His salty perspiration caused his lacerations to sting. But he did not notice. He was numb — inside and out. Tommy just looked straight ahead, the shotgun in hand.

And then he saw it. The airboat was in front of him. It seemed to be slowing down. When the driver saw that Tommy had caught up, he sped up again.

Tommy nodded. "Okay, pal, let's get to it."

Karb craned his head around and saw Tommy's airboat close behind him. *It's about time.* Karb smiled. He pushed the engine to its limit as the boat skidded on top of the water. He whipped the stick to one side, and the boat sailed over a small isle. He laughed as he saw Tommy do the same. He maneuvered the boat around several heads, the water spraying his face and clothes.

He headed straight towards the high, thick grass up ahead.

"This should make it more interesting . . ."

Tommy followed the airboat into the high grass. The boat disappeared into the bush. The reeds and vegetation tore by him, hitting him across the face. His eyes were stinging again. But this time it wasn't from sweat. It was from blood. His face was lined with gashes. But the pain urged him on . . .

Suddenly the other airboat appeared out of the bush and came up beside him.

Karb sneered at him as their boats bumped side to side, his sardonic grin glowing in the darkness.

Tommy steered into the other boat, the violent clash sounding loudly in the night.

Karb fired a shot. Tommy veered the boat away to avoid the bullet. He continued to drive erratically to make himself a difficult target.

When he saw an opening, Tommy squeezed off a charge that sent buckshot ricocheting off Karb's boat.

Then they came upon a small head. Tommy rode around it. But Karb skimmed on top of it. Tommy twisted his neck around and saw Karb's boat coming at him off the elevated island. Tommy dived into the water just as the boat crash-landed on top of Tommy's boat. The fan ate into it; smoke poured forth.

Tommy broke the surface and watched as the airboat mangled the skiff. Karb spotted him and fired a round. Tommy went below once again. He could hear the grinding noise even under the water.

Tommy saw bubbles on top of the water. Then silence fell over him. He broke the surface and saw that Karb's airboat had vanished. He swam to his boat. It was beginning to sink, the deck filled with water. He climbed up to the seat and looked all around. The other airboat was gone. The early morning sun was breaking on the horizon.

He started up the engine. Maybe if he went easy, the boat would be able to make it back.

He wiped his bloody face with his wet sleeve and took off.

He thought about poor Gator. How was he going to tell Betty that he was dead? He felt like a fool for coming to the cabin. He knew it was a trap. He knew it was for revenge. Why did he have to drag old Gator into it? How many more innocent people would die because of him? It had to stop.

He was even more determined to get to the bottom of this. He had to track down Cardinal. To get the truth out of him. And he would use any means to do so.

Tommy recalled where Cardinal lived from Mandy's file on him. Palm Beach. That was where he would most likely be. Tommy hoped Cardinal thought he was dead. Then his visit would be a surprise.

He pulled his pistol from his pants.

Maybe he wouldn't have to use it this time around.

He put it away. But the cold metal against his skin reminded him of its presence. It was the only possession he had left. One he would use — if he had to, to kill.

The thought brought on a feeling of remorse. He felt so wasted. All chewed up. His bones ached. His wounds stung. He was desperate. A hunted animal.

And he still didn't know why.

Bigelow and McGuane stood before the receptionist's desk. The blonde smiled and asked if she could help them. Bigelow said yeah — is your boss in? She shook her head, still smiling. That smile was getting to Bigelow. It was so fake. He hated insincere people. What about Mr. Bava? he asked. She nodded. More teeth.

They went into Bava's office, just off to the side of Cardinal's door. He was big and fat and sat behind his big, fat desk nibbling on a pencil eraser.

Bigelow was still steaming from the day before when Mandy had given him the slip. He was glad McGuane was able to join him today after passing his physical. If he had been along with him yesterday, she wouldn't have gotten away.

"Well, well, well . . . if it isn't my old friend, Frank Bigelow." Bava giggled his squeaky laugh. "Have a seat, gentlemen."

Bigelow had met Bava once before. In a courtroom. He had been charged with drug smuggling off the Rock. Bigelow had been the agent who brought him to court.

The judge had thrown the case out due to lack of evidence. Bigelow never forgot the shit-eating grin on Bava's face afterwards. It had haunted him ever since. He'd vowed that next time he would nail his ass to the wall and put him away for a very long time. Maybe now was his chance.

Bigelow put his hands on top of Bava's desk, leaning over to peer into his face. "How's it going, Bava?"

"Very well. We closed with a ten-point gain yesterday."

"I'm referring to your *other* business, Bava," Bigelow said, smiling.

"I'm afraid I don't understand," he smirked, still chewing on the eraser.

"The business you and your friend got going in Hammett."

Bava blinked a few times, then said, "Hammett?"

Bigelow straightened up. "I'm onto you and Cardinal. I know about the dioxin. I have a reporter who has told me quite a story."

"A reporter?" Bava asked. "You mean that dipstick redhead who writes for that Commie paper?"

"How do you know about *her*?"

"She's been pestering poor Mr. Cardinal with all her wacko accusations for the past week. A real sickie."

"I expect when we catch up with Tommy Shepard, he will verify her story."

"*If* you catch up with him." Bava smiled, his teeth yellowed from smoking.

Bava's tone gave Bigelow a chill. "You plan on getting to him *before* we do?"

He shook his head and stroked his mustache. "I really don't know what you're talking about. I'm the Business Manager for Cardinal Airlines. Why would I care about this fugitive?"

Bigelow shifted his gaze to his partner. "Do you believe this guy?"

McGuane smirked.

"Who the hell do you think you're fooling, Bava?" Bigelow asked.

"The whole world," he said, waving his arms.

"Where's your boss?"

"Mr. Cardinal's out of town."

"How the hell did he ever get tied up with you?" Bigelow asked distastefully.

"I saved his company."

"You never made it past the third grade, Bava. How could you save his company?" Bigelow said, then thought it over. He decided to add what Mandy had told him. "Okay, I got it. You turned Cardinal onto drugs. Pumped in some bucks for his ailing company. I get it now."

Bava sobered up. "I'm really very busy, gents."

"You're coming with us," Bigelow ordered.

Bava beheld them with contempt. "On *what* charge?"

"On anything I feel like charging you with," Bigelow said defiantly.

Bava stood up and sucked in his gut, throwing his chest out. "My lawyer will have you grounded for this. Didn't you learn anything from the *last* time, Bigelow?"

"Why don't you stand up and say that?" Bigelow snapped.

McGuane covered his mouth to laugh.

"Very amusing."

"Get your things together," Bigelow commanded.

"You have no right to do this!" Alarm appeared on Bava's face when he realized that Bigelow was serious.

"McGuane — read him his rights."

McGuane began to speak in a monotone voice.

Bigelow went behind the desk and grabbed Bava. He threw him against the wall and cuffed him.

Bava stared up at him through brown slits. "You're finished, Bigelow."

"Yeah, yeah, yeah . . ." Bigelow pushed Bava into McGuane.

McGuane grabbed hold of him and said, "Do you understand your rights?"

Mandy was on the phone to Manville in King's apartment. She was leaning against the refrigerator, the phone tucked between her neck and shoulder. She was writing notes on a yellow pad. King sat on the edge of the kitchen table. He was shaking his head. He couldn't believe what was happening.

"Didn't I tell you, Rob? Huh? Remember? I told you this was going to be big. But *noooo*, you wanted your stinking piece on Rick 'who remembers?' Marlowe. Well, I'm going to sell this on the open market. Come off it, Rob, I don't owe you anything. HA! You can't sue. I don't care if the article could save the paper. You should've thought of that before." Mandy raised her eyes. "How much are you willing to pay? HA! Well, you better come back with a better offer or bye-bye story. Yeah. The same to you, grouch!" She hung up the phone on the wall mount.

King laughed. "You're really sticking to your guns on this one, aren't you?"

"After what I've been through — *damn straight.*" Mandy picked up the can of Diet Pepsi and threw her head back to drink it.

King picked up a bag of Fritos and started munching on them. "How're you going to get around town without getting picked up?"

"Under the cover of darkness," Mandy announced as she snatched the Fritos away from him.

"I wonder how your friend is doing?"

Mandy stopped chewing. She was trying to conceal her concern for Tommy. She knew deep down he had been right about Cardinal. He was involved. He had tried to dissuade her and did a damn good job of it. It was just like King had told her about knowing your limitations. She now was aware of her own. She wanted to improve upon some of her shortcomings. Writing an exclusive article about all this was just a start.

"Aren't you listening to me?" King asked, annoyed.

She nodded, snapping out of her thoughts.

"Now what's your next move?" King asked.

"Tonight, I go visit Cardinal."

"How do you know he didn't skip the country already?"

'No, you don't know Cardinal like I do," she said. "Where can a man of his stature escape to? I just want to see his face when I tell him what I told that Federal agent. He'll shit in his pants."

"He still might be holding the winning hand in this game."

Mandy said, "There's only one way to find out."

chapter 24

Bava was sitting at the huge conference table with his arms folded, his mouth sealed. He reminded Bigelow of a spoiled brat who wasn't getting his way. Bigelow sat across from him, staring directly at him. Bava wasn't saying anything until his lawyer got there. McGuane stood by the closed door, his eyes on the blinking fluorescent ceiling light. The stenographer, a pretty brunette, smoked a cigarette while she waited for something to happen.

There was a three-inch-thick file on the table. It was Bava's file. Years and years of records, court hearings, and photographs. All this and Bava had yet to spend a single day behind bars. That irked Bigelow. He, alone, had been trying to nail him for over five years. Enough was enough.

Bigelow put his chin on top of the file, his eyes burning into Bava.

Bava averted his eyes. "Give me a break, Bigelow."

"Never."

"You ain't got anything on me, pal. Face it," Bava hissed. "I've had it with your harassment."

Bigelow pouted and shot a glance at McGuane. "You got a box of tissues?"

"Want me to go get them, Frank?" McGuane played along.

Bava shook his head. "Games. All games. When're you guys going to grow up, for chrissakes?"

"When there're no more bad guys out there, Bava."

"You really believe that, Bigelow?"

Bigelow smirked. "I believe you're the bad guy, if that's what you mean."

Bava shook his head and laughed. "Un-*fucking*-believable."

"Hey-hey-hey . . . we have a lady present," Bigelow snapped.

Bava nodded at the girl. "Sorry."

She shrugged. She heard enough of that stuff around here.

Suddenly, there was a knock on the door. McGuane opened it. A short, balding man in a brown pinstripe suit hurried in. He placed his briefcase on the table. He scanned the faces and said, "Why're you holding my client here, Bigelow?"

Bigelow sat back in his chair and put his hands behind his head. "Because he's the bad guy."

Mandy drove up to Cardinal's gateway in her Avis-rented white Camaro. She leaned out the window and stared into the video camera. She waved. "Guess who?"

Cardinal stood behind Karb who sat before the six black-and-white monitors. He smiled when he saw Mandy wave to him on one of the screens. "Nice of her to drop in like this."

"Saves me a helluva lot of trouble," Karb said with a snicker.

"Open the gates," Cardinal ordered.

The doors slowly eased open, and Mandy drove in. The gates closed behind her. The driveway was lined with palm trees. She pulled up in front of the mansion and got out of the car. She took in the white glow of the house. She had read that he owned two tennis courts, a swimming pool, and a private dock where he kept his three boats. His garage housed a Mercedes, a Porsche, and a Rolls. His grounds were protected by an electrified fence and video-surveillance system. As Mandy had said, it was a fortress.

She walked up to the front door. Before she had a chance to knock, the door swept open, and Cardinal stood before her. He was dressed in a pair of white linen trousers and a red polo shirt. Sunglasses were pushed back on top of his head. "Good evening, Ms. Cronenberg. Come on in."

"I expected a maid or butler," Mandy said as she entered.

"Ah, I gave all my servants and groundskeepers the night off."

"Including your security force?"

"Yes." Cardinal waved her into his study. The room was decorated in earth tones and wood. There was a large mahogany desk against one wall. A wet bar was built into another wall. Bookcases, stocked with leatherbound editions, enhanced the room. "Sit down . . . make yourself comfortable."

Mandy sat down on a thick brown-leather chair. She noticed the Oriental rug on the floor. Cardinal went to the bar. "What'll it be?"

She didn't like the way she was feeling. The thought that she let this man . . . touch her sent a chill up her spine. "A gin and tonic."

He mixed her the drink and poured himself an apple juice. He handed her the drink and went behind his desk. He sat down, the smile never leaving his face.

"How is it I got the feeling you were expecting me?" Mandy asked.

Cardinal laughed. "Actually, I was expecting someone else."

"Oh, I hope I'm not interrupting anything."

"No. Not at all. We'll have a nice little get-together," Cardinal said.

"I had a good, long talk with a Federal agent yesterday."

The smile vanished from Cardinal's face. He thought it over for a few moments, then said, "You're trying to spook me, again." The smile reappeared. "I thought we had made amends . . . that we were *friends*." He winked.

"His name is Frank Bigelow," she said.

Cardinal sipped his juice. "Oh? Can't say I ever had the pleasure."

"You *will*."

"I really can't figure you out, Mandy." Cardinal leaned over in his chair, his hands on top of the desk. "One day you sleep with me, and the next day . . ." He shook his head and sighed. "Besides, you have no evidence . . . not a shred of proof. If the authorities listened to every crackpot's story, they'd never be able to get their work done."

Mandy ignored his comment about their personal encounter. "Yeah, but this Bigelow guy became real interested in my tale. He especially appreciated Bava's involvement in it. Seems they had a run-in before." Now Mandy was smiling.

Cardinal sat back in his chair with a sigh. "You're either incredibly stupid or very naive, Mandy."

"Oh?"

"Have you any idea how much *power* and influence a man like myself has?" he asked.

"Money can't buy everything, Cardinal."

"*Really?*" He arched his eyebrows, smiling.

"They'll catch up with you. There's no doubt in my mind. You can't mess around with dioxins and murder and expect to get away with it."

"I never killed a single living thing in my life — man or animal!" Cardinal exclaimed.

"You don't have to," she said. "You *pay* someone to do it for you."

Cardinal laughed. "You're really very entertaining, Mandy. I'm sorry we couldn't meet under better circumstances. You were good the other day. A *real* woman. Compassionate. How can you shut it off so quickly?"

Mandy finished her drink and stood up. She walked to his desk and put down her glass. "A job is a job."

He smirked. "Are you trying to say that was all an act? You were just trying to get into my confidence?"

"It worked, didn't it?" she said confidently.

That made Cardinal laugh even louder.

Mandy was feeling very uneasy in his presence. She felt he knew something that she didn't. "I think I'd better leave."

Cardinal began another robust round of hysterics. Mandy picked up on a sadistic streak she had not noticed before. Perhaps Cardinal was not just in this for the money. Maybe he was a sicko. That really got Mandy worried. She turned and hurried to the door. She opened it and Karb was bearing down on her. He was dressed in all black — jeans, tee shirt, and sneakers.

"Excuse me." She tried to push him out of her way, but he was cemented to the floor. His lips curled into a crooked grin as she turned bright red from the exertion. She started to pull on his clothes. "Get the fuck outta my way, stone face."

She turned around and saw Cardinal wiping the tears from his eyes. "I'm sorry, Mandy. Come back in and sit down. I'll make you another drink."

She faced Karb again and came to the conclusion she wouldn't be able to tackle him. She went back to her chair and plopped down.

Cardinal handed her another drink. "Now all we have to do is wait for your friend Tommy," he said. "And then Karb will take care of *both* of you."

Bigelow left Bava and his lawyer in the room when McGuane summoned him. They stood outside the door in the quiet hallway. McGuane leaned his hand against the wall as he spoke softly to Bigelow. "A new development in the Oates case."

"A *new* development? He already confessed to killing Higgins."

"Ahh! But he didn't act alone," McGuane pointed out.

"*What?*"

"You always said he was a jerk," McGuane said. "His old lady found a knapsack filled with one-hundred-dollar bills. She thought if she handed it in and Oates came clean, we could make a deal."

"Yeah?"

"It seems these two guys gave Oates the money the very night he blew Higgins away. They told him if he knocked off the sheriff and Tommy in one clip, he would get another sack of bread and become the sheriff to boot."

"Who were these two men?" Bigelow asked.

"Two kids. A blond and a redhead. The blond did all the talking. He told him that Carpenter had worked for them," McGuane related.

"The mayor worked with them?" Bigelow asked, then thought it over. "I like it. Too bad we don't have any names." Then the expression on Bigelow's face changed in an instant. Nulls was coming down the hall with Mike Bishop.

Their greeting was cool and sober. "How's it going in there, Bigelow?" Nulls asked.

"We have no grounds to hold Bava any longer," Bishop added.

"It's going," Bigelow answered curtly.

"Nowhere," Nulls snapped.

"I'll get him to talk," Bigelow said assuredly.

"All I want from that man is one name — *Pope.*" Nulls stared at Bigelow menacingly.

"It sounds *personal.*" Bigelow saw the desperate look in the Assistant Attorney General's eyes. "I can understand that. I've been after Bava for many years now. It's become personal with me, too. Just one thing — there're more people involved in this than just Pope."

"I don't care about anyone *else,*" Nulls emphasized. "I want it on the record that Pope was the mastermind of this operation."

Bigelow nodded. "Don't worry, I'll get him to talk."

"And don't do anything illegal, Bigelow," Bishop interjected. "We don't want this case thrown out of court on a technicality."

Bigelow glared at his boss angrily. "If you think *you* can do a better job, Mike."

Bishop held up his hands. "Just don't blow it, Frank."

Bigelow said, "Give me fifteen minutes — that's all I need."

Karb's eyes were peeled on the monitors when he spotted the bearded man by the west gate. It was Tommy. He grinned. He shut off the electrified fence so Tommy could climb over and enter the grounds. Karb picked up his Walther P-38 that was resting on the table. He stood up and tucked the pistol into his jeans.

It was time to introduce Tommy to Jonathan Cardinal.

chapter 25

Tommy scaled the fence and dropped down onto the green grass. He stayed there for a while to catch his breath. He was exhausted. What he really needed was a couple of days in the sack. He got to his feet and, staying low to the ground, skirted through the trees and across the lawn. There were spotlights scattered along the way. He tried to stay out of their glare. He got to a thick cluster of bushes and saw the house before him. He pulled out his pistol and took a few moments to compose himself.

He wiped the sweat from his brow as he thought about his next move. His eyes were on the dark window. He wondered if it was hooked up to an alarm system. Most likely it was. He shrugged. He would deal with that when it happened. Perhaps if he acted quickly enough, he could still catch Carpenter off guard.

He looked around, then ran to the window. He squatted down and started to examine it.

That was when he felt the cold barrel of Karb's gun in his ear. "Drop it, Shepard, or I'll clean the wax outta ya ears."

Tommy shifted his gaze and saw the white-haired man holding the gun on him with two hands in the combat position. He recognized him as the airboat driver.

Tommy exhaled loudly and dropped his gun. He watched Karb scoop it up in his hand. Tommy rose and put his hands in the air.

"You had us going there for a while, buddy." Karb smiled.

Tommy nodded.

"You handled yourself real nice with that airboat," Karb complimented him.

"Not as well as you."

Karb shrugged, "Got a few more years on you." He waved his gun. "Let's go see Mr. Cardinal."

Tommy walked off with Karb's gun against the base of his skull. They entered the front door and went through the hallway into another room.

Tommy saw Cardinal sitting behind the desk. He looked even more handsome in person.

Cardinal stood up. "Well, well, well . . . come on in and join the party, Tommy."

Karb pushed Tommy ahead while he shut the door.

Tommy took a few steps before Mandy got up from the chair. They exchanged glances. "Are you okay, Mandy?"

"I'm fine, Tommy."

"We finally meet," Cardinal said.

Mandy turned around and glared at Cardinal. Tommy brushed his hair back with his hand. "Mr. Cardinal, I presume."

Cardinal nodded.

"Why is she here?"

"She came by to visit me. We were just having some drinks. Isn't that right, Mandy?"

She said, "You son of a bitch."

Cardinal took a deep breath. "I'm sorry, guys. *Really.*"

"Now what?" Tommy asked.

"What did you have in mind for me, Tommy?" Cardinal asked.

"I only wanted to hear the truth . . ." Tommy said.

"The truth?" Cardinal said. "What difference does it make now?"

"It makes a big difference to me."

"You know most of the story already."

"I want to hear it from *you*," Tommy said.

"Is that the *only* reason you came here?"

Karb said, "He had this on him." He held up Tommy's pistol.

Cardinal nodded. "I guess the truth wasn't the only thing you had in mind, Tommy."

"That gun belonged to my brother, Elmore," Tommy said. "He was one of the people you murdered."

"As I told Mandy, I'm no killer. I'm a businessman. I had nothing to do with that mess in Hammett. Believe me."

"I think he has a guilty conscience," Mandy told Tommy.

"Perhaps," Cardinal said. "I never wanted it to go this far. If I had known, I would never have gotten involved."

"A lot of people look up to you, Cardinal. *Why* did you do it?" Tommy asked sincerely.

Cardinal didn't answer. He nodded to Karb.

Karb came up to Tommy and Mandy. "Let's go for a little boat ride."

"I would like an explanation, Cardinal," Tommy said.

Karb grabbed his arm. "Let's go."

Tommy pulled his arm away. "Come on, Cardinal, you owe us *that* much."

Karb wrapped his arm around Tommy's neck and put the barrel of his gun against his temple. "Don't fuck with me, Shepard!"

"Karb!" Cardinal shouted. "Release him. He's right.

I owe him at least my side of the story."

Karb pulled his arm away and backed away. 'If you think you can afford the time. The sooner we terminate these two, the safer we'll be."

"I understand that, Karb. It will only take a few minutes." He eyed his two captives. "Please sit down."

He went around to the front of his desk and leaned against it. He watched Tommy and Mandy sit down. He shook his head. "I just want to tell you up front that this wasn't my idea."

And with that he began his story.

Bigelow returned to the room and sat down in his chair. He could feel eyes on him. He looked up and saw Bava and his attorney waiting impatiently for an explanation. He twisted his head around and smiled at the steno-grapher. Then he eyed his partner who was at the head of the table. He saw the nervous perspiration on McGuane's brow. He nodded. He faced Bava again and sighed.

"We're waiting, Mr. Bigelow," the lawyer said.

"I want to make a deal with your client."

Bava covered his mouth and laughed. "I don't believe this turkey."

"Why would my client have to make a deal with you if he's not charged with anything?"

"*Yet,*" Bigelow added with a smile.

Bava shook his head. "I want you to bust his ass," he told his attorney. "I want him on the fucking street selling pencils!"

The lawyer calmed him down, then said to Bigelow, "You're finished."

"All I want to do is make a deal with Mr. Bava," Bigelow said calmly. "That's all. If he talks . . . maybe we can do something for him. It'll be tough. I mean, look at this file. Big as a fucking phone book."

Bava stood up and slammed his fist onto the table.

"I'VE HAD IT! IF YOU DON'T GET ME OUTTA HERE REAL SOON, I'M GOIN' TO KICK YOUR ASS RIGHT HERE AND NOW!"

Bigelow stood up. "Anytime, cowboy." He pulled his gun out of the holster and slapped it down on the table. "Let's do it!"

McGuane shot up and put his arm around Bigelow. "Cool it, Frank."

The lawyer got Bava back to his seat. "Sit down — let me handle it."

Bigelow sat down while McGuane stood behind him, both hands resting on his shoulders. "Pete, go make a long-distance call to Washington, Dee-Cee."

"I have to protest your treatment of my client . . ." the lawyer said.

Bigelow continued, oblivious to the attorney's comments. "If this bozo won't play ball maybe *Hank Pope* is interested in saving his own ass."

A silence fell over the room. Bigelow observed Bava's reaction.

Bava faced his lawyer. "What is he talking about?"

The attorney shrugged.

Bava stood up and eyed Bigelow. "What did you just say?"

"Go on, Pete. Call him."

McGuane left the room.

Bava sat down again, sweat beading on his forehead. He couldn't keep his composure. His hands were everywhere. Scratching his nose. Adjusting his necktie. He took out a handkerchief and blew his nose. He whispered something to his lawyer.

The attorney said, "My client has to make a phone call."

Bigelow smiled. "He already made a phone call. He's only entitled to *one*."

"Do I have to remind you he's not under arrest?"

"Who says he isn't?" Bigelow asked, then eyed Bava.

"We read you your rights — isn't that correct?"

McGuane tucked his head into the room. "I have that call for you."

"Great." Bigelow stood up and walked towards the door.

"WAIT!" Bava shot up. "Okay — I'll make a deal."

Bigelow froze, his back to Bava. He winked at McGuane with a shit-eating grin on his face. He turned on the balls of his feet. He put his hands on his hips. "Who says I want to make a deal with you anymore?"

Bava and his lawyer had their heads together in a hushed conference. The attorney said, "My client will agree to talk only if you don't prosecute him."

"HA!" Bigelow said. "I can make a better deal with Pope."

Bava ground his teeth. "You bastard."

"I'll agree to lessen your charge to a few clicks. But that's the best I can do. I know you're not the mastermind behind this. So that reduces you a notch right off the bat."

The lawyer whispered something into Bava's ear. Bava nodded and said, "I still haven't seen a single piece of evidence."

"Come on, Bava, make up your mind. If you don't play with me, I always have Pope and Cardinal. Either one is a lot more intelligent than you. And they don't have a criminal record as big as a telephone book."

"That file is useless . . . Mr. Bava has never been charged with a single crime," the lawyer said. "He has only been under suspicion. Not one single case has ever been processed in a court of law . . . that book of yours would be thrown out by the judge."

"*Still* . . ." Bigelow looked into Bava's eyes. "Come on, Tony, you know they'll sell you out when I pour the heat on. How the hell are you going to get out of this one? Dioxin poisoning, for chrissakes!"

"That was Pope's idea!" Bava cried out candidly.

Then realizing what he had said, he faced his lawyer for assistance.

His lawyer gripped his arm. "You don't have to say anything."

Bigelow nodded to the stenographer. She started to type. Bigelow pulled a chair up and sat down. "Okay, let's hear it, Tony. It's self-preservation time, so make it good."

Bava covered his face with his hands.

He remembered the details all too well. Especially the first time he had met Hank Pope. Bava was staying at his favorite Key West resort. He liked it because it was right on the water. His terrace faced the beach and all those topless beauties. He was sitting on a lounge chair on the terrace. It was three o'clock in the afternoon of a beautiful day. The sun was bright and hot, not a cloud in the sky. He left the glass door open so the air conditioner could blow outside and keep him cool. He was working on his fourth beer and needed to relieve his bladder when he heard a knock on his door. His bodyguard answered it and a few minutes later came outside on the terrace. "There's a guy here to see you, boss."

Bava, his brown, hairy belly glistening with suntan oil, was annoyed by the intrusion. "What guy?"

"He says his name is Hank Pope."

"Hank Pope?" Bava kicked the name around inside his head but came up with a blank. "Does he look okay?"

The bodyguard shrugged. "He looks like a businessman."

Bava laughed. "Or a fed."

"He says he only wants to talk."

"Okay, show him in," Bava said. "But make sure he's clean."

"Right." The bodyguard left.

A few moments later Pope came out on the terrace. The bodyguard stood by the door. "He ain't holdin', Mr. Bava."

Bava stood up. "Don't think I ever had the pleasure."

They shook hands.

"My name is Hank Pope." He was about Bava's height. Not as heavy.

"What can I do for you, Mr. Pope?"

Pope eyed the bodyguard. "I'd like to talk over some business matters with you . . . *alone*."

Bava said, "My man stays close to me at *all* times."

"Not this time, Bava," Pope said with an authoritarian tone.

"Okay, take a walk," Bava told his bodyguard. "Just outside the door."

Pope nodded.

"Can I offer you a drink?"

"A beer will be fine."

Bava went inside and took a beer out of the small refrigerator. He popped it open and handed Pope the can.

Pope smirked as he took the can and sipped it. He obviously wasn't used to drinking out of a can.

Bava plopped down in his chair, "Sit down."

Pope leaned against the terrace railing and looked out at the ocean. "Beautiful view."

"What's on your mind, Pope?"

Pope faced him. "Okay, I'll get right to it. Do you know me?"

Bava took off his sunglasses and squinted up at him. "Were you in one of those American Express commercials? No, that's not it." The expression on his face brightened when the light bulb lit up inside his head. "I think I remember reading about a Pope with the C.I.A."

"That's right. I'm out of that now. I head the President's drug enforcement program," Pope told him.

Bava cleared his throat. "The *what*?"

"Don't worry, I'm not here to bag you. Sure, I'm well aware of your background. And I admire you for getting away with it for so long," Pope added with a wink.

Bava sat up in his chair. "What the fuck is this?"

"I'm not speaking as a government employee. I come to you for myself."

"Well, get to it," Bava said impatiently.

"You make a lot of money."

"Yeah." Bava spoke softly, still not sure if Pope could be trusted.

"I want to make you some more money."

"What?"

"Well, let's just say, *I* want to make a lot of money," Pope explained.

Bava laughed. "You must be putting me on . . . is this your idea of entrapment?"

"I said I'm here for myself . . . I'm acting alone." Pope sounded sincere.

"Sure you are." Bava was still not buying it.

"Listen, Bava, I'm not that stupid. And I know you're not stupid. I'm here to offer you a deal."

"What kind of deal?"

"I can't discuss it unless I know you're with me one hundred percent," Pope said.

"How the hell can I promise you that?"

Pope sat down at the foot of Bava's lounge chair. "Listen, I want you to be my partner in a little business venture I dreamed up. I can offer you unlimited legal protection in exchange. I could pull any Federal agent off your back. I have that authority. With what I have in mind, we could rake in more capital than you ever dreamed possible."

Bava studied him closely. He seemed trustworthy. But could he trust him? "Why me, Pope?"

"Because you run one of the largest drug operations on the east coast. You have the know-how I need. I've done my homework. I know the business well. The C.I.A. has their hand in a few operations. But I don't have the firsthand knowledge you have. You know it from the ground up."

"That's because I started from nothin'. I was just

somebody's gopher. I picked it up real fast. I made myself
rich in the process. Growing and growing. Everyone
knows who controls the Gold Coast — am I right?"
Bigelow asked.

"Unfortunately, so do the local drug enforcers."

"They can't touch me," Bava proclaimed.

"You work with me . . . and I'll clear your name.
You'll not only get respect from the locals, you'll get it
from the whole country. You will be above the law."

Bava thought it over. "I have so much money now,
I don't need to make any more."

"That doesn't sound like the Bava I read about, "
Pope said. "Man, are you ambitious."

Bava nodded. "And you're in this for the bread?"

"I'm going to make it work for me *both* ways."

"Whaddaya mean?"

"You'll have to hear me out . . . but first you must
agree."

Bava stuck out his hand.

Pope shook it. "I hope you're a man of your word."

"That's the only way I ever do business, Mr. Pope.
There're no signed contracts in my line of work."

Pope smiled.

"Whaddaya have in mind?"

Pope filled him in on his scheme. Using Pope's
government-sponsored program, Grim Reaper, as a
cover, the two men could wipe out the competitors. Shut
down as many drug-smuggling operations as they could,
except Bava's. Pope also wanted to put a squeeze on the
domestically grown marijuana enterprises. Destroy their
crops. Bava knew where to find his competitors. He
would inform Pope of their whereabouts. And Pope, in
return, would send his men in. In that way, the avail-
ability of drugs would tighten, causing the market price
to skyrocket. Bava could sell his products at the new in-
flated rates and make a fortune.

Pope also devised a method of crop destruction by

secretly spraying them with a new chemical solution. Not only would it destroy the plants, but it would contaminate the soil so no new crops could grow there for years to come.

Then Pope told him how he could clean up Bava's reputation. He had a corporate friend who needed capital to help save his ailing company. A man who was above suspicion — Jonathan Cardinal. He would appoint Tony Bava as Cardinal Airlines' Business Manager.

Bava was overwhelmed by Pope's proposal; it sounded too good to pass up. He couldn't believe that Cardinal was a partner. That made him feel better. If a legitimate businessman like him was involved, it had to be a sure thing.

"Then what happened?" Bigelow interrupted his story.

"The fucking dioxin." Bava said. "Pope used this experimental chemical without properly testing it. Asshole."

Bigelow could not hide his admiration. "What an operation."

"It was brilliant except for that experimental herbicide."

"So you locked in with Cardinal."

"Yeah, I pumped some capital into his company. Pope managed to shut down a few smugglers . . . that hiked the price a bit. But he sure blew it with the local marijuana growers. Hammett was just a test town. Small, out-of-the-way. No man's land, y'know? He figured let's try it out in this redneck town first. If it worked, start spraying all the crops in the state. Then branch out from there."

"The whole country?"

"Pope's one hungry dude."

"And what about *you*?" Bigelow asked.

"If Pope had listened to me, we wouldn't be sitting here right now," Bava said repugnantly.

"What was your idea?" Bigelow wondered aloud.

"Let's just say I could've handled this mess more efficiently."

"With more *bloodshed?*" Bigelow grinned.

"Whatever it takes . . . " Bava said as he stared deeply into Bigelow's eyes.

"Getting back to Pope, couldn't he have covered it up?"

"Believe me, he tried *every*thing. He pulled you out. That was before the spraying. Then that hick stumbled onto it."

"What hick?'

Cardinal finished his apple juice. He rubbed his eyes, went behind the desk, and sat down. He eyed his two captives. He cleared his throat and continued. "Then your brother, Elmore, discovered the dioxin. We figured after Carpenter told him that the stuff was safe — just a sap — he would drop it. But, as you know, he didn't. He went to you for help."

"You should've seen him . . . he was all bloated and sick," Tommy said.

"Yeah, that was a side-reaction that Pope didn't bother to tell us about. He claimed he didn't know about it. But I think he did. He was just in a hurry to get on with the operation. It was working smoothly until the Hammett incident. Again we thought we were in the clear until you showed up. We didn't count on that. And then you brought in Mandy and her husband. It was spreading like wildfire. Pope acted quickly instead of cautiously. He couldn't use his own men, so he brought in mercenaries and Bava's hoodlums. All of them were ineffectual. Except for our Mr. Karb." He acknowledged Karb standing at the door. "He's a real pro. A stuntman. This guy takes chances no one in his right mind would take. That right, Karb?"

Deadly silence.

"You don't like me, do you?" Cardinal asked Karb.

"Then again, you probably don't like anybody."

"So now you take care of us. But they're onto you — why bother?" Tommy asked.

"They don't have much without your testimonies."

"But you said you're not a killer," Mandy reminded him.

Cardinal closed his eyes. "Karb."

"Well, I guess there's a first time for everything, you coward," Mandy snapped.

Karb stood by them, gun in hand. "Let's go."

"You still didn't tell me *why*, Cardinal." Tommy said.

Cardinal looked up. "My whole life is tied up with my success story. It wasn't for the money. I really don't care about the money anymore. I just have this thing about failure."

"So you're willing to succumb to murder because you're a sore loser," Mandy said. "That's beautiful."

Cardinal swung around in his chair, his back to them. *"Karb."*

Karb waved his pistol. "Up."

They both stood up and walked to the door. Karb came up behind them. "Let's keep this nice and simple. I promise to make it painless. So no funny business, okay?"

Tommy shrugged. "What choice do we have?"

He waited in his car until he saw the ragged young man climb over the fence. That must have been Tommy Shepard. Mandy had been in there for hours. He was getting worried. He got out of the car and scaled the fence. He stayed close to the outer area of the grounds, creeping along the fence.

When he got to the house, he decided to swing around to the back. He ventured past the two tennis courts and hid behind the bush by the rear door. He figured he had a better chance of getting into the house from there.

He sat down on the ground and lit up a cigarette. He hoped a smoke would settle his nerves. He held a tire iron in his hand. It was times like these that he wished he owned a gun. But it went against his whole philosophy.

He stamped out the cigarette and took in the surroundings. He saw the big cruiser tied up to the dock. And there were a couple of speedboats next to that. Then he shifted his gaze to the kidney-shaped swimming pool off to the other side of the house. Man, did this guy know how to live. All it took was money. *And* drugs.

He sat there for three-quarters of an hour. He thought about breaking in but he was worried about the alarm. He wasn't the heroic type. He just hoped something would happen for him so he could act.

And sure enough, he heard someone at the door. He got up on his knees and listened closely.

The door sprang open, and Mandy and Tommy walked out.

Then he heard a man's voice. "Out to the dock."

A tall, white-haired man came into view. He was holding a pistol.

He gulped and tightened his grip around the tire iron. He waited until they took a few steps.

Then he sprang into action. He ran up to Karb with the tire iron raised above his head. He brought it down, but Karb moved out of the way. It hit his shoulder. Karb managed to squeeze off a shot that hit him in the arm.

Mandy turned around and cried out, "DAVE!"

King hit the ground in a daze.

Tommy rushed up behind Karb and wrapped his arm around him. The two men struggled. Karb still held the gun.

Mandy ran to King. He was stretched out on the ground holding his wounded arm. She picked up the tire iron and swung it at Karb, knocking the gun from his hand.

Karb bent over and flipped Tommy over his back. Tommy landed on the ground on top of the gun.

Karb pulled out Tommy's gun that was tucked in his pants.

Mandy whipped the tire iron across Karb's face, shattering his dentures. He fell back, shook his head, and took aim with the gun.

Mandy shut her eyes when she heard the gunshot. She waited to feel the pain in her stomach. But there was none. She opened her eyes and saw Karb squirming on the ground, blood seeping from his chest. She looked down and saw Tommy sitting up with Karb's smoking pistol in his hand.

Tommy's eyes rolled to the back of his head and he passed out. Mandy went to him. "Tommy — are you okay?"

Then she felt a hand on her shoulder. She turned around and saw the bloody hand and followed the arm up to Karb's wrinkled face. He held a gun in his other hand. "You bitch!" he snapped with a bloodied mouth.

She poked the tire iron into his crotch and he backed away, his hand clutching his testicles. She saw he still held the gun.

She had to act quickly.

She pulled the gun from Tommy's hand and aimed it at Karb.

Karb recovered and was just about to go after Mandy when he saw her with the gun.

She pulled the trigger.

The bullet ripped into Karb's neck.

She fired again and again until the gun was empty.

Karb took each bullet while still on his feet. He finally collapsed to his knees, his chest and face pitted with bullet holes.

He gazed at Mandy one last time, the pistol in his hand. He opened his mouth to speak and blood sprayed out. He fell forward to the ground.

Mandy sighed, "Holy shit!" She turned her attention to Tommy. She held his head in her lap, slapping his face.

"Is he okay?" King asked as he sat up.

"Never mind him — how are you?"

"I never did go in for this hero crap." King grimaced from the pain.

"I'm sure glad you did this time, Dave." Mandy managed a smile.

"You sure did a number on that poor bastard." King beheld Karb's body. "I thought I would have to get up again."

"Tommy — Tommy!" She shook him.

Tommy opened his eyes. "Mandy."

"Oh, Tommy, are you okay?"

Tommy sat up, holding his head. "What the hell happened?"

"Mandy just wasted 'The Terminator'," King said excitedly.

Tommy saw Karb's body, then looked at King. "Who are you?"

"I'm Superman. I came here to rescue Lois Lane and Jimmy Olson."

Tommy eyed Mandy. "Is he *okay*?"

"Just a little overzealous."

They stood up. Tommy went to Karb and turned him over. He ripped the gun from his hand.

Cardinal was standing in the doorway.

Tommy raised the gun.

"Tommy — *don't!*"

Cardinal raised his hands.

Mandy went up to Tommy. "Let him live to stand trial."

Tommy's arm was still stretched out. Sirens were shrieking in the background.

"The disgrace alone will kill him," Mandy said.

"She's right, Tommy," King said.

Tommy dropped his arm.

Cardinal gazed up into the clear night sky and sighed.

Pope had trouble falling asleep as it was. He hadn't heard from Bava or Cardinal, and that troubled him. He finally managed to doze off when his doorbell stirred him. He sat up and rubbed his eyes. *What the hell?* He scanned the alarm clock. It was two o'clock in the morning. He put his feet on the carpeted floor and slipped into his leather slippers. He stood up and pulled on his silk robe.

The doorbell sounded again.

"OKAY!" He shuffled out of the bedroom, went down the stairs, and opened the front door. Two tall men wearing conservative gray suits stood before him.

"Yes?"

"The President would like to see you, Mr. Pope," one of the Secret Service men said.

"The President — at this hour?" Pope asked in a sleepy voice.

"We're here to escort you."

"Escort me?" It finally sank in. Pope nodded. "I have to get dressed."

"Make it fast." The two men came in and shut the door.

Pope went up the stairs to his bedroom. One of the agents followed him.

"You don't have to watch me get dressed, for chrissakes."

"I have orders not to let you out of my sight," the clean-cut young man said.

Pope gulped nervously. He quickly put on his navy blue suit. He went into the bathroom and gazed at his reflection in the mirror. He had a five-o'clock shadow. "May I shave?"

The agent nodded.

Pope wrapped a towel around his neck and worked up a lather with the brush. He began to shave with a barber's razor. His hand was trembling. He nicked himself and drew blood. The agent came up to him and took the blade away from him. "We better go."

Pope eyed the blade in the agent's hand. "You didn't think I was going to . . ."

"Let's go, Mr. Pope."

The two men took Pope to their car and drove off.

They arrived outside the main gate of the White House. The gates swung open and the two men flashed their identification. The car journeyed down the driveway and pulled up before the front door. They escorted Pope into the house. Nulls was descending the stairs just as they were entering.

"Nulls." Pope was surprised to see him.

Nulls smiled broadly. "The President's awaiting you impatiently, Pope."

"So it was *you* . . ." Pope said. "I just knew someone with clout was working against me." Pope gazed upon Nulls with disgust.

The smile never leaving his face, Nulls said, "Alexis was a great help to me."

"You bastard!" Pope had to be restrained by the Secret Service men.

They accompanied him forcefully up the stairs and into the Oval Office where the President sat behind his desk in his pajamas.

The President gazed up at Pope when he entered the room. The President's brown hair was a mess. He had dark rings around his eyes and appeared older than the last time Pope had seen him.

It was the first time Pope had seen him without makeup.

Pope sat down and smiled coyly at the President.

The President cleared his throat and leaned over his desk, his eyes penetrating Pope. He said in a soft but agitated voice, "What in God's name have you done, Pope?"

Pope dropped his head.

It was over.

epilogue:
CASUALTIES

Dunne stood outside the station house and watched the trucks pull out. He removed his helmet and went inside. Doc Crichton was sitting at Higgins' old desk sipping bourbon from a flask. Dunne stepped out of his protective suit, bundled it up, and sealed it inside a plastic bag. He wandered over to Crichton and sat down on the edge of the desk, "Well, that's that."

Crichton handed him the flask. "Is it?"

Dunne threw his head back to drink. "Yep. We cleaned up the four infected areas. Luckily, they didn't spray all the patches. Otherwise the residents wouldn't be able to return so soon."

"I don't know, Lieutenant." Crichton shook his head. "Only a few people were infected with the disease, but what about the long-range effects?"

Dunne shrugged. "They cleared the area . . . the scientists know what they're doing."

"Yeah, I heard that before. Ten years down the line people start developing cancer . . . giving birth to deformed children. We heard it all before."

"I don't know what to tell you, Doc." Dunne stood up. "I only know my job is finished here."

Crichton grinned. "Until the *next* time . . ."

Dunne said, "You shouldn't be so pessimistic, Doc."

"I know I shouldn't be. I'm an old man. I'll probably be long gone when the repercussions from this nightmare start appearing. By that time, most of the people behind this crime will probably be dead, too. Nobody seems to be concerned about the future. It's all live-for-today. Well, Lieutenant, I care. But I feel very alone at the moment."

Dunne nodded. "I suppose you're right. But what can you do?"

Crichton laughed. "That's right — *what can you do?* You can't sue City Hall."

Bigelow woke up before the alarm clock. He gazed over at his wife. She was sound asleep. He smiled. He got out of the bed and went into the bathroom. He turned on the water in the sink and washed his face.

He took in his face in the mirror. He now had two pimples on his nose. He started to squeeze one, but it hurt like hell. *Where're these things coming from?*

Then he flashed on the oozing sores on Nick Hill's face.

He examined his pimples again.

No, they're just pimples . . . aren't they?

The guard escorted the lawyer into Cardinal's jail cell. He was a tall, distinguished man in his mid-fifties. He sat down on the chair next to Cardinal's bunk. He opened his briefcase on his lap and brought out a yellow legal pad. He brushed his gray, bushy sideburns with a pencil and took in his client.

Cardinal was dressed in blue prison clothes, a number on his shirt pocket. He appeared tired. There were deep creases around his mouth. He looked at his attorney with pleading blue eyes.

"Is there any way of getting me out of this?" he asked the highest-paid lawyer in America.

The attorney's thick eyebrows came together in deep thought. "Have you ever thought about becoming a born-again Christian?"

Mandy watched Tommy as he stood on the terrace looking out over the ocean. His long, blond hair was blowing in the strong, cool breeze.

King sat on the edge of the bed, his arm in a sling, his eyes on Mandy's profile as she lingered in the doorway, a gin and tonic in her hand.

They remained that way in deadly silence for quite some time in Mandy's hotel room

Mandy had just heard that *R & R Express* was bought out by a notorious Australian media magnate. He had already canned Manville and most of the staff. Mandy had been ordered to return to New York to face the music. With her sitting on this big story, she doubted she would be given walking papers.

"What are you going to do, Mandy?" King's voice broke the solitude.

She shrugged. "Fuck 'em." She drained her glass with an insincere giggle. "I think I'll sell my co-op and move down here . . . write a book on this whole affair."

King beamed. "Hey, that'd be great."

Mandy eyed King with a crooked grin. "Yeah, you would like that, wouldn't you?"

"What about . . . ?" He motioned to Tommy out on the terrace.

"Let's find out." She marched out on the terrace and stood next to Tommy. King stood quietly behind them.

"How're you doing?" Mandy asked.

Tommy nodded.

Tommy shifted his gaze to her. "What else? I have a home and family to take care of."

Mandy squinted at him in confusion. "You mean . . ."

"Yeah, I'm going back to Hammett. Take care of Deb and Sage."

"And the *family business?*"

"Yeah — that, too."

Mandy glanced back at King who stood there shaking his head. "You think that's a sensible idea?"

Tommy smirked. "I best be goin'."

"Did you hear that I'm planning on moving down here and writing a book on all this?" Mandy asked.

"That's nice," Tommy said.

"I may need your help."

"You know where to find me," Tommy said as he shook both their hands. "Take care."

Mandy and King watched Tommy as he slipped out the door.

"I don't believe *that* guy," King said.

"A lone wolf," Mandy added.

She went back inside and fell back on the bed with a sigh. She looked up at the ceiling. She wondered what old Rob Manville and the rest of the guys would do now. A lot of papers had folded over the last few years. It was going to be tough.

At least she would not have to listen to Rob bark at her ever again. Funny. She would miss it. He really was an okay guy. Which brought to mind how she got involved in all this in the first place. . .

What the hell happened to Rick Marlowe, anyway?

About the Author

Born and raised in Brooklyn, New York, **Michael Serrian** is the published author of the mysteries *Captured and Night Runners.* The suspense thrillers *Mirage* and *Fatal Exit*, soon followed, published by Bantam Books. Macmillan published his first nonfiction hardcover book, *Now Hiring: Film*, for young adults, focusing on careers in the film industry. Later novels, *An Empty Sky* and *Breakers: High Surf Warning*, appeared in 2010 and 2023. His early books have all been republished in hardcover and Kindle formats in 2023. *Edgeplay* is his latest novel published in 2023.

Currently, Michael Serrian lives in Los Angeles and is working on his next novel.

The Neo Noir
Press Hardcover
& Kindle
Editions of
Michael Serrian's
other books are
available on
Amazon.

NEO NOIR
PRESS

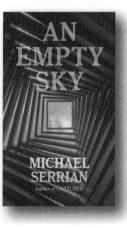